SO-AJF-194

Medicine Creek

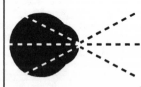

This Large Print Book carries the
Seal of Approval of N.A.V.H.

WIND RIVER SERIES

MEDICINE CREEK

JAMES REASONER
& L.J. WASHBURN

THORNDIKE PRESS

A part of Gale, Cengage Learning

GALE
CENGAGE Learning

Farmington Hills, Mich • San Francisco • New York • Waterville, Maine
Meriden, Conn • Mason, Ohio • Chicago

GALE
CENGAGE Learning

Copyright © 1995 by James M. Reasoner and L. J. Washburn.
Thorndike Press, a part of Gale, Cengage Learning.

ALL RIGHTS RESERVED
This is a work of fiction. The characters, incidents, and dialogues are products of the author's imagination and are not to be construed as real. Any resemblance to actual events or persons, living or dead, is entirely coincidental.
Thorndike Press® Large Print Western.
The text of this Large Print edition is unabridged.
Other aspects of the book may vary from the original edition.
Set in 16 pt. Plantin.

LIBRARY OF CONGRESS CATALOGING-IN-PUBLICATION DATA

Names: Reasoner, James, author.
Title: Medicine Creek / by James Reasoner.
Description: Large print edition. | Waterville, Maine : Thorndike Press, 2017. | Series: Thorndike Press large print western
Identifiers: LCCN 2017012152| ISBN 9781432838508 (hardcover) | ISBN 1432838504 (hardcover)
Subjects: LCSH: Large type books. | GSAFD: Western stories.
Classification: LCC PS3568.E2685 M43 2017 | DDC 813/.54—dc23
LC record available at https://lccn.loc.gov/2017012152

Published in 2017 by arrangement with James and Livia Reasoner

For Jessica Lichtenstein

1

Frenchy LeDoux reined in at the top of the rise, leaned forward in his saddle, and narrowed his eyes as he studied the rugged Wyoming Territory landscape in front of him. A moment later an angry curse burst from his mouth.

No doubt about it. That dust floating in the air about half a mile away didn't lie.

Those damned Latch Hook punchers were moving Fisk's cows toward one of the waterholes claimed by the Diamond S — again.

Frenchy whirled his horse around and heeled it into a gallop. They'd just see about this.

He was riding a big buckskin gelding, and its long-legged stride carried him quickly toward the spot where the rest of the crew was doing some of the spring branding. There were about a dozen men in the bunch, more than enough to deal with some

Latch Hook riders. Austin Fisk's men would soon regret trying to move their stock onto Kermit Sawyer's range.

Frenchy had been out scouting for just such trouble as this. More and more this spring, cowboys and cattle from the neighboring spread had been encroaching on Diamond S territory. It was time to put a stop to it before it got any worse.

He had ridden over a couple of hills when he saw the smoke from the branding fire. The fire itself came into view a minute later as he topped another rise. Down below were the makeshift corrals where the gather was taking place, filled with cattle that had been combed from the pastures and gullies of the broad valley where Kermit Sawyer had established his ranch. Near the corrals was the branding fire, and gathered around it were several of Sawyer's punchers. Frenchy heard the bawl of the calf that was being branded at the moment, and as he rode up he smelled the familiar scent of singed hair and burned hide. The young man holding the branding iron stepped back from the fire and looked up at Frenchy in surprise.

"Something wrong, Frenchy?" he called. "The way you came tearing over those hills, it looked like something must be after you."

"No, but I'm goin' to be after something

in a few minutes, Lon," Frenchy replied. "Namely a bunch of Latch Hook polecats. They're moving stock toward that waterhole over by Wildcat Ridge."

"Damn!" Lon Rogers exclaimed as he tossed the branding iron down. "What're we going to do about it?"

"What do you think?" Frenchy asked with a glare. "I reckoned we'd go disabuse 'em of that notion."

Several of the Diamond S cowboys nodded in grim agreement. They headed for their horses while Frenchy took off his hat and sleeved some of the dust and grime from his face.

He was a tall, lean-bodied man in his late twenties, with a thick shock of black hair and a naturally dark complexion made even darker by years of exposure to the elements. His black hat was wide-brimmed and had a pinched crown. He wore a cowhide vest and leather wrist cuffs, and batwing chaps — not really necessary in this part of the country but a habit from his days of riding the range in Texas — were strapped to his long legs. A holstered Colt rode on his right hip. Anyone looking at him now would have hardly taken him for anything other than a cowboy, and only a faint accent, as well as the nickname he had carried ever since drifting from Louisiana to Texas as a young man, revealed his Cajun heritage.

Lon Rogers, who was some seven or eight years younger than the hard-bitten *segundo*, was the first man in his saddle. His open, innocent face and curly brown hair made him look even younger. But he was all business, and grim business at that, as he rode up alongside Frenchy. "Let's go teach those Latch Hook skunks a lesson," he said curtly.

The other men were ready to ride, too. Texans all, by either birth or choice, they had accompanied their boss, Kermit Sawyer, all the way up to Wyoming Territory from Texas when Sawyer had brought a herd along the trail to establish a new ranch here. The middle-aged cattleman had left his ranch in Texas to his daughter and her husband following the death of his wife, and the challenges of the arduous trail drive, not to mention the problems of starting up a new ranch, had been just the tonic he needed to get over his grief.

Other ranchers had other reasons for coming to Wyoming, though, not the least of which was the fact that this was prime country for a cattle spread. A few years earlier, there hadn't been anything out here except a few army posts, the remnants of the once-flourishing fur trade, and the

Oregon Trail, which carried hundreds of thousands of immigrants farther west. Now, with the ending of the Civil War and the arrival of the railroad, people were beginning to realize that Wyoming Territory itself was ripe for settlement. Kermit Sawyer had been here less than a year, and already he was saying that the country was getting downright crowded.

And the fella doing the most crowding, the way Sawyer saw it, was Austin Fisk.

Frenchy thought about that as he led Lon and the rest of the punchers over the rolling hills toward Wildcat Ridge and the waterhole there. Sawyer and Fisk hadn't gotten along right from the start. Fisk was a Kentuckian, for one thing, and Sawyer just naturally didn't fully trust anybody who wasn't from Texas. And Fisk was pushy, too, accustomed to getting his way. The man had arrived only a month earlier, with his herd about a week behind him. The cattle had been gaunt and worn-out when they showed up, having been driven west during the winter, stopping only when the weather was too bad to proceed. The graze along the way hadn't been good, of course. Any fool could have told Fisk that. But he had wanted to arrive in the spring, and so by God, he had gotten here in the spring, no matter how

11

hard it was on his animals!

Those Latch Hook cows would fatten up again, probably already had. Frenchy knew that. But he still couldn't imagine putting men and cattle through the hardships of such a drive, just out of sheer cussedness.

That was typical of Fisk, though. What he wanted, he went after, and devil take the hindmost!

"Frenchy," Lon said, sounding a little more nervous now that they were drawing near the disputed waterhole. "Do you reckon there'll be any trouble with Fisk's men?"

"Gun trouble, you mean?" Frenchy asked. Lon nodded.

"Could be," Frenchy said. "Only if they start it, though. Mr. Sawyer told us not to slap leather on those boys unless they go for their guns first."

He glanced over at Lon, wondering just how badly scared the young man was. Lon was brave, but he wasn't much more than a kid. Sure he was nervous; only a fool wouldn't be when there was a chance of trouble like this. And Lon had been green as grass when they'd started up here from Texas. He had toughened up some since then. He'd been mauled by wolves the previous winter and had recovered completely from that ordeal, and that showed what sort of man he was. But he might not know that yet. There might still be some self-doubts.

The only way to get over those, Frenchy figured, was to grab by the throat whatever life threw at you and keep going. He figured Lon would be all right. But as foreman of Sawyer's crew, it was his job to keep an eye on all of the men. He would watch Lon especially close, he decided.

The haze of dust in the air that Frenchy had spotted earlier was gone now. That probably meant the cattle had arrived at the waterhole. As he and the other men came in sight of the long, pine-dotted Wildcat Ridge, Frenchy saw that his guess was correct. The waterhole was at the base of the ridge, and he could see the cattle surrounding it. Some of the cows had waded out into the water, roiling the surface. A fresh surge of anger went through Frenchy. Those were Latch Hook cows down there, not Diamond S, and they had no right to be there.

The interloping cattle were accompanied by six or seven of Fisk's punchers. The men moved out away from the waterhole to meet the newcomers, leaving the cattle there to drink. Frenchy led his men on, not stopping to draw rein until only about thirty yards separated him from the first of the Latch Hook cowboys. The rest of the Diamond S punchers halted, too, spreading out on either side of Frenchy.

Fisk's men followed suit, stopping in a ragged line with one man in the center, sitting his horse a little ahead of the others. He started forward slowly, and Frenchy did likewise. As he drew nearer, he recognized the other man as Wilt Paxton, Fisk's foreman. That was good, Frenchy decided. He could talk to Paxton as an equal, *segundo* to *segundo.*

Paxton cuffed his hat back on his blond hair. He was a good-looking man about Frenchy's age. Frenchy remembered hearing that Paxton had not come all the way from Kentucky with Austin Fisk; he had signed on in Kansas, and already he had worked his way up to foreman of the outfit. That was ample evidence that he was a top hand.

He was supposed to be good with a gun, too, and Frenchy kept an eye on Paxton's right shoulder, watching for a telltale twitch, as he said, "Sort of off your range, ain't you, Paxton?"

"Not so's you'd notice," Paxton replied easily.

"This is Diamond S land," Frenchy said,

14

more impatient now. "Mr. Sawyer has the whole valley, from that range of mountains on the east side to the ones in the west."

Paxton grinned. "Sort of greedy, wouldn't you say? Of course, that's just like a Texan. . . ."

Frenchy could sense the tension gripping his companions. It grew even tighter at Paxton's mocking words. Holding his own temper in check, he said, "You'd best tell your boss that we won't stand for his stock on our range. If you get those cows out of the waterhole and drive 'em back over to the Latch Hook, there won't be any trouble."

"Won't be any trouble anyway," Paxton drawled. "This is open range, free to anybody who wants to use it."

Frenchy shook his head stubbornly. "Your boss had better check again on that. Mr. Sawyer bought this valley from McKay and Durand, the fellas who founded the town of Wind River and started the settling of this part of the territory. And they got the land from the Union Pacific after it'd been granted to the railroad by the government when it wasn't for sure which route the railroad would take. It's all legal and above board, Paxton. Plenty of Wyoming Territory *is* open range, I reckon — but not this valley!"

The smile dropped off of Paxton's face as he said, "Mr. Fisk tells it different, LeDoux. And I go by what my boss says. So we're going to graze our stock on this range and let 'em drink this water until Mr. Fisk says different. Understand?"

Frenchy's teeth grated together as his jaw tightened. He forced it open to say, "I understand you're goin' to get yourself and your crew shot all to hell if you ain't careful, mister."

For a long moment, Paxton didn't say anything. During the tense silence, Frenchy heard a few soft coughs coming from behind him, the occasional stamp of a hoof as a horse moved, the creak of saddle leather. The same noises were coming from the Latch Hook punchers. It was amazing how quiet it could get just before guns started to go off. A man could hear the tiniest sounds — as well as some louder ones like his own pulse hammering in his head.

Finally, Paxton said, "There's twice as many of you as there is of us. That's not a fair fight."

"Nobody said anything about fair," Frenchy grated. "All I said was that this is Diamond S land, and you'd better get the hell off."

Paxton hesitated a couple of seconds longer, then nodded abruptly. "All right," he said curtly. "I reckon you've got us outgunned this time, LeDoux. But it won't always be that way. I wouldn't mind seeing how we'd stack up against each other, just you and me."

"Any time," Frenchy told him.

Paxton turned his horse and jerked his head at the other Latch Hook riders. "Get those cows started back toward home," he ordered. With a mixture of reluctance and relief on their faces, the punchers moved to comply. They had to have known that if shooting had broken out, most of them likely would have died. But they were men who rode for the brand, and they would have run that risk if Paxton had forced the issue.

Frenchy, Lon, and the rest of the Diamond S men watched in grim silence as the Latch Hook riders choused the stock out of the waterhole and got it moving back toward the east, around Wildcat Ridge toward the broad canyon that had given them access to the valley. The Latch Hook spread lay beyond those mountains to the east, in another valley that was smaller and less fertile than the one in which the Diamond

S was located. It was still pretty good range, though, Frenchy knew. The only real reason Fisk was trying to push into this valley was sheer cussedness.

When the cattle were out of sight and all that was left of their presence was another haze of dust and the still-muddy waterhole, Lon edged his horse up alongside Frenchy's and said, "I thought for sure there was going to be some shooting that time."

Frenchy leaned forward in the saddle and rolled his shoulders, trying to ease the tenseness there. "For a minute, I thought so, too. But Paxton's no fool. He knew the odds were too high against him. If things had been even, well . . ." Frenchy shrugged. "No tellin' what might've happened."

"You going to tell Mr. Sawyer about this?"

The foreman nodded. "He's got a right to know. This ain't the first time we've had to chase Latch Hook stock off his range. This was the biggest bunch so far, though, and the first time Fisk's punchers just drove 'em over here out in the open. Always before there was the chance they'd just strayed."

"Not this time," Lon said.

"Nope. Not this time." Frenchy drew a deep breath. "You and the boys get back to the brandin', Lon. I'll ride back to headquarters and talk to Mr. Sawyer."

"What do you reckon he'll do? He's going to be pretty mad."

"Mad as hell is what he'll be. But he won't load all the rifles and go chargin' over to the Latch Hook to start a war. Not yet. I reckon he'll go to town and try to straighten this out legal-like. He'll need to talk to Mrs. McKay and maybe the marshal."

"You think Marshal Tyler will do something about Fisk?" Lon asked.

Frenchy rubbed his lean jaw. "Don't know if he will. Don't know if he *can*. But one thing's for certain — somebody had better do something . . . or there's going to be hell to pay around here."

2

Cole Tyler felt like a schoolboy. He felt downright foolish, in fact. But that didn't stop him from standing here on the big porch of the Wind River Emporium, waiting for Simone McKay to come out.

He had seen her go into the block-long general store a few minutes earlier, when he was walking down the other side of Grenville Avenue, Wind River's main thoroughfare. Without really thinking about it, he had crossed the broad street and stepped up onto the porch. He hadn't talked to Simone in several days, and he wanted to remedy that situation.

Not that there was anything deliberate about it. It was just that they were both busy people. Simone owned practically the entire town, which she had inherited from her late husband, Andrew, and his equally deceased partner, William Durand, so she had business matters demanding a great deal of her time and attention. And Cole was the settlement's marshal, which meant he had to deal with proddy cowboys, rambunctious railroad workers, saloonkeepers who were only as honest as they had to be, and all the hardcase drifters who naturally gravitated toward the largest settlement in this part of the territory. It was a big job, which was why he hadn't wanted it in the first place.

Cole had been a buffalo hunter, providing meat for the thousands of Union Pacific workers, when the leading citizens of Wind River had prevailed upon him to pin on a badge and become their lawman. Almost a year had passed since then, and in that time Cole had learned that the chore was every bit as troublesome as he had expected it to be — and then some.

But he was still here and still had that badge pinned to his buckskin shirt, partially because he'd found that he liked living in town more than he thought he would, and partially because of the friends he had made here in Wind River.

He was a medium-sized man with thick brown hair that fell to his broad shoulders. His face was clean-shaven, and his eyes were keen and alert. He wore a broad-brimmed brown hat, which usually dangled on the back of his neck from its chin strap, as well as denim pants and high-topped boots. A cartridge belt was strapped around his hips, and in its holster rode a well-cared-for Colt .44. On his left hip was sheathed a heavy-bladed Green River knife. He had the look of a seasoned, competent frontiersman who could handle just about anything life might throw his way.

Anything except falling in love with a woman who was much too good for him.

Of course, it was too early to even be thinking about love, Cole told himself sternly. He liked and admired Simone McKay, and anybody with eyes could see that she was beautiful, but she had never indicated that she might feel anything toward him other than friendship and respect. And she was, in a manner of speaking, his boss, which complicated things even more. She was a widow, too, and might still be grieving for her loss . . . although it had been a long time since her husband had been killed.

As he stood with his shoulders against the wall of the emporium, he took a deep breath and told himself that maybe this wasn't a good idea after all. Maybe he ought to just go on about his business —

"Hello, Cole. Goodness, I just realized I haven't seen you in several days. What have you been doing with yourself?"

He stepped away from the wall, nodding to the woman who had just emerged from the building. Simone McKay was around thirty, but unlike many frontier women who were worn out by that age and looked twenty years older, she had spent all of her life except for the last year in the east. Her skin was clear and pale, and it contrasted with the lustrous, raven's wing hair that surrounded her features. She wore a light-brown skirt and jacket over a green blouse, and a green scarf was fastened around her throat with a pearl pin. She was so pretty she just about took Cole's breath away.

"Morning, Mrs. McKay," he greeted her, then replied to her question by continuing, "I haven't been up to anything in particular. Just keeping the peace around here. That's what the town pays me for."

"Yes, I know," she said with a smile. "And you're doing an excellent job of it. I read in the paper this morning that there were only three killings in town last week."

"Yes, ma'am, I read that, too. Of course, I knew about 'em anyway, what with being the marshal and all."

"Yes, I'm sure you did," Simone said gently. "Is something bothering you, Cole?"

"Well, I was just wondering . . ." Damn,

he'd rather have faced a gang of outlaws or a bunch of angry Sioux than do this! But something kept prodding him on, and he said, "There's going to be a dance tomorrow night, the first dance we've had here in town, and I was wondering if you'd like to go with me. I know I used to be a buffalo hunter, and I still don't look like much, but I don't clean up too bad."

The words came out of him in a rush, and he felt more foolish with each one that popped out of his mouth, but he couldn't seem to stop them. When he finally reined in his tongue, he halfway expected Simone to laugh at him.

But instead she just smiled some more and said, "Why, I'd be happy to go with you, Cole. I'd planned to go, of course, but I was beginning to wonder if I was going to have an escort. It seems there aren't very many men in town who, ah, desire the pleasure of my company."

"Then they're a bunch of damned fools —" Cole began, then stopped short and grimaced. "I beg your pardon, Mrs. McKay."

"Simone," she reminded him. "You keep forgetting."

"Yes, ma'am . . . Simone."

She took a deep breath. "Well, I feel better now. And I'm looking forward to going with you to the dance. But I have to get over to the land office now. I was going over the books with Harvey here at the store, and I have to do the same thing in the office with my clerks there."

"Sure, I understand," Cole nodded. "I'll walk with you. Got to go that way to get back to my office, too."

That was a foregone conclusion, since the marshal's office and the headquarters of the Wind River Land Development Company shared the same building. Cole was debating whether or not he should take Simone's arm when a voice with a British accent hailed them from the boardwalk down the street.

Dr. Judson Kent, Wind River's only physician, was coming toward them, his long-legged strides covering the distance quickly. The medico was tall and distinguished in his dark suit and vest and bowler hat. He wore a close-cropped dark beard that was shot through with gray. He was smiling as he came up the steps onto the porch of the general store. He tipped his hat to Simone.

"Good morning, Simone. Hello, Marshal. I'm not keeping you from something, am I?"

"Nothing that can't wait a few minutes,"

Simone smiled back at him. "What can we do for you, Judson?"

"Well, actually, it was you to whom I wished to speak, my dear." Kent glanced at Cole. "No offense, Marshal."

"None taken," Cole assured him. "I've got to be getting back over to the office anyway." He tried not to show his disappointment at not being able to walk with Simone. Kent obviously wanted to speak to her in private, however.

Cole nodded pleasantly to both of them and stepped down off the porch. He had only gone a few feet when he heard Kent say, "I was hoping that you might do me the honor of accompanying me to the little soirée that's planned for tomorrow evening, Simone."

Cole stopped and swung around.

Simone looked a little flustered, which was unusual. She was normally just about the most self-possessed person Cole knew. She glanced at him, then back at Kent, and managed to smile as she said, "I'm sorry, Judson. But I've already promised someone else that I'd go with him. I certainly didn't expect to have *two* invitations so close together."

"Oh, I see." Kent made a visible effort not to appear too crestfallen. He went on,

"Would you be offended if I asked who the lucky man was?"

Cole said, "Me."

Kent looked at him and arched an eyebrow. "Indeed?" he murmured.

Now what the hell did he mean by that? Cole wondered. It was just like a damned Englishman to pack so much insinuation into one little word. And that eyebrow — !

Maybe Kent thought he wasn't good enough to go to the dance with Simone. Kent probably figured that Simone ought to be with somebody more cultured and sophisticated, somebody more experienced in the ways of the world instead of some rough-handed frontiersman. Somebody like Doctor High-and-Mighty Judson Kent himself . . .

Cole caught himself as those thoughts flashed through his mind in an instant. He had no right to think such things about Kent. The doctor was a good man, a friend as well as a fine physician. And there was no way Cole could blame him for being attracted to Simone.

"Perhaps another time, Judson," Simone was saying to him. "This won't be the only dance we ever hold here in Wind River, you know. I expect there will be a great many of them in the future."

"Certainly," Kent said with a nod. "Well, I hope you have a good time." He glanced at Cole and added, "Both of you." He reached up to tip his hat again. "I'm sure I'll see you there —"

"M-Marshal!"

Cole stiffened and turned quickly at the sound of the voice calling him. The word had been croaked out painfully, but Cole recognized the voice anyway. He saw his deputy, Billy Casebolt, stumbling across the street toward him, coming from the direction of the office.

Cole's first thought was that Casebolt had been hurt somehow. The deputy's shambling, uncertain gait seemed to indicate that. Casebolt was a tall, gangling, middle-aged man with a lean face and iron-gray hair. At the moment, he wasn't wearing his battered old hat, and his thin hair was askew. Cole hurried to meet him.

"What is it, Billy?" Cole asked as he grasped the deputy's arm. "Are you hurt?" There hadn't been any gunshots in the past few minutes, Cole was sure of that.

Casebolt managed to shake his head. "Not h-hurt," he said. "Reckon I'm just . . . sick."

Now that he was closer, Cole could see how flushed Casebolt's face was. The deputy sagged against him, and Cole suddenly became aware of heat coming through the sleeve of Casebolt's shirt. Cole brought his other hand up and laid the back of it against Casebolt's leathery forehead.

"Damn it, Billy, you're burning with fever!" Cole exclaimed.

"Knew I felt poorly when I got up this mornin'," Casebolt muttered, "but I never figgered it'd get this bad."

Cole turned his head and saw Simone and Kent still standing on the porch of the store, watching with frowns of concern. He called, "Doctor! Can you come over here?"

"Certainly." Kent came quickly down the steps and trotted across the street to join them. Simone trailed him by several feet. Without slowing down, Kent added over his shoulder to her, "You'd better stay back until I find out what's wrong, Mrs. McKay."

She nodded and slowed down, giving the three men some distance.

"He's burning up with fever," Cole said as Kent came up to them.

Kent touched Casebolt's forehead as Cole had done. A couple of seconds later, he nodded. "Indeed he is. We had better get him down to my office."

Cole lifted Casebolt's right arm and draped it across his shoulders. He put his left arm around Casebolt's waist. "Come on, Billy. We'll take you to Dr. Kent's office."

" 'S all right," Casebolt said. "I can walk —"

With the first step he took, however, he fell forward and would have pitched to the ground if Cole had not had hold of him. Kent moved up on the deputy's other side and grasped his left arm. "Let us help you, Mr. Casebolt," he said firmly. "Doctor's orders, you know."

"Is there anything I can do?" Simone called.

Kent shook his head. "Not right now, my dear."

"Let me know how he's doing."

"I will," Cole promised her.

Together, Cole and Kent got the older man down the street to the physician's office. They drew a lot of stares along the way from pedestrians on the boardwalks and passersby on the street. Quite a few of the people looked worried when they saw how ill Casebolt appeared. The deputy was well-liked in the settlement.

Cole and Kent helped Casebolt through the door and down the hall to one of the examination rooms. They assisted him onto the table there, and Casebolt lay back gratefully on the pillow at the head of the table.

"Room's spinnin' like I been on a three-day bender," he said.

"I should imagine so, with a fever like that," Kent said. "Just lie still and allow me to examine you."

Cole stepped back to give the doctor some room. All of the resentment he had felt when Kent asked Simone to the dance had vanished. At the moment, all Cole was worried about was his deputy.

Kent used his stethoscope to listen to Casebolt's chest, then examined his eyes, ears, and throat. He followed that with some prodding of the deputy's torso and a few questions about what hurt and what didn't. After several minutes, he patted Casebolt on the shoulder and said, "You just lie there and rest, Deputy. I want to talk to the marshal now, but I'll be back in a moment."

Cole didn't need to be hit over the head. He backed out of the room and stood waiting anxiously while Kent came out and closed the door softly behind him. The doctor was frowning as Cole asked, "What is it? Something pretty bad?"

"I wish I knew," Kent replied quietly.

"You mean you don't know what's causing the fever?"

"I haven't the slightest idea."

"Well . . . well, what are you going to do

31

about it?" Cole demanded.

Kent's voice was grim as he replied, "I'm afraid I don't know *that,* either."

3

Cole stared at the physician for a long moment. Finally, he demanded, "What do you mean, you don't know?"

"I can't treat a condition properly if I don't know what's causing it," Kent said. "I can try to deal with the symptoms, of course, and I intend to do that. I'm going to attempt to bring Deputy Casebolt's temperature down with some cool baths. Perhaps whatever is causing his illness will run its course and allow him to recover quickly. But even if I'm successful in reducing the fever, it could come back immediately."

"Well, that's no damn good at all!" Cole burst out. His earlier anger and resentment returned. "Maybe you just don't know enough about medicine."

Kent stared at him coldly. "I dare say I know more than anyone else in this settlement, including you, Marshal. But if you

wish to treat the patient, by all means go ahead."

Cole felt frustration clogging his throat. He swallowed hard and said, "Hell, I didn't mean it like that, and you know it, Doctor. I'm just worried about Billy."

"As am I," Kent assured him. "Why don't you allow me to get started with what I *can* do? You can stop by later to check on Deputy Casebolt, and if I have need of you, I shall send for you immediately."

"Can't complain about that," Cole admitted. "I'll see you after a while."

With that, he left the doctor's office, a worried frown on his face.

Billy Casebolt had saved his life more than once, Cole thought as he walked distractedly up the street toward the marshal's office. Casebolt had served as town constable here in Wind River during the early days of the settlement, before Cole had arrived and been persuaded to accept the newly created position of marshal. He had acquired a reputation as something of a bumbler, a garrulous old man who didn't have any business trying to be a lawman. It was true that Casebolt liked to talk, and he *was* getting a mite long in the tooth, but Cole had found him to be a dependable ally in the task of bringing law and order to the region. In

fact, Casebolt's friendly relations with the Shoshone Indians who lived in the area had even helped avert an Indian war.

Cole's job was going to be a lot harder if Casebolt didn't recover from this sickness. And there would be something even more important missing from his life if anything happened to Casebolt: a good friend.

Simone must have heard him come in, because she walked down the hall from the offices of the land development company and paused in the doorway of Cole's office. As he dropped his hat on the scarred top of the old desk and sat down, she asked, "Did Judson find out what was wrong with Deputy Casebolt?"

Cole shook his head. "Only that he's got a bad fever, and Kent's not sure what's causing it or what to do about it."

"Poor Billy," Simone sympathized. "But if anyone can help him, it's Judson. I've never known a finer doctor."

"No, I don't reckon I've ever run across a better sawbones, either." Cole shook his head bleakly. "But there's some things that can't be helped, no matter how good a doctor you have."

Simone nodded. "I'm afraid you're right. But there's no point in giving up so soon,

35

Cole. You need to be hopeful. Billy Casebolt is a tough old bird."

"He is that," Cole agreed with a slight smile. "You're right, Simone. I'll go back over there and check on him in a little while."

"Let me know if there's anything I can do to help."

"Sure thing."

She went back through the foyer to her own offices, leaving Cole to brood in his.

He tried to study some of the reward dodgers that had been sent to him, which was usually a productive way of passing the time, but he found it difficult to concentrate on the descriptions and crude sketches of men who were wanted for various crimes. After a few minutes he put the wanted posters aside, picked up his hat, and stalked out of the office. He felt like he had to be moving right now, so he decided to take a turn around town.

He had just stepped out onto the boardwalk when he saw Kermit Sawyer reining to a halt in front of the building.

Sawyer grunted as he saw Cole at the same time. The cattleman swung down from his saddle, looped his horse's reins over the hitch rail, and said, "Just the man I was lookin' for. I got a complaint to register."

"Something happen here in town, Sawyer?" Cole asked.

"Nope. Out at my ranch."

Cole shook his head. "I don't have any jurisdiction out there."

"That ain't never stopped you from buttin' in any time there's trouble. You're the only law we got around here, Tyler, and if you're goin' to use that as an excuse for stickin' your nose in where it ain't wanted, you got to remember it when folks bring their troubles to you."

Cole frowned. There was some undeniable logic in what the Texan said, but that didn't mean he had to like it. And he didn't have to like Kermit Sawyer, either. Cole knew from experience that the feeling was mutual.

Sawyer was a powerful looking man, a little taller than Cole and just about as broad in the shoulders. Age had thickened his middle some, but he still cut an impressive figure in an outfit that was all black from his boots to his hat. The pearl-handled butt of his Colt and his thick shock of snow-white hair were the only things that relieved the blackness. His rugged features were seamed and weathered and permanently tanned to the color of saddle leather. To give the devil his due, Sawyer was one of the toughest men Cole knew — and also one of the most arrogant and unpleasant.

"All right, Sawyer," Cole said with a sigh. "What sort of bur's under your saddle now?"

"It's that damn Kaintuck, Fisk. His men have been pushin' his stock over onto *my* range."

"You know that for a fact?"

"My *segundo* and some of the boys caught 'em with some Latch Hook cows at that waterhole over by Wildcat Ridge. You know damn good and well that's part of the Diamond S — and so did they." Sawyer snorted in disgust. "Fisk's foreman tried to tell Frenchy that they were on open range. You know that ain't true."

Cole nodded slowly. He might not like Sawyer, but the valley where the Texan's ranch was located *did* belong to him, right enough. "Was there any shooting?"

"Not this time, but only because my boys had Fisk's bunch outgunned by two to one. Next time, if it ain't that way, there'll likely be blood spilled."

"What do you want me to do about it?"

"How about arrestin' that land hog Fisk?"

"I can't do that," Cole said. "Like I told you before, I don't have any legal jurisdiction outside of town. And even if I did, I'm not a judge. That's what you need, Sawyer. You need a lawyer and a judge to settle this."

Sawyer grimaced, as if the very thought of dealing with lawyers and judges left a bad taste in his mouth. "That's what I was afraid you'd say, damn it. Where I come from, a man settles his own problems without havin' to go through all that legal foofaraw." He sighed. "But I reckon what I'd best do is talk to Miz McKay and line up whatever I'll need to prove that valley's mine."

"Good idea," Cole told him. He was surprised — but glad — that Sawyer was prepared to be reasonable about this.

"Fisk better watch out, though," the Texan went on. "I'll only be prodded so far." With that, he stalked into the building without looking back.

The encounter with Sawyer had distracted Cole for a few minutes, but as soon as the cattleman was gone, Cole's thoughts returned to Billy Casebolt. He wasn't going to wait any longer. He strode down the street toward the building which housed Judson Kent's office, examination rooms, and living quarters.

When Cole reached the neat, little building, he found Kent in the office, seated at the desk with the human skeleton called Reginald hanging from its stand in its ac-

39

customed spot nearby. Kent had a thick book open on the desk in front of him. He looked up when Cole entered the room.

"I know I haven't been gone long," the lawman said, "but how's Billy doing?"

"He's resting as comfortably as can be expected," Kent replied. "I'm going back to look in on him in a moment, but I wanted to check some things in my medical books while I had the chance."

"Well? Did you figure out anything?"

Kent shook his head. "I'm afraid Deputy Casebolt's condition is as much of a mystery as ever. He has no other symptoms of the grippe, which sometimes produces a high fever, nor of dropsy or ague or croup. It isn't scarlet fever, either." The doctor sighed and closed the medical book. "I fear this is some sort of new ailment, the likes of which I've never seen before."

"That's not very encouraging."

"No, it's not. But Deputy Casebolt is in good health for his age, and I believe it's quite likely he'll pull through this on his own if we keep him comfortable and try to cool off that fever."

"I thought a fever had to burn itself out," Cole said.

"Many doctors believe that to be so, perhaps even most of them. In a situation like this, they would pile quilts on a feverish patient and try to bring the temperature up even more. But I've never found that to be a particularly effective solution. When a fever gets too high, it does much more harm than good."

"In other words," Cole snapped, "you're treating Billy different than most doctors would."

Kent shrugged. "You could look at it that way, if you wish."

"I don't like it, Doctor. I'm going in to see him."

Kent stood up and squarely met Cole's stare. "Go ahead. But please don't upset him."

Cole nodded curtly and left the office, heading down the hall toward the examination room where he had last seen Casebolt. None of the other rooms were occupied at the moment; it was evidently a slow day for Kent's practice.

Which must have been why he had time to ask Simone McKay to go to that dance with him. . . .

Cole shook off that thought. He needed to concentrate on Casebolt's problems now, rather than his own.

The deputy's eyes were closed, but they flickered open when Cole came into the

41

room. "H-howdy, Marshal," he said weakly. "Sorry I'm . . . laid up like this. I know I ought to . . . ought to be doin' my job. . . ."

"Don't you worry about that, Billy," Cole said, squeezing the older man's shoulder. "Things are pretty peaceful around here right now." He didn't say anything about Kermit Sawyer's trouble with Austin Fisk. No point in worrying Casebolt about that.

"They don't . . . stay peaceful for long . . . in Wind River," Casebolt said.

"Well, that's usually true," Cole admitted. "But maybe they'll surprise us this time. Is there anything I can do for you?"

"I been thinkin' . . . When I was out at Two Ponies' camp, I met this feller . . . a shaman, he was . . . called Black Otter . . . claimed he could cure most any sickness . . . He took care of me . . . when I had that bullet hole in me."

From behind Cole, Judson Kent said, "Absolutely not. I won't allow some Indian medicine man to treat one of my patients."

Casebolt blinked and frowned. "Oh, hell, I . . . I'm sorry, Doc . . . didn't see you come in . . . and I don't mean no disrespect . . . but sometimes them Injuns, they know . . . they know a heap more'n we give 'em credit for. I thought it wouldn't hurt nothin' —"

Kent came up on the other side of the

table and laid a hand on Casebolt's arm. "No, Deputy, I don't think that would be wise. Some savage who's spent his entire life in the wilderness can hardly be expected to know as much about medicine as a man educated at Oxford, wouldn't you say?"

"I . . . I reckon so."

"I don't see anything wrong with letting this fella Black Otter have a look at Billy," Cole said. "Couldn't do any harm, could it?"

"It might," Kent said stubbornly. "It certainly could if Black Otter proposed some course of barbaric treatment that would result in Deputy Casebolt's death. Pardon me for speaking so bluntly, but you'd be risking his life to expose him to such a thing, Marshal."

Casebolt reached up and caught the sleeve of Cole's buckskin shirt. "Jus' never you mind, Marshal," he said. "Doc Kent's the smartest feller I ever seen . . . He'll take good care of me."

Cole leaned over the table and peered down into the gaunt, flushed face of his deputy. "I'll fetch Two Ponies and Black Otter if you want me to, Billy," he offered.

Casebolt shook his head. "Nope. We'll go along . . . like we been doin'."

Reluctantly, Cole said, "Well, all right. If

you're sure."

"I'm sure," Casebolt said.

Cole looked at the physician. "You keep me posted," he said.

Kent nodded. "Of course."

Cole patted Casebolt's shoulder again. "I'll be back by in a little while, Billy. You just take it easy until then."

"Reckon I will," Casebolt said. "Don't feel up to doin' much of anything else."

Cole left the room. He hoped Kent was right and that Casebolt had made the correct decision not to seek help from the Shoshones. If anything, Casebolt looked worse than he had before.

Casebolt had been to see the elephant a time or two, Cole thought as he left the doctor's office. The leathery old man had faced more than his share of dangers and come through all of them. But now he might be struck down for good by something so mysterious that nobody even knew what it was.

It wasn't fair, Cole told himself bitterly. It just damned well wasn't fair. . . .

Judson Kent bathed Casebolt's face and chest with cool water once more, then left one of the damp cloths lying on the deputy's forehead. "I'll be right back," he told Casebolt.

"I'll be here, Doc," Casebolt said weakly.

Deep trenches appeared in Kent's cheeks above the neatly trimmed beard as he left the room and walked slowly back to the office. He sighed heavily as he looked at the skeleton hanging there. "Ah, Reginald, what am I to do now?"

Reginald didn't say anything.

Was he just playing God? Kent thought. Had he so stubbornly refused to even consider seeking help from the Shoshone shaman because of vanity? Or even worse, had he refused because his nose was still out of joint about Simone McKay going to the dance with Marshal Tyler? If that was the case, he was a disgrace to his profession and to the title of "Doctor."

"That's what's wrong with the world, old boy," Kent said to Reginald as he slumped into the chair behind his desk. "Too many questions . . . and not nearly enough answers."

4

It was late that afternoon, and Kent had just finished wrapping up the sprained ankle of a twelve-year-old boy, whose mother hovered anxiously nearby, when he heard a commotion outside. Quite a few people were shouting, and when he glanced out the window of the examination room, he saw several men running past in the alley outside, heading for Grenville Avenue.

"There you are, Tom," Kent said as he stepped back. "You need to stay off that ankle for a few days, but I'm confident it will be all right. Have your father make a crutch for you, so that you can get around if you need to while the sprain is healing."

The boy nodded, and the mother said, "I'll sure tell my husband to do that, Dr. Kent. What do we owe you?"

"Fifty cents will do nicely," Kent told her. His mind was on what was going on outside; he could still hear quite a bit of shouting, and it seemed to be getting closer. The sounds had a touch of fear to them.

The woman dug a fifty-cent piece out of her bag and dropped it in Kent's outstretched hand. "Thank you kindly, Doc," she said. Then she turned to her son and went on, "and if I ever catch you up on top of that chicken house again, Tommy, I'll whale the livin' tar out of you!"

"Aw, Ma, I didn't mean to fall off," the youngster protested.

"Come on," she said as she helped him down from the table and then led him out while he hopped on his good leg. "I got to get home and do your chores as well as mine, now."

Kent followed along behind them, anxious to see what was happening outside. The sight that met his eyes as he stepped out onto the porch of his office was one of the last things he would have expected to see, and yet he shouldn't have been surprised at all, he thought, as he frowned in disapproval.

Cole Tyler was riding down the street toward the doctor's office with a couple of Indians beside him and four more warriors trailing along behind. Several dozen people were hurrying along the boardwalks on both sides of the street, staying roughly even with

Cole and the Indians and shouting questions at the marshal.

Kent strode angrily into the street to meet them. He looked up at Cole as the lawman drew rein. "You just couldn't leave well enough alone, could you, Marshal?" Kent asked. "You had to involve these . . . these . . ."

"I'd watch what I said if I was you, Doctor," Cole told him in a cool tone of voice, as if knowing that Kent had been about to use the word *savages.* He went on, "Two Ponies and Black Otter have been kind enough to come into town to visit their friend, and I reckon we ought to respect that."

Kent took a deep breath and managed to control his emotions. He said, "You're right, of course. Please, tell your companions to come in."

A slight feeling of nervousness went through Kent as the two Indians with Cole swung down from their ponies. His lack of familiarity with Indians would have made it impossible for him to identify them by tribe had he not already known they were Shoshones. They had never come into town before, although there had been talk during a time of troubles the previous fall about Two Ponies coming to Wind River to talk

48

peace with an army officer. That meeting had not been necessary after all, as it turned out.

Kent wasn't the only one who was anxious. Most of the townspeople who had gathered around to stare at the visitors looked worried, even though the Shoshone had never bothered the settlers. Kent hoped everyone kept a level head and that no one would start any trouble.

"This is Two Ponies," Cole said as he indicated the larger of the two men who had dismounted with him and joined Kent in front of the building. The Shoshone chief was a large, powerful man of middle age, with streaks of gray in his long, dark hair, which was pulled back and tied behind his head. He wore buckskin leggings, moccasins, and a chest piece made of animal bones. He nodded gravely to Kent.

Cole went on, "And this is Black Otter." The shaman was smaller than Two Ponies and more twisted with age. His hair was completely gray, and he wore a buckskin shirt in addition to leggings. His dark eyes were bright and alert as he said something to Kent in the Shoshone tongue.

Two Ponies translated. "Black Otter says he is honored to meet another healer. He has heard much about you, Doc-tor Kent."

"And I've heard a great deal about him," Kent replied, trying to be polite. He didn't add that he'd heard more than he ever wanted to know about the Shoshone medicine man. He turned to Cole and went on quietly, "I thought we had agreed —"

"I got to thinking about it," Cole said curtly, "and I didn't see any reason why Black Otter shouldn't at least take a look at Billy."

"I advise against it, as a doctor and as Deputy Casebolt's friend."

"Billy is friend of the Shoshones," Two Ponies said emphatically. "Shoshones want to help him."

"I'm sure you do," Kent told the chief, making an effort to remain calm and patient. "But he's already under medical care —"

Black Otter spoke up again, and Kent couldn't help but glare at the interruption.

"Black Otter says Shoshone medicine can help Billy, can make him well again," Two Ponies translated.

"How can he know that?" Kent demanded. "He hasn't even seen the patient yet!"

"That's right," Cole put in. "So how do you know that he *can't* help Billy?"

They weren't going to be satisfied until

they had gone through with this spectacle, Kent saw. Grudgingly, he nodded. "All right, come in, come in," he said, not bothering any longer to hide the asperity in his voice as he turned to climb the few steps to the porch.

Cole glanced at Two Ponies and said, "Will your men be all right out here?"

"My warriors will cause no trouble," Two Ponies replied. "Can you say the same for the people of your town?"

"I'll make sure of it," Cole said. He lifted his voice and called out, "Listen up, folks! Two Ponies, Black Otter, and I are going into the doctor's office with Doc Kent. The rest of Two Ponies' men are going to stay out here, and I don't want anybody bothering them."

One of the citizens shouted, "What about *them,* Marshal? How do we know they won't go on some sort of rampage?"

"Yeah!" another man added. "You know you can't trust any of them redskins!"

As a few angry catcalls echoed those concerns, a new voice boomed out even louder. "I'll keep an eye on things out here, Brother Tyler," a huge man in a blacksmith's apron said as he moved easily through the crowd. Jeremiah Newton was not only Wind River's blacksmith, he was also a preacher,

51

and he had no trouble making himself heard above the hubbub. The protesting voices died away as Jeremiah glared around at the townspeople. Tall and as powerfully built as a buffalo, Jeremiah could generally quell arguments with his sheer presence.

"Thanks, Jeremiah," Cole told the massive blacksmith. "The Shoshone don't mean any harm, and I'd like to think the same of the folks here in town."

Jeremiah folded his arms like the trunks of small trees across his broad chest. "There'll be no trouble here, Brother Tyler," he promised. "To make sure of that, I'll witness to our red brethren while you're busy inside the doctor's office."

Kent was growing impatient. "I'll take you to see Deputy Casebolt now," he said crisply to the Shoshone visitors. If he had to do this, he wanted to get it over with.

Cole and the two Shoshones stepped up onto the porch. Kent ushered them inside and took them down the hall to the room where Billy Casebolt was resting.

The deputy was awake. He was too weak to sit up, but he managed to grin as he saw Two Ponies and Black Otter come into the room behind Kent. "Howdy, fellers," he greeted them, his voice shaky but cheerful. "Didn't . . . didn't expect to see you here."

52

"Marshal Tyler came to our village," Two Ponies said. "He told us that our good friend Billy was very sick. We would have come to visit you, even if we did not believe that Black Otter's medicine can help make you well again."

"Please try not to disturb him too much," Kent said. "Deputy Casebolt needs his rest."

Black Otter spoke to Two Ponies in Shoshone, and the chief replied. Black Otter nodded and stepped forward. He reached out with a gnarled hand to press his palm against Casebolt's forehead. He pulled back with an exclamation.

"Y-yeah," Casebolt grunted. "Hot enough to . . . fry an egg on . . . ain't I?"

Black Otter reached underneath his shirt and brought out some sort of gourd with eagle feathers tied to it. He began to shake it over Casebolt's head, causing a loud rattling sound. Kent realized the gourd had been hollowed out and something — probably beans or pebbles — had been placed inside it. Black Otter continued shaking the rattle, moving it slowly from Casebolt's head down over his body to his feet. As the shaman shook the rattle, he also stamped his feet lightly on the floor and chanted something.

"Oh, really!" Kent said, unable to suppress the exclamation.

Cole and Two Ponies both shot glares of disapproval at Kent, but Black Otter seemed to ignore him. The Shoshone medicine man brought the rattle back up Casebolt's body, holding it so close to the deputy as he shook it that several times it touched Casebolt's lanky frame. All the while, Black Otter continued his stamping and chanting. Casebolt watched the proceedings with wide eyes, occasionally swallowing hard.

When Black Otter reached Casebolt's head a second time with the gourd rattle, he put it aside and leaned over the deputy, cupping his hands together and placing them on Casebolt's forehead. Kent stepped forward, saying, "Here now, what's he doing?"

Cole put a hand on the physician's arm to stop him from interfering. "I reckon Black Otter knows what he's doing," Cole said.

"Yes, but I don't," Kent protested. There was nothing he could do, however. Between Cole's hand on his arm and the hard stare Two Ponies was giving him, he realized it might be dangerous to intrude on the ceremony Black Otter was carrying out.

The shaman had formed a tube of his cupped hands as he pressed them to Case-bolt's head. Now he leaned over even more and put his mouth to the end of that make-shift tube. He inhaled loudly.

In a quiet voice, Two Ponies said, "Black Otter is trying to suck out the evil ghost that is causing the sickness in our friend Billy."

"Of all the utter balderdash —" Kent subsided again as both Cole and the Shoshone chieftain glowered at him.

But it was insane, he thought. Not only the theory that some sort of evil ghost was causing Casebolt's illness, but the idea that it could be sucked out of his body like that. It was all a lot of pagan, unscientific mumbo-jumbo as far as Kent was concerned. Two Ponies and Black Otter evidently had complete faith in the method, however. And as for Cole, well, the marshal was worried enough about his deputy to try anything.

Kent restrained his impatience only with an effort as several minutes went by and Black Otter continued what he was doing. Finally, the old man straightened and stepped back with a shake of his head. A few sentences in Shoshone rapped out from him.

"Well, now that he admits he's not going to be able to help Deputy Casebolt —" Kent began.

Two Ponies interrupted him. "Black Otter says that the ghost inside friend Billy is strong, very strong. The ghost has hold of Billy's spirit and will not let go."

"That's ridiculous," Kent snorted.

"Have you got a better idea of what's causing his fever?" Cole asked angrily. "You haven't had any more luck curing him than Black Otter did."

"He's been under my care less than six hours," Kent shot back. "That's hardly a fair test of my skills as a doctor."

Casebolt lifted a trembling hand. "Fellers, fellers, I wish you wouldn't . . . fight over me. . . ."

Black Otter spoke quickly, the words tumbling out of his mouth. Two Ponies listened, then turned to Cole. "He says that he can drive the ghost out of friend Billy's body, but to do it we must take him to our village."

"Absolutely not!" Kent burst out. "This man cannot be moved."

"Why would Billy have to go to your village?" Cole asked, ignoring Kent's protest.

"This is something I cannot say," Two Ponies replied with a frown. "Some medicine must not be spoken of."

Cole turned to Black Otter and looked intently at him. "You're sure you can help

56

Billy?" he asked. Two Ponies translated the question.

Black Otter replied with a firm nod and another burst of Shoshone. Two Ponies said, "As sure as I am that all rivers flow to the Father of Waters and all spirits flow to the Great Spirit. These are the words of Black Otter."

Cole drew in a deep breath, then nodded abruptly. "Might as well give it a chance."

Kent stared at him, open-mouthed. He could not believe what he was hearing. "You can't be serious, Cole," he said when he was able to overcome his surprise enough to speak again. "Deputy Casebolt is under my care, and I forbid that such an utterly ludicrous course of action be followed."

"Why don't we ask Billy?" Cole suggested.

"He's in no shape to make a decision like that."

Casebolt said, "Beggin' . . . your pardon . . . Doc. But I reckon I . . . I trust ol' Black Otter. If he says he can . . . can fix me up . . . I don't mind him tryin'."

"That settles it," Cole said before Kent could say anything else. "You reckon you can ride, Billy?"

"There is no need for friend Billy to ride," Two Ponies put in. "We will make him a travois."

Casebolt nodded. "Sounds all right . . . by me."

They were all ignoring him now, Kent realized. It wasn't a good feeling. And yet he could tell from the expressions on the face of Cole and Two Ponies, as well as the determination of Casebolt's weathered features, that it would do no good to argue. Still, he couldn't allow them to go through with this without saying anything.

He folded his arms across his chest and told them sternly, "You're doing this over my objections and against my best medical judgment, gentlemen. I won't be responsible for what happens."

"Don't worry . . . Doc," Casebolt said. "I'll be all right."

"I pray that you're correct, Deputy Casebolt. Because if you're not, you won't need a doctor anymore. You'll need an undertaker."

With that, Kent turned on his heel and stalked out of the examining room. There was nothing left for him to do except to wash his hands of the entire matter.

That, and hope that somehow Black Otter's barbaric "medicine" would do the trick after all.

5

Frenchy hauled back on the reins and brought the team of horses pulling the ranch wagon to a halt in front of the general store. Kermit Sawyer was on the seat beside Frenchy, and he stood up to step directly from the wagon onto the raised porch of the emporium. Sawyer turned and spoke to Frenchy and the men on horseback who had accompanied the wagon from the Diamond S into Wind River.

"It'll likely take me a while to get this order filled," Sawyer said. "You boys can go get a drink, but no gamblin' and no fightin', savvy?"

"Sure, boss," Frenchy said. "I'll keep an eye on 'em, don't you worry."

Sawyer grinned. "If you're tryin' to make me feel better, you ain't succeedin', Frenchy. When you first signed on with my crew, you were the biggest hell-raiser west of the Trinity, you ol' Cajun."

"That was a long time ago, boss," Frenchy protested as hoots of laughter came from Lon Rogers and the other hands. Most of the crew had been left on the ranch, but in this rugged territory, even a routine trip into town to buy supplies could lead to trouble. Sawyer insisted that a few of the Diamond S punchers come along with the wagon whenever it headed for Wind River.

Besides, a trip to town was a good way to reward hard work. This wasn't payday, but the men could all afford a couple of shots of whiskey apiece.

Sawyer turned and went into the general store, taking from his coat a piece of brown paper with this month's order scribbled on it. The emporium's manager, Harvey Raymond, and his clerks would fill the order and load it onto the wagon while Frenchy and the other men went over to one of the saloons.

There were plenty of those to choose from in Wind River. Some of the saloonkeepers had moved on when the railhead of the Union Pacific was transferred farther west, but others had stayed, and in fact even more had arrived in the intervening months. As the only good-sized settlement for eighty or ninety miles around, Wind River was a prime location for drinking establishments of every sort. There were regular saloons, gambling dens, dance halls, and out-and-out brothels. Businesses that had once been housed in large canvas tents were now permanent.

Frenchy set the brake on the wagon and hopped down from the seat as the other men dismounted and tied their horses to the hitch rail. One of the cowboys suggested, "How 'bout we head on over to Parker's place, fellas?"

"Sounds all right to me," Frenchy nodded. "One place is as good as another."

Spurs jangling and bootheels clomping on the broad planks of the boardwalk, the men strolled toward a big building with an impressive three-story false front and a large sign with curlicued letters emblazoned across it. *PARKER'S PRONGHORN SALOON,* the sign read. Smaller, plainer letters beneath the name proclaimed, WIND RIVER'S OLDEST AND FINEST.

Bragging about being the oldest saloon in a town established less than a year earlier wasn't much of a boast, Frenchy thought with a grin. But Parker's was a good place anyway, with relatively honest games of chance, dance floor girls that weren't completely worn out and were even occasionally pretty, and whiskey that a man could drink without worrying overmuch about getting the blind staggers or falling down dead. Of course, the visit today would be a quick one, but later in the month, when payday rolled around, some of the Diamond S punchers would spend the night at the Pronghorn and come out the next morning broke and hung over — but somehow satisfied.

Lon and the other cowboys were laughing and talking, but although Frenchy walked alongside them, he didn't really take part in their ribald banter. For one thing, he was a few years older than the rest of them, and for another, he was the foreman. He had to hold himself a little apart, so that the men would respect him and know that he meant it whenever he gave an order. It was sort of a burden, and sometimes he missed the days when he could be as carefree as the rest of them, but Kermit Sawyer had made him the *segundo.* Sawyer was counting on him.

That was why Frenchy didn't hesitate to say sharply, "Hold it, boys!" when he spotted some horses with a familiar brand tied up in front of the Pronghorn. "Maybe we better find someplace else to drink."

"Aw, why, Frenchy?" Lon wanted to know. The other men echoed the question.

Before Frenchy could answer it, several men pushed through the batwinged entrance to the saloon and came out onto the boardwalk. The man in the lead froze, and the others followed suit. The Diamond S punchers saw the newcomers, and everyone stiffened in sudden anticipation of trouble.

The man who had just led half a dozen cowboys out of the saloon smiled, but it wasn't a very pleasant expression. "Hello, LeDoux," Wilt Paxton greeted Frenchy. "You're not fixing to tell me that the Pronghorn belongs to the Diamond S, too, and that Latch Hook riders aren't wanted there?"

"Take it easy, boys," Frenchy said under his breath to his companions. "Mr. Sawyer said no fightin', remember?"

To Paxton, he went on, "I reckon you Latch Hook boys can drink anywhere you want to, long as the other people in the place don't mind."

"What about you?" Paxton asked. "You heading for the Pronghorn?"

One of the other men answered before Frenchy could. "We were," he called out, "but I don't reckon it's had long enough to air out just yet. We'll come back later when the stink's gone."

Frenchy bit back a curse. "We're not lookin' for trouble," he said quickly, but he knew it was too late. The gibe from the

63

Diamond S rider had struck its targets, and the Latch Hook cowboys all looked tense and angry, ready to stab their hands toward their guns.

Another man pushed through the batwings and said curtly, "What's going on here?"

Without looking around, Paxton replied, "Just a little run-in with some of those Texas boys, Mr. Fisk."

Austin Fisk was tall and slender and held himself upright in a stiff, military carriage. He wore a dark suit and hat and had a neatly trimmed, gray mustache underneath his prominent nose. He looked at Frenchy and the other Diamond S riders and said, "You're some of Sawyer's men, eh?"

"That's right," Frenchy said.

"That one's called LeDoux," Paxton told his boss. "He's Sawyer's *segundo* and the gent who ran us off from that waterhole after you told us to take the cattle over there, Mr. Fisk." Paxton's grin was ugly as he went on. "Him and the others were mighty brave when there were twice as many of them as there was of us. Now that the odds are even he starts yelping about how they ain't looking for any trouble."

"Is that so?" Fisk murmured. "Well, we're not looking for trouble, either, but we won't run from it. I think it's time we settled this problem, if we can. LeDoux, where's your boss?"

Frenchy hesitated, not knowing if he should get Sawyer involved in this or not. But Sawyer was already involved, of course, when you got right down to it. Frenchy inclined his head toward the emporium and said, "Back yonder in the general store."

"Fetch him," Fisk rapped in the tone of a man who expected unquestioning obedience, even from men who didn't work for him.

Frenchy's anger bristled, but before he could say anything, Lon Rogers spoke up. "Mr. Sawyer's already on his way down here, Frenchy."

The foreman glanced over his shoulder and saw Kermit Sawyer striding briskly along the boardwalk toward the confrontation. The ranks of the Diamond S punchers parted to let him through.

"What's goin' on here, Frenchy?" Sawyer asked curtly as he came to a stop beside his *segundo.*

"I can answer that, Sawyer," Austin Fisk said before Frenchy had a chance to reply. "I'm glad you're here. Now we can get to the bottom of that ludicrous claim of yours about owning that entire valley."

Sawyer's eyes narrowed. "Howdy, Fisk. I sort of figured you'd be around if there was some sort of trouble goin' on."

Fisk's lean features flushed with anger. "Your men are the ones who have been causing trouble, Sawyer. Just the other day they threatened some of my riders who were merely following my orders."

"Well, then, that'd be your fault, because your orders took 'em onto Diamond S range," Sawyer shot back.

"Open range, you mean."

Sawyer shook his head. "Not a bit. That valley's mine and has been for almost a year. I've got papers and witnesses to prove it."

"I haven't seen any papers, nor heard from any witnesses."

"No, and you won't unless you take me to court."

Fisk snorted in contempt. "The nearest court's in Cheyenne."

"That's right. You want to hash this out legally, that's where you'll have to go, I reckon." Sawyer paused, then added in a harder voice, "Where I come from, men usually take care of their own disputes without a bunch of damned lawyers and judges."

Fisk smiled thinly. "Possession is nine-tenths of the law, eh?"

"So I've heard. And if you don't keep your men and your stock off my land, you're likely to find out just how Texans settle things."

This wasn't going very well, Frenchy thought. Sawyer and Fisk had started out talking rationally enough, even though it was obvious that neither man was going to budge an inch in his beliefs. But they were getting edgier now, and the Latch Hook crew standing behind Fisk all had their hands close to their guns. Frenchy didn't have to look around to know that the Diamond S cowboys were also ready for shooting to break out. Hell, for that matter his own right hand was only inches away from the smooth walnut grips of his Colt.

"I don't take kindly to being threatened, Sawyer," Fisk said sharply.

"And I don't like it when some bastard tries to push his way onto my range!" Sawyer answered, even more harshly.

Fisk pulled his coat back. He was wearing a pistol in a cross-draw rig, the holster tilted forward to the left of his belt buckle. Frenchy was vaguely aware that all the other pedestrians had cleared the boardwalk on this side of the street, and even folks on the other side of Grenville Avenue were ducking into doorways. Somebody shouted

67

somewhere, but Frenchy was too wrapped up in what was about to happen to understand the words. He had taken part in showdowns like this before, and he had the uncomfortable feeling that somebody was about to die. . . .

Suddenly, alarm in his voice, Fisk said, "Hold it!" He lifted his arms, moving slowly so as not to spook anyone on either side into reaching for a gun. He went on, "Wilt, take the boys, mount up, and get out of here. Go back to the ranch."

"But, boss —" Wilt Paxton began.

"Just do as I say, damn it! Now!"

Paxton grimaced, then said grudgingly, "All right, Mr. Fisk. I reckon you know what you're doing." To the other Latch Hook riders, he added, "Come on, boys."

Sawyer, Frenchy, Lon, and the rest of the Diamond S men stood there and watched warily as Paxton and his fellow cowboys stepped off the boardwalk, went to their horses, and swung up into their saddles. Everyone from the Diamond S suspected that this might be a trick of some sort. But when Paxton looked one more time at Fisk, the Kentuckian made a curt gesture, indicating that they should go. Paxton called out, "Let's ride." He and his companions moved off down the street, heading east.

Austin Fisk was still standing in front of the saloon, gazing stonily at the Texans. Frenchy wondered what in blazes was going on, but then, the next moment, a female voice said from behind him, "Excuse us, please. Can we get through?"

Once again the tight knot of Diamond S punchers parted, and this time two young women walked past them. Both of them were wearing expensive dresses and were quite attractive. The older one, whom Frenchy judged to be in her early twenties, was a green-eyed brunette, tall and lithe. The second young woman, who was probably no more than eighteen or nineteen, had blond hair and blue eyes, was shorter and more lushly curved than her companion. There was a resemblance between them despite their differences, and Frenchy realized they were likely sisters.

Austin Fisk's features remained an inexpressive mask until the brunette came up to him and said, "We're finished with our shopping, Dad. Are you ready to go?"

Fisk's expression softened slightly as he nodded and said, "You and your sister go on down to the wagon, Alexandra. I'll be there in a moment."

The young woman called Alexandra looked over her shoulder at the group of

Diamond S men, and for an instant, her eyes met Frenchy's. He read suspicion and dislike in her gaze, as well as a keen intelligence. Alexandra Fisk was smart enough to realize that she and her sister had just interrupted something, Frenchy thought.

The blonde paid no attention to the Diamond S cowboys, however, other than to glance at them and give them an innocent smile. Several of Sawyer's punchers reached up hurriedly to tug their hats off and nod politely to her.

"Go on, Catherine," Fisk said to her, his voice stem.

Catherine Fisk appeared not to have noticed the warning tone. She smiled at the Diamond S riders again, then moved off down the boardwalk after her sister. They headed toward a big wagon parked in the next block.

Frenchy understood now what had happened. Fisk's daughters had emerged from the general store down the street and started toward the saloon, obviously intending to meet their father there. Fisk had seen them coming and realized that if any shooting broke out, the two young women would be in imminent danger of being struck by stray bullets. That was why he had called off the confrontation so abruptly.

But the showdown had merely been postponed, Frenchy knew. Fisk confirmed that by saying in a low voice, "I'll be seeing you again, Sawyer."

"Don't doubt it," Sawyer grunted. "I just hope I see you first, otherwise I might wind up with a bullet between my shoulder blades."

Fisk flushed again. "I'm no backshooter," he declared icily. "We'll settle this man to man."

"Until then, keep your damn cattle off my range."

Fisk made no reply. He turned and walked stiffly toward the wagon where his daughters were waiting.

The tension on the boardwalk eased. Sawyer turned to his men and said, "Go get your drinks. We'll be pullin' out for home in a little while."

The Diamond S men started into the Pronghorn. As they did so, the wagon driven by Austin Fisk rattled past. Frenchy hung back from the others and watched it roll by. Fisk was pointedly staring straight ahead, and Catherine was talking animatedly to him. Alexandra, though, turned her head and coolly returned Frenchy's look.

She was mighty nice-looking, Frenchy mused. Too bad she was Fisk's daughter.

"Frenchy." Sawyer's voice broke into his thoughts. "You comin' or not?"

"I'm comin', boss, I'm comin'," Frenchy replied. He pushed through the batwings after the others and entered the cool, dim interior of the Pronghorn, which had the typical saloon smell of liquor, smoke, and sweat.

But as he did, he was still thinking about a tall young woman with dark brown hair and the most striking green eyes he had ever seen.

6

Cole hoped he hadn't made the worst mistake of his life. If he had, it wouldn't be him paying the price for his mistake in judgment.

It would be Billy Casebolt.

A night and a morning had passed since they had left Wind River to journey here to the village of Two Ponies and his band of Shoshones, and still Casebolt burned with fever. So far the old shaman Black Otter had done nothing except rattle gourds and bang on a little drum and dance around while he chanted monotonously. All of that was so Casebolt would be prepared to accept the healing medicine that Black Otter would soon perform, Two Ponies had explained to Cole.

But as far as the marshal could see, Casebolt was just getting worse. The deputy was weaker today, less coherent when he spoke.

They had left Wind River late the previous afternoon. After Black Otter had examined Casebolt, the Shoshones had ridden out, much to the relief of the citizens, and Cole and Casebolt had met the Indians later, outside of town. Casebolt had been able to ride that far. The two lawmen had left town by way of the back alleys, so that no one knew where they were going except Dr. Judson Kent and Jeremiah Newton. Kent had promised that he would tell Simone McKay what was going on.

And since he wasn't going to be there for that dance, Cole had reflected, it looked like Kent might get to accompany Simone after all. That was a stroke of luck for the physician, but it gnawed at Cole.

Leaving Wind River surreptitiously was Cole's idea. Given the distrust that most of the townspeople still felt for the Shoshones — even though they had never been given any real reason to feel that way — Cole had thought it was best that no one except for a few know where he and Casebolt had gone. If Black Otter was able to cure Casebolt, all well and good; if not, the citizens wouldn't have the opportunity to leap to the conclusion that the Shoshones were to blame for the deputy's death. Of course, the plan depended on Judson Kent keeping his mouth shut, and Cole wasn't completely sure he could rely on the Englishman any-more.

By the time Cole and Casebolt rendez-voused with the Shoshones a couple of miles southwest of town, Two Ponies and his warriors had felled several small trees and constructed a travois out of them, trim-ming the branches and lashing the slender trunks together with rawhide. Casebolt lay down gratefully on the travois, the side poles of which were tied to Two Ponies' horse, and the group had set off for the Shoshone village.

Night had fallen before they reached the cluster of lodges along the banks of a small creek. Casebolt had immediately been taken into one of the lodges, and Cole had fol-lowed. Black Otter brought out his gourds and drum and launched into whatever it was he was still doing now, more than twelve hours later.

Cole didn't know if the old shaman had slept during that time; he didn't much think so. Two Ponies had taken Cole to his lodge the night before, had given him food and a place to sleep, but the chief's lodge was near the one where Casebolt had been taken, and Cole's sleep was restless. Every time he roused wakefully, he had heard the rattling and drumming.

Now it was afternoon of the next day, and as Cole watched unobtrusively from the side of the lodge where Casebolt lay on a pile of buffalo robes, he wondered how much longer this could possibly go on.

Two Ponies was seated cross-legged next to Cole. As Black Otter lay down his gourd and drum, the chief leaned closer to Cole and said, "This part of the ritual is finished."

Cole suppressed the impulse to say that it was about time. Offending his hosts wouldn't be a very smart thing to do. Instead, he said, "Billy doesn't look any different. What happens now?"

"Now we must take him to the place of healing."

Cole frowned. "You didn't say anything about having to go somewhere else. Or is this place of healing here in the village?"

Two Ponies shook his head and said, "Not in the village. But near. It will not take long."

"Can I talk to Billy before we go?" Cole asked with a nod toward the sick man.

Two Ponies spoke to Black Otter in Shoshone, and the old shaman nodded. Cole got to his feet, his muscles a little stiff from sitting for so long, and went over to kneel beside Casebolt. The deputy's eyes were closed. Cole said, "How are you doing,

76

Billy? Can you hear me?"

Casebolt's eyes flickered open weakly. "I . . . I hear you, Marshal," he said. "I don't . . . feel so good. . . ."

"I know," Cole told him, resting a hand on Casebolt's shoulder and squeezing reassuringly. "Two Ponies says they've got to take you somewhere else close by. They call it the place of healing. I reckon that means you'll be all right soon."

"Sure . . . hope so. I feel . . . downright poorly."

Two Ponies said quietly, "We will take him now."

"I'll be right beside you, Billy," Cole promised. "Don't forget that."

He straightened and stepped back while several burly warriors lifted Casebolt and carried him out of the lodge. Cole followed. The Shoshones placed Casebolt on the travois again. Instead of riding, this time Two Ponies led the horse as it pulled the travois. Black Otter walked along on the other side of the horse, moving more spryly than a man of his age should have been able to after a night and a good part of a day spent dancing and chanting. The shaman was obviously a lot stronger than he looked.

Either that, or he really did have the help of the spirits, Cole thought, as he followed along behind.

Casebolt had a lot of friends among the Shoshones, and there was quite a procession following the travois as it left the village. There was a range of small but rugged hills nearby, and Two Ponies headed directly for them. The group had gone about a mile, Cole estimated, when Two Ponies brought the horse to a stop at the crest of a rise and pointed into a narrow valley below them.

"There," the chief said. "The place of healing."

Black Otter spoke, too, in hushed, reverential tones. Cole couldn't understand the words, but the meaning was clear enough. This was a sacred place to the Shoshones.

To Cole, it just looked like a little valley between some hills. A creek ran down the center of it, spilling from a pool at the far end of the valley. The pool had formed against a sheer, rocky bluff that brought the valley to an abrupt end. The pool and the creek were probably fed by underground springs, Cole thought.

But there was something strange about it, he realized as he looked closer. The surface of the pool seemed somehow to be moving, although it should have been calm and placid. And there was a peculiar haze in the air above it, a sort of perpetual mist.

"That pool," Cole said, understanding dawning in his brain, "it's fed by a hot spring, isn't it?"

"The spirits of the earth rise there," Two Ponies said. "That is why it is a place of healing, a place of great medicine. In your tongue, the Shoshone name for that stream would be Medicine Creek."

Cole looked over at Two Ponies. "What's Black Otter going to do, let Billy drink some of the water from the creek?"

"No. We will bathe him in the waters of the pool."

His eyes widening in surprise, Cole couldn't hold back the words that sprang to his lips. "Wait just a blasted minute! Billy's already got fever, and that pool's probably boiling hot. You put him down in that water, he'll burn up for sure!"

"You said that you trusted us, Cole Tyler," Two Ponies said, his voice formal enough for Cole to know the chief had been insulted. "Even more important, our friend Billy trusts us. The waters of Medicine Creek are his only hope."

"Cole . . ." Casebolt's voice came from the travois, and he struggled to lift a hand. "I reckon we better . . . let 'em do . . . whatever they want. I . . . I'm willin' to . . . take a chance. . . ."

Cole knelt beside the travois. "You sure about this, Billy?"

"I'm . . . sure." Casebolt managed to nod his head as he spoke.

Cole straightened and drew a deep breath. He looked at Two Ponies and nodded. "Go ahead. Do what you think is best."

Two Ponies led the horse down the hill toward the creek. Black Otter went with him, and after a moment, so did Cole. The other Shoshones stayed where they were, on top of the hill, as if they were afraid to come any closer to the stream but wanted to see what was about to happen.

When Two Ponies reached the creek, he turned the horse and headed toward the pool at the head of the valley. Cole reached down and dipped his hand into the creek, aware as he did so that some surprised muttering came from the Shoshones looking on. He supposed what he was doing bordered on sacrilege of some sort, but he lifted his hand to his mouth anyway. The water was quite warm, and it had a strong, unpleasant taste to it. He spat it out and tried not to make a face.

They reached the pool, which was surrounded by rock. Although there were trees and bushes along the banks of the creek, not much grew around the pool itself. Two

Ponies and Black Otter helped Casebolt up from the travois. He stood between them, swaying unsteadily.

"You must take your clothes off now, Billy," Two Ponies told the deputy.

Casebolt nodded, and with the help of the two Indians, he stripped off his boots, shirt, pants, and long underwear. He was too sick for any false modesty. His face, neck, and forearms had weathered over the years to a deep permanent tan, but the rest of his body was fish-belly white.

"Now what?" Casebolt muttered when he was naked.

"Step into the pool," Two Ponies said. He grasped one of Casebolt's arms while Black Otter held the other.

Gingerly, Casebolt extended a foot and let it sink down into the water. He pulled it back as quick as he could and said, "That water . . . is mighty hot."

"It is the place of healing," Two Ponies urged.

"Well, I reckon . . . I can only get . . . boiled once."

Casebolt walked out into the shallow pool, wincing as he did so. Two Ponies and Black Otter went with him part of the way, then stepped back. From where he was standing nearby, Cole thought he could feel the heat coming from the pool, but that might have been his imagination, he told himself. Slowly, following the orders that Black Otter relayed through Two Ponies, Casebolt sank down into the pool, letting the water rise around him until only his head was showing. Within minutes, his features turned a bright red.

"Damn it, you're killing him!" Cole burst out. He took a step toward the pool. "Billy, I'm coming in there to get you out."

Casebolt lifted an arm and held up a hand, the palm turned toward Cole. "Wait, Marshal," he said. "It ain't quite so hot . . . once you . . . get used to it. I reckon I can . . . stand it."

The hand and arm that Casebolt had lifted out of the water to forestall Cole's reaction were even more red than his face. Cole knew that sitting in that pool had to be like sitting in a pot of boiling water. It was like a gigantic pot of son-of-a-bitch stew — and Casebolt was the son of a bitch.

Long minutes passed, and Cole had to admit that the flush on Casebolt's face was fading. Great beads of sweat formed on his forehead to roll down his cheeks and drip from his chin. He shook his head slowly.

"How are you doing, Billy?" Cole called out anxiously to him.

"Well, it ain't as bad as what you'd think. You get a little used to it after a spell."

Casebolt's voice sounded a little stronger, Cole thought. Maybe the Shoshones were right. Maybe there *was* something special about this pool and the creek that it fed, besides the fact that the water was as hot as hell's hinges and tasted bad.

Black Otter began shaking a rattle and chanting again, and Two Ponies told Cole to sit down. "It will take some time for the healing to be complete," the chief explained.

Casebolt didn't seem to be in any particular distress, so Cole sat down with Two Ponies, both of them moving back off the rock that bordered the pool. The rock was hot, too, since it was heated by the water it enclosed.

Cole thought about the hot springs that must feed this pool and remembered the area called Colter's Hell, up north of the Tetons. There were hot springs up there, too, as well as pits of boiling mud and geysers of steaming hot water that shot from cracks in the ground. As a young man, Cole's mountain man father had known old John Colter and had heard all the stories about the region that was also sometimes known as the back door to hell. Those yarns had been passed down to Cole, who had been there later in his own wanderings and knew the stories to be true. It stood to reason that if such things were possible in one place, they could be possible in another, especially somewhere relatively close like this. It was a reminder that the earth was alive and ever-changing, especially below the surface.

More time had passed than Cole was really aware of. He only realized how late it was when he looked up and saw how much the sun had sunk toward the western horizon. Casebolt was still sitting in the pool, his eyes closed now and a look of contentment on his face. Cole felt a sudden stab of worry. What if Casebolt had died out there?

"Billy?"

Casebolt's eyes opened, although he had trouble for a moment focusing them on Cole. "What is it, Marshal?" he asked groggily.

"How do you feel? Are you ready to get out of there?"

Black Otter spoke before Casebolt could say anything, and Two Ponies translated, "It is time to leave the pool."

Cole got to his feet. "I'll come out there and give you a hand."

"Don't reckon you need to do that," Casebolt said. He stood up, water streaming from his spindly shanks.

His skin still shone a bright pink. He shuddered a little as he walked out of the pool. To him, even a warm spring late afternoon had to feel cold after a couple of hours in that hot water. Black Otter met him with a buffalo robe and wrapped the thick hide around him.

"Lie on the travois," Two Ponies instructed him. "We will take you back to the village."

Cole asked, "Will he be all right now?"

Black Otter said something, and Two Ponies translated, "Only time — and the spirits — will tell."

7

Casebolt had fallen into a deep sleep by the time they reached the Shoshone village. Two Ponies barked some orders, and several men carried the deputy back into a different lodge from the one where he had spent the previous night. That lodge, Two Ponies explained to Cole, would have to be cleansed before it could be used again, just in case some of the evil spirits that had caused Casebolt's illness had escaped from his body while he was there.

That made just about as much sense as anything else Cole had heard over the past couple of days, so he nodded and went on into the lodge with Casebolt, who was still sleeping. Black Otter knelt beside the deputy and chanted softly.

When Two Ponies joined him, Cole gestured toward the shaman and said quietly, "I thought everything was finished."

"A few more songs of prayer will not harm

our friend," Two Ponies replied with a faint smile. Cole nodded.

Once again, Cole ate supper with Two Ponies and his family in the chief's lodge, leaving Black Otter to continue watching over the sleeping Casebolt. It was difficult for Cole to leave his friend's side, but Casebolt seemed to be breathing deeply and regularly and resting comfortably. There was nothing Cole could do for him, so it didn't make any sense to go hungry.

He enjoyed the stew with big chunks of buffalo meat floating in it that Two Ponies' wife dished up for him in a wooden bowl. While he was eating it, however, his thoughts turned back to Casebolt and the idea that had gone through his head earlier in the day. From now on, Cole figured, stew was always going to remind him of Billy Casebolt sitting in that pool of hot water.

When the meal was over, Two Ponies brought out his pipe, but before the smoking ritual could get underway, Black Otter came into the lodge and spoke hurriedly to the chief. Two Ponies listened with a solemn expression on his face and finally nodded to Black Otter. Cole leaned forward anxiously, fearing the worst, as Two Ponies turned toward him.

"Our friend Billy is awake," Two Ponies

said. "He wishes to speak with you, Cole Tyler."

A wave of relief washed through Cole. Quickly, he got to his feet and left the lodge, followed by Two Ponies and Black Otter. When he thrust aside the flap of hide that hung over the entrance of the other lodge, he saw Casebolt sitting up, still wrapped in the buffalo robe. The deputy held a bowl of broth in his hands and sipped from it. He looked up and smiled at Cole.

"Howdy, Marshal. Sorry I had everybody so doggone worried about me."

Cole dropped to one knee next to him. "Are you feeling better, Billy?" he asked.

"A whole heap better," Casebolt confirmed. "I reckon I'm still about as weak as a little ol' kitty cat, mind you, but my head's clear again."

"That's good," Cole said. "Mighty good. The fever's gone?"

"Seems to be. You can check for yourself."

Cole held his hand to Casebolt's leathery forehead. The skin was cool. Casebolt's eyes were brighter and more alert than Cole had seen them since before the sudden illness had struck. The deputy seemed to be well and truly on the way to recovery.

"You go ahead and drink that," Cole told him, "then get some more rest. I reckon you need that about as much as anything right now."

"You're right," Casebolt nodded. "I feel like I could sleep for nigh on to a week. Reckon I won't, though, because I want to get on back to town soon's I can. Got to thank Doc Kent for tryin' to help me."

Cole couldn't stop himself from grunting. "You'd probably be dead by now if we'd left you in Kent's hands," he said.

Casebolt frowned. "Aw, now, don't go sayin' things like that, Marshal. The doc, he done as much for me as he knowed to do. Wasn't his fault that whatever laid me low was something he didn't know nothin' about."

"Well, you're more generous than I might be," Cole said as he patted Casebolt's shoulder and stood up. "I'll see you later. Rest."

"Intend to," Casebolt nodded.

Cole strode out of the lodge into the night and took a deep breath, feeling better than he had since leaving Wind River. Casebolt was alive and evidently well on the way to recovery.

And back in Wind River tonight, Cole suddenly realized, the dance was likely going on as planned. At this very moment, Judson Kent might be taking a turn around the floor with Simone. Cole's jaw tightened at the thought.

Then he made himself relax. Saving Casebolt's life was more important than any dance. And there would be other nights, he told himself, nights that *he* could spend with Simone McKay.

It was going to be hard to wait for Casebolt to grow strong enough to return to Wind River, Cole realized dismally.

To Cole's surprise, Casebolt was ready to ride the next morning.

"I can't get over how good I feel," the deputy said as he and Cole ate breakfast together in Two Ponies' lodge. "I slept mighty good last night, and this mornin' I feel downright perky."

"Well, we don't want to take any chances," Cole said. "You don't need to go wearing yourself out by trying to do too much too soon. It won't hurt for you to rest a day or two more before we start back."

Casebolt frowned. "I don't much like leavin' Jeremiah there to take care of any trouble that comes up. He ain't even an official deputy. Folks might not pay him no mind, was he to tell 'em to do something."

Cole thought about how the citizens of Wind River regarded Jeremiah Newton, not only because of his massive size but also because he was the town's only minister. Dryly, Cole said, "I don't think anybody's going to give Jeremiah too much trouble."

"You're likely right about that," Casebolt admitted. "But there still ain't no reason to wait." He leaned closer to Cole and went on in a quieter voice, "It ain't just the fever breakin'. I had some other problems, and the water in that pool 'pears to have cleared them up, too."

Cole frowned. "What are you talking about, Billy?"

"Well, my rheumatism, for one. The stuff's plagued me for years, but this mornin' . . . shoot, my joints don't hurt a lick! I can move around better and easier than any time since I was a young pup!"

Cole's frown deepened as he said, "How could that pool help anybody's rheumatism?"

"Don't know," Casebolt said with a shake of his head. "But I know I sure don't hurt like I normally do in the mornin's, after my bones've had a chance to stiffen up."

Cole wasn't convinced. "You said you had some other problems that have gotten better . . . ?"

Casebolt's tone became even more hushed and confidential. "A feller who's been sittin'

91

a saddle for as many years as I have just naturally has some other complaints. . . ."

"Say no more," Cole told him, holding up a hand to forestall any further explanations. "I'll take your word for that one, Billy. Fact is, I'll take your word for all of it, and I suppose if you're convinced that you're strong enough to ride back to Wind River, I shouldn't argue with you. I'll get our horses saddled up as soon as we're finished with breakfast."

That appeared to satisfy Casebolt. When they were done eating, Cole left the lodge and found Two Ponies outside, told the chief they were going to leave the village and ride back to Wind River. Two Ponies nodded solemnly and said, "The place of healing is strong medicine. That is why we gave the name to the creek."

Cole saddled his golden sorrel, Ulysses, and the chestnut mare that Casebolt had been riding when they slipped out of Wind River. Casebolt came striding out of the lodge a few minutes later, fully dressed and moving easily and confidently. Cole thought about the jerky gait his deputy usually affected and realized it had been due to the rheumatism that had made Casebolt's joints so painful. Cole would have been convinced of the pool's healing capabilities by the breaking of the fever alone; the easing of Casebolt's other aches and pains was just more confirmation.

Casebolt clapped his battered old hat on his head. "Reckon I'm almost ready to ride, Marshal," he said. "Just one more thing I got to do first."

He strode over to Two Ponies and Black Otter. Looking as serious as Cole had ever seen him, Casebolt said, "You fellas saved my life, and that's twice now. I'd've been a goner for sure if it hadn't been for you, Two Ponies, and you, Black Otter. I ain't goin' to insult you by offerin' to pay you for givin' me back my life, but I want you to know that if there's ever anything I can do for you or your people, all you got to do is ask."

"This thing we already know, friend Billy," Two Ponies told him. "You have been a good friend to the Shoshones."

"Well, just don't you forget, I owe you a whole heap."

Casebolt and Two Ponies clasped wrists, then Casebolt came back over to join Cole. As the whole village looked on, the two lawmen swung up into their saddles and started toward Wind River, turning to wave their farewells as they rode away.

The journey back to the settlement was uneventful. Cole kept a close eye on Casebolt to make sure the ride wasn't too much of a strain on the deputy, but Casebolt's recovery seemed complete. After they had been on the trail for over an hour, Casebolt admitted he was a little tired, but he wanted to push on.

As they neared the town, Cole brought up another subject that had been on his mind. "I've been thinking, Billy," he began. "It might not be a good idea for you to talk too much about what happened out there with the Shoshones."

Casebolt looked over at him and frowned. "Why not, Marshal?"

"Well, some folks might not believe that sitting in a pool of hot water could cure whatever was wrong with you and even clear up your other medical problems."

"Don't care if anybody believes me or not," Casebolt snorted. "You an' me both know what really happened."

"Yep, we sure do. But the people who don't believe aren't really the ones I'm worried about."

Casebolt shook his head. "Don't reckon I know what you're gettin' at."

"If folks hear about Medicine Creek and that pool, they're liable to want to go out there and see if the water can heal their illnesses and solve their problems, too," Cole said bluntly.

Casebolt thought about that for a moment, then nodded. "Could be, but I don't see what's wrong with that."

"That's a sacred place to the Shoshones, Billy," Cole said gently. "They only took you there because they think so highly of you. They wouldn't like it if suddenly there were dozens of people tramping around that creek."

"Yeah, I reckon you're right," Casebolt said after a moment. "I hadn't looked at it from that angle. I'll try to keep quiet about it."

A few minutes later, they reached the settlement, once again sticking to the back alleys as they made their way toward the marshal's office. They tied their horses behind the building and went through the rear door.

That took them past the offices of the Wind River Land Development Company, and Simone McKay stood up from behind a desk and hurried out into the corridor when she saw Cole and Casebolt passing by. "Billy!" she exclaimed. "You're back! And I must say you look much better than when you left."

"Yes'm, I feel a heap better," Casebolt said as he tugged his hat off.

"But how in the world —" Simone began.

"I'll tell you all about it later," Cole promised. He could trust Simone with the secret of Medicine Creek. "Right now, Billy and I just want things to get back to normal around here as soon as possible."

"I think that's what we all want," Simone said, and something about her tone made Cole look intently at her.

"Has something happened?" he asked.

"Nearly. And there may still be some trouble brewing. I'll let Jeremiah Newton tell you about it, though, since you left him in charge while you were gone." Simone looked at Casebolt again, smiled, and shook her head. "It's so good to see you healthy again, Deputy. Judson and I were so worried about you. Have you seen him yet?"

"No, ma'am, we haven't," Casebolt replied. "We came here to the office first."

"Well, I'm certain he'll be as happy to see you as I am."

Cole wasn't so sure about that. Kent might be jealous of the success Black Otter had had in curing Casebolt.

There were other things to deal with first. Cole said, "If you feel up to staying here in the office in case of trouble, Billy, I'll hunt up Jeremiah and find out what's going on."

"Sure, Marshal. I don't mind."

Simone added, "And I'll be right here if Billy needs anything."

Casebolt grinned sheepishly. "Shucks, with all you folks worryin' about me and tryin' to do for me, I'm liable to get downright spoiled."

"Don't concern yourself with that," Simone told him. "Why don't you go on in the office and sit down? You must be tired."

"A mite," Casebolt admitted. He headed on into the marshal's office.

Cole started toward the front door, but he turned back and said quietly to Simone, "How bad is this trouble Jeremiah's going to tell me about?"

"I don't know," Simone said. "But Kermit Sawyer is involved —"

Cole grimaced and held up a hand. "Don't say any more. Let Jeremiah break the bad news to me."

He made it to the door of the building before Simone said quietly, "Cole . . . I'm glad you're back."

The tenderness in her voice made his heart leap, made him forget the weariness of the ride from the Shoshone village. He smiled and nodded and said, "I'm glad to be back."

Then he went in search of Jeremiah Newton to find out what sort of trouble had cropped up in his absence. Once he did, he thought, he might not be quite so happy to have returned to Wind River.

8

The mountains that formed the eastern boundary of the Diamond S were to Frenchy's left as he rode along, his eyes watching alertly for any stock that might have strayed over here into this rugged terrain. Several miles to his right, the last of the spring branding was going on, and members of the Diamond S crew were spread out all across the valley, combing it for any calves that might have escaped the first sweep.

Frenchy had assigned the area that each man would cover, and he had taken this part of the valley for himself, since it was closest to the pass where Austin Fisk's Latch Hook stock had intruded before. Wildcat Ridge was not far off. If there were going to be any more confrontations with Fisk's men, Frenchy wanted to keep them from getting out of hand. After the near-shoot-out in Wind River the day before, he knew that a level head would be required to keep violence from erupting the next time riders from the two ranches chanced to meet.

He hoped he was level-headed enough to keep that from happening.

On the other hand, since he was alone, if he ran across Wilt Paxton or any of the other Latch Hook punchers, they might take that as an invitation to bushwhack him.

Maybe Fisk had gotten smart and decided not to push in where he wasn't wanted anymore. That was what Frenchy was going to hope for, anyway.

It was only a few minutes after that thought went through his head that he saw the cattle grazing on the side of a hill.

Frenchy grimaced and reined in. It had taken him only a second to see that those weren't Diamond S cows. For one thing, they weren't longhorns, which made up the huge majority of Sawyer's stock. For another, they were still sort of skinny, and that, too, marked them as belonging to Austin Fisk. Fisk's cattle were only now beginning to recover from the long, hard drive west.

Quickly, Frenchy's eyes scanned the slopes above and below the cattle. He didn't see any riders. It was possible that the Latch Hook stock hadn't been driven over here at all but had simply strayed through the pass and onto Diamond S range instead.

Well, Mr. Sawyer's orders in a case like that were clear enough. Strays were to be run in with the Diamond S stock, and if Fisk wanted them back, he would have to pay for the privilege.

Frenchy heeled his horse into a trot. There were only about twenty of the cows. He could handle that many by himself. He would round them up and drive them into the center of the valley where the branding was going on.

He had reached the base of the hill where the cattle were grazing when he saw a rider appear at the top of the rise. The other horsebacker started down when Frenchy started up. Too much distance separated them for Frenchy to be able to tell much about the other man, except for the fact that he rode well. Frenchy knew every member of his own crew, though, and this wasn't one of them, which led to the obvious conclusion: the rider was from Fisk's spread.

Frenchy's right hand went to the butt of his Colt, checked that the gun slid easily in its holster. He was pretty fast on the draw when he needed to be. That wasn't boasting, just a matter of fact.

He hoped he wouldn't need to be fast today.

The other rider was close enough now for Frenchy to tell that he wore a denim jacket and pants, as well as a flat-crowned brown hat. There was a cartridge belt strapped around the man's hips, too, supporting a pistol in a tied-down holster. Frenchy didn't recall seeing this hombre during either of the two recent confrontations with Latch Hook punchers, but that didn't mean anything. Fisk likely had quite a few men Frenchy had never run into.

Both Frenchy and the other man had almost reached the cattle by now. If Frenchy could see the other gent, then the other gent could certainly see him. Nobody was going to be taken by surprise here. And from the looks of things, nobody was going to back down, either. Frenchy rode straight through the widespread herd, scattering a few of the cows. A glance at their brands as he passed confirmed what he already suspected — they were Latch Hook stock, all right.

He reined in as the other rider came to a stop about thirty yards in front of him. "This is Diamond S range," Frenchy called as he leaned forward in the saddle. "State your business here."

"I came to get those cattle. *They* don't belong to the Diamond S."

Frenchy stiffened, his nostrils flaring as he

drew in a sharp breath. The voice was *female.*

And he could see now that the other rider possessed a lithe slenderness that also betrayed her sex, despite her garb and the fact that she was carrying a gun. Her hair must have been tucked up underneath the hat. He swallowed hard and said, "Would you be one of Austin Fisk's daughters, ma'am?"

"I'm Alexandra Fisk," she answered coldly. "And those are my father's cattle. I saw their tracks while I was out riding and followed them through the pass. They seem to have strayed over here. Are you going to allow me to recover them?"

"Strayed . . . or were driven onto the Diamond S?"

It was Alexandra Fisk's turn to stiffen and rise up a little straighter in her saddle, but her reaction was due to anger instead of surprise. "I said they strayed, and that's what I meant," she called. "My father gave orders not to force any more confrontations."

"What do you reckon you're doin' right now, ma'am?"

"Trying to retrieve what rightfully belongs to my father," she snapped. "And if you interfere with me, mister, you're nothing but a lowdown cow thief!"

Frenchy couldn't suppress the grin that tugged at his mouth. When he had seen her in town, Alexandra Fisk had seemed mighty cool and collected, but she was sure enough full of fire today. He halfway expected her to haul out that hogleg on her hip and start blasting away at him. Thankfully, she didn't do that but settled for glaring at him instead.

He edged his horse closer to hers so that he wouldn't have to raise his voice so much to be heard. "Look, Miss Fisk," he said. "I've got my orders. Strays are supposed to be run in with the Diamond S stock. If your daddy wants them back, he'll have to talk to my boss."

"You're the foreman, aren't you, the one called Frenchy?"

He blinked, surprised that she would know him. "Yes, ma'am, that's who I am."

"Then surely your employer gives you some latitude in your orders. He expects you to deal with situations that may arise by using your best judgment, otherwise he wouldn't have given you the responsibility of being foreman."

"If you mean Mr. Sawyer don't keep me on a tight rein, I reckon you're right," Frenchy admitted. "He still wouldn't like it if I was to go against a direct order of his."

"He wouldn't mind if he didn't know about it," Alexandra pointed out.

Frenchy frowned. What she was asking him to do was tantamount to a betrayal of Kermit Sawyer and the Diamond S, and where Frenchy came from, a man rode for the brand and didn't allow himself to be swayed by such things as a pretty face.

Even as pretty a face as that of Alexandra Fisk. . . .

However, she was right about Sawyer giving him some leeway in his actions. He was the *segundo,* accustomed to making some of his own decisions based on what he thought would be best for the ranch. If he drove these Latch Hook cattle in among the Diamond S stock, that would lead inevitably to another confrontation between the two spreads, because Fisk wouldn't take such a move lying down. With any luck, Fisk would be reasonable and offer to pay for the return of his cattle. But such a stroke of luck was improbable; it was more likely Fisk and his men would ride over to the Diamond S and try to take back the cows at gun point. And of course, Sawyer would fight back. A lot of good men would die.

"You swear these cattle just strayed through the pass?" Frenchy asked abruptly.

"That's twice you've asked me that," Alexandra replied coolly. "I'm beginning to think you don't trust me. But, yes, I swear they just strayed over here."

"Wouldn't have if your daddy's punchers didn't have 'em grazin' so close to the pass," Frenchy muttered. He held up a hand to forestall her protest as a look of anger flashed across her face. "All right, all right. You can have 'em back, I reckon."

"Thank you." Her voice was icy, without a hint of real gratitude in it.

"You can't handle so many of these critters by yourself, though. I'll give you a hand."

"I don't need your help," she shot back.

"Well, you're gettin' it, whether you need it or not," he said stubbornly. "I want all these cows off of Diamond S range as soon as possible. Don't want any of 'em strayin' off again."

Alexandra glowered at him for a couple of seconds, then nodded in resignation. "All right. Thank you." This time the words sounded a little more sincere, although still grudging.

Frenchy turned his horse. "I'll ride around that end of the bunch," he said, waving his arm to show her what he meant. "You head the other way. We'll push 'em together and head 'em back to the pass."

Alexandra nodded her understanding and urged her mount into a quick trot. She handled the horse well, Frenchy thought, as he watched her over his shoulder. Rider and mount moved almost as one. Obviously she had been riding for a long time, back there in the bluegrass hills of Kentucky. One of those kids who could ride before they could walk, he supposed.

Rounding up the Latch Hook cattle was a relatively easy chore, and within a few minutes, Frenchy and Alexandra had the stock bunched and moving toward the pass in the mountains that led to the next valley. The young woman proved to be as adept at handling cattle as she was with her horse. Every time one of the cows tried to move off from the herd on her side, Alexandra was there immediately, blocking the path of the recalcitrant critter and prodding it back in the direction it was supposed to go. Frenchy kept an admiring eye on her while he pushed his own side of the small herd toward the pass.

They reached it in less than an hour. As the cattle started through the narrow passage between steep, thickly wooded slopes, Alexandra reined in and called to Frenchy, "I can handle them from here. We'll be back on Latch Hook range once we get through the pass."

He rode over to her and shook his head. "I'll go with you until you get where you're goin'. Wouldn't want any of those cows to get it in their heads to turn back."

"It's really not necessary. The pass is narrow enough so that I won't have any trouble —"

"No point in takin' any chances," Frenchy broke in. "Shoot, I've already come this far. Might as well go a little farther."

"Well, if you insist. . . ."

Together, they rode into the pass behind the little jag of cattle. Frenchy would be glad when they got to the other side of the pass. He was relieved that they hadn't run into any other Diamond S riders while they were driving the Latch Hook cows back to the pass; he would have been damned hard put to explain just what in blazes he was doing.

Heading off more trouble before it started, that's what he was doing. That was what he told himself, at any rate.

But in the back of his mind, he had to wonder if he would have done the same thing if Wilt Paxton or one of the other Latch Hook cowboys had come onto Diamond S range to retrieve that stock. Somehow, he doubted it.

The cattle cooperated, as if sensing that

they were headed back to their home range, and it wasn't long before the end of the twisting pass came into view. Frenchy and Alexandra prodded the cows out into the next valley, back onto land claimed by Fisk's Latch Hook spread. Once again, Alexandra reined in and looked over at Frenchy.

"Thank you," she said, and this time he could tell the expression was genuine. "You could have caused some trouble about this, but instead you were quite reasonable. Not at all like Father —" She stopped abruptly and caught her bottom lip between even white teeth.

Frenchy grinned. "What'd your pa say? That all of us over on the Diamond S were a bunch of crazy, trigger-happy Texans?"

Alexandra had to laugh. "Something like that," she admitted.

"Well, we're not. A mite proddy some-times, maybe, but not crazy. No offense to your pa, Miss Alexandra, but if *he* would just be reasonable, likely him and Mr. Sawyer could settle this wrangle without anybody gettin' hurt."

Right away, he saw that he had gone too far. The hint of friendliness he had seen in her eyes had vanished instantly at his words. Her stare was once again cool and apprais-ing and a little bit hostile.

"Reasonableness works both ways, Mr. LeDoux," she said. She dug the heels of her boots into the flanks of her horse and sent the animal forward.

Stubbornly, Frenchy bit back a curse and rode alongside her. "I can go a mite farther with you, just to make sure —"

Alexandra interrupted the offer. "Not necessary. And might I remind you, we're on Latch Hook now. You'd better make yourself scarce before we run into some of my father's riders. I don't think they'd like to find you here."

Frenchy was about to tell her that he wasn't afraid of any Latch Hook riders when a group of men suddenly emerged from a line of trees about three hundred yards ahead of them. There were at least a dozen of them, Frenchy saw, and they had to be Fisk's men.

Alexandra saw them, too, and brought her horse to an abrupt halt. "What did I tell you?" she snapped. "Now get out of here while you still can."

Frenchy had reined in as well, and he studied the approaching cowboys as he sat his saddle tensely. They had been ambling along when they came out of the trees, not in any hurry, but now they seemed to be moving faster. They must have spotted the cattle, as well as him and Alexandra. And she was right — they wouldn't like it if they found him here.

"All right," he said. "Only reason I helped you bring those cows back over here was to head off trouble, so I reckon it wouldn't do to start any now. I'll go."

"Thank you. You can reach the pass and get back through it before my father's men can catch up to you."

"Yep. There's just one more thing I got to do first."

It was an impulse, pure and simple, and Frenchy couldn't have come up with even one good reason for doing it — except that he wanted to.

He reached over, caught the reins of Alexandra's horse, and leaned toward her. She had time to say, "What —," before his lips met hers.

The kiss was hard and fast, but even though it didn't last very long, it packed a wallop. Frenchy was breathless and his pulse hammered in his head when he pulled back. Her lips had been soft and warm and sweet as strawberries, just as he expected. And also just as he expected, she was staring at him through eyes wide with surprise.

He let go of her reins, ticked a finger against the brim of his hat, and said, "So long, Miss Alexandra."

As he wheeled his horse, he glanced at the oncoming riders. They must have seen what he had done, because he heard faint shouts of anger, and suddenly guns began to pop as they drew their pistols, fired into the air, and galloped forward at a breakneck pace. Frenchy dug his heels into the flanks of his horse and sent it into a gallop. He tugged off his hat, slapped it against his mount's rump, and gave a high-pitched Texas yell. A last glance over his shoulder showed him Alexandra still staring after him, her face pale with shock.

It had been a crazy stunt, he thought with a reckless grin. Those Latch Hook cowboys must have recognized their boss's daughter, and they had seen one of the hated Diamond S men kissing her. His life wouldn't be worth a plugged nickel if they caught up to him.

But he had a good horse under him, and the mouth of the pass was right ahead, and besides, the risk had been worth it, Frenchy thought.

Kissing Alexandra was worth just about any risk he could think of.

9

"Nobody got shot?" Cole asked.

Jeremiah Newton shook his head. "Not this time. One of the citizens who saw the trouble brewing ran down to the blacksmith shop to fetch me, but by the time I got there, Brother Sawyer's men were drinking in the Pronghorn, and Brother Fisk and his men had ridden out of town. I'm not sure what stopped them from trying to kill each other. The Lord was provident, I'd say."

"You're probably right," Cole said. "I knew there were plenty of hard feelings between those two, but I didn't figure it would break out into gunplay right here in town."

"It didn't," Jeremiah pointed out.

"Not *this* time. Not yet."

The blacksmith shrugged his massive shoulders in acknowledgment of Cole's point.

"Reckon I'll have to ride out to the Diamond S and have another talk with Sawyer," Cole said with a sigh. "I'll pay a visit to Fisk, too, but he strikes me as being just as mule-headed as Sawyer. Probably won't do any good to talk to either of them."

"You have to keep trying, though, just like I continue to spread the Word of God despite the fact that some simply won't allow themselves to hear it."

Cole nodded. When Jeremiah put it like that, he had to admit there were some similarities between lawmen and preachers.

Jeremiah changed the subject by asking, "How is Brother Casebolt?"

"Better," Cole said. "Just about over whatever was ailing him, in fact." He didn't think Jeremiah knew where they had been, so he didn't say anything about the Shoshones and the visit to Medicine Creek. Jeremiah would probably consider everything that Black Otter had done to be pagan and sinful. Cole didn't care about that, as long as it worked.

"Well, I'm glad that you've returned to town, Brother Tyler. Between the blacksmith shop and my ministry, keeping the peace isn't that easy."

"I know, Jeremiah, and I sure appreciate you helping out the way you have. As fast as Wind River is growing, I'm going to have to start giving some thought to hiring another regular deputy . . . if the town will go along with paying for one, that is."

Jeremiah nodded and said, "That's a good idea, especially since I'm soon going to be even busier once I start building the church."

"Fixing to start pretty soon, are you?"

"I hope so," Jeremiah said fervently. "Wind River needs a house of worship."

Cole couldn't argue with that. When he had first met Jeremiah, almost a year earlier, the big blacksmith had already been talking about building an actual church so that he wouldn't have to continue holding services in empty stores or under trees, the way he had been doing. Jeremiah had even started a collection of money for just such a purpose. However, the contributions hadn't come in as quickly as he had hoped, and so far, nothing had been done about the construction of a church.

Religion wasn't the only area Andrew McKay and William Durand had neglected when they were developing the settlement, either. There was no school in Wind River, although some of the parents had taken to sending their children over to the boarding-house run by Lawton and Abigail Paine, who had a considerable brood of kids. Abigail taught her own children and any others who showed up, but the town needed a real school and a real teacher. McKay and Durand had been interested only in things that would make money and increase their own fortunes, and religion and education hadn't fallen into that category.

As those thoughts went through Cole's mind, he told himself he would have to discuss both issues with Simone McKay sometime. Cole had always thought many of the so-called benefits of civilization were overrated, but if they were going to have a settlement here, they might as well go ahead and do it right.

"Well, I'd better get back to the office," he told Jeremiah. "Thanks again."

The blacksmith nodded, and Cole left the squat, thick-walled building where Jeremiah plied his trade. The marshal strode along the boardwalk, looking up and down Grenville Avenue. The town was fairly quiet today, folks going about their business, a few riders and wagons moving along the street. He heard the whistle of a locomotive as it pulled into the depot a few blocks away. That would be the westbound, heading for the railhead at Rock Springs, Cole judged.

The tranquility of the town was deceptive, though, Cole knew. It could shatter in an instant, without even a moment's notice. All it would take would be for Kermit Sawyer's men and the crew from Austin Fisk's Latch Hook spread to run into each other again, and the air could suddenly be filled with the crash of guns, the stink of gunsmoke, and the whimpers of dying men.

But not if he had anything to say about it, Cole told himself grimly. Not in his town. . . .

Casebolt had the chair tilted back and his booted feet resting on the desk in the marshal's office. His hat was tipped down over his eyes. It felt mighty good to just sit here like this and relax, he thought. The ordeal of the past few days had taken a great deal out of him. He felt better than he had any right to feel, though, and he figured that was due to whatever special quality that pool at the head of Medicine Creek possessed.

The sound of footsteps on the boardwalk outside made Casebolt raise his head and open his eyes. He saw a sandy-haired young man in a town suit and string tie passing by the window, and a moment later that same young man came through the foyer and appeared in the door of the marshal's office. "Hello, Billy!" Michael Hatfield said enthu-

117

siastically. "I didn't know you were back in town."

Casebolt sat up and nodded. "Got back a short spell ago," he told the young editor of the *Wind River Sentinel.*

Michael pulled up a chair and sat down without waiting to be invited, saying, "I knew you and Marshal Tyler were out of town, but I wasn't sure where you had gone."

The youngster was fishing for a story for his paper, Casebolt realized. And Cole had warned him about revealing too much. So he said, "The marshal and me had some business to take care of, that's all. Weren't much to it."

"I heard you were sick," Michael said.

Casebolt shrugged. "I felt a mite poorly. Doin' a lot better now."

"The way I heard it, you almost died."

Somebody had been doing some gossiping, Casebolt thought. He didn't figure Dr. Kent or Simone McKay had spread any stories, at least not on purpose, but Wind River was still a pretty small town, relatively speaking. Word got around, and there didn't seem to be anything anybody could do to stop it. But that didn't mean Casebolt had to confirm any rumors Michael had heard.

"I feel mighty spry now, better'n I have in

a long time," he said. "Looky here."

Casebolt stood up and came out from behind the desk. He did a little jig, moving his feet fast and flapping his arms. Michael laughed out loud, and Casebolt grinned.

"That look like somethin' a feller on death's door could do?" Casebolt asked.

"No, I suppose not. Those Shoshones must have worked some real magic."

"Wasn't magic," Casebolt said without thinking. "Just —"

"Just what, Billy?" Michael asked as Casebolt stopped in mid-sentence and grimaced.

"I didn't say nothin'," the deputy insisted.

"Yes, you did. I said the Shoshones must have worked some magic on you, and you said they didn't. So what did they do?"

"Don't know what you're talkin' about. I ain't seen no Shoshones in a month or more."

Michael leaned forward. "Now, Billy, you know that's not true. Everybody in town saw them ride in the other day, and a couple of them went into Dr. Kent's office. I hear tell you were in there sick. That's why the Shoshones came into town, to see you. And then, later the same day, you and Marshal Tyler vanish mysteriously." Michael shrugged and spread his hands. "It seems obvious to me that you went back to the

Shoshone village. Did their witch doctor cure you?"

"Black Otter ain't no witch doctor," Casebolt said hotly. "He's a shaman, a medicine man." Too late, he realized that once again Michael had prodded him into saying more than he wanted to.

Michael opened his mouth to say something else, but Casebolt made shooing motions with his hands. "You best go on and get out of here, Michael," Casebolt said firmly. "I got law business to tend to."

The young newspaperman looked around the otherwise empty office. "What law business?"

"Just . . . just never you mind about that."

Michael stood up, but he didn't turn to leave. "Was it some sort of potion this medicine man Black Otter gave to you? Or did he just chant and dance and wave talismans over you?"

"You been readin' too many o' them penny dreadfuls, boy," Casebolt told him.

"Or maybe he sacrificed something," Michael prodded. "An animal, maybe? Or . . . a *virgin,* like the ancient Aztecs down in Mexico?"

"It wasn't nothin' like that!" Casebolt exploded. "He sat me down in a pool o' hot water at a place they call Medicine Creek, all right? And that's just all he —" Casebolt clapped a hand to his forehead as he closed his eyes in dismay and muttered, "Oh, hell!"

"Thanks, Billy," Michael said as he headed for the doorway.

"Hold on there a minute! You can't print none of that! You got no right —"

"You're a public official, Deputy Casebolt. What you and the marshal do is news. And my job is to print the news."

Casebolt's hand closed around the butt of the old Griswald & Gunnison revolver on his hip, but then he sighed and let go of the gun. Short of shooting Michael Hatfield, there wasn't much he could do. Cole might be unhappy about him spilling the story to Michael, but Casebolt figured the marshal would like it even less if he was to go gunning down uppity, young newspapermen.

Casebolt waved a hand at the door. "You got what you came for," he said. "You best get on out of here now."

"I'm sorry, Billy," Michael said, and he sounded sincere. "The people have a right to know what's going on, though."

"Sure. I reckon you're right."

But that didn't make Casebolt feel any better as he stepped out onto the boardwalk and watched Michael hurry toward the newspaper office.

Marshal Tyler wasn't going to be happy about this, Casebolt thought. No, sir, he sure wasn't.

Michael Hatfield wasn't very happy with himself as he entered the office of the *Wind River Sentinel*. In fact, he felt positively guilty for badgering the deputy into giving away what had happened to him. Michael liked Billy Casebolt, he truly did, and Casebolt had once saved the life of Michael's daughter, Gretchen.

But news was news, and every journalistic instinct in Michael's body had told him there was a hell of a story waiting there in the marshal's office. Sure enough, he had been right.

He took off his coat, sat down at his desk, and pulled a pad of paper over in front of him. Picking up a pencil, he began to write. The next edition of the *Sentinel* would be printed the following day, and there was just enough time to write this story, set the type, and get it into print.

As often happened when he was working intently on something, Michael lost track of time. So he wasn't sure how much of it had passed when he heard a footstep and looked up to see Cole Tyler coming into the office. The marshal looked angry.

"I thought you and I had gotten to be friends, Michael," Cole said without preamble.

Michael placed his pencil on the desk. "I think we have, Marshal," he said. "We still are, aren't we?"

"Not if you print that story about how the Shoshones cured Billy of whatever was ailing him, along with his rheumatism."

"His rheumatism is cured, too, eh? I didn't realize that. But I should have known, from that jig he did for me."

Cole came closer to the desk and slapped a palm down on top of it. The sharp crack made Michael jump a little.

"Blast it, boy, aren't you listening to what I'm saying? You'll cause more trouble than you know if you put in your newspaper that Billy was cured by some sort of magic water."

Michael grinned. "I like the way you phrased that, Marshal. Magic water . . . mind if I use it?"

Cole's jaw tightened and his eyes blazed, and for a second Michael was afraid he had pushed the lawman too far. He dropped the grin and stood up so that he could meet Cole's angry glare on a more or less equal level.

"Look, Marshal," he said seriously. "I'm

sorry if you're upset about this. And I'm sorry I sort of tricked Deputy Casebolt into telling me what happened. But this is news, and it's my job to print it." He waved a hand at the racks of type he had already set up. "There's a story about the trouble between Kermit Sawyer and Austin Fisk. That could cause more problems, I suppose, once the people involved read it. But I don't hear you asking me not to print that story."

"Yeah, well, I don't much like the idea of you running it," Cole said. "Don't reckon I can talk you out of that one, either."

"No, you can't. A newspaper has to operate independently of governmental intrusion, no matter how well-intentioned. It's called freedom of the press, and it's one of the foundations of our democracy."

Cole looked at him for a long moment, then said, "Maybe you're right. But a bunch of words set down by some high-toned politicians nearly a hundred years ago don't always mean as much out here on the frontier. The Shoshones never heard of the Bill of Rights or any so-called freedom of the press."

"You're saying the Shoshones will be upset about this newspaper story? I didn't even know any of them could read!"

"You're an arrogant little son of a bitch

sometimes, you know that?"

The young editor paled in anger, but he didn't move out from behind the desk. Throwing a punch at Cole Tyler would be one of the stupidest things he could do, and he knew it.

After a moment, Cole asked again, "You won't stop this story?"

"No," Michael said flatly. "I won't."

"Then you remember one thing, mister. If there's trouble that comes from this, some of it — all of it! — is on your head."

With that, Cole turned and stalked out of the office.

When the marshal was gone, Michael heaved a long breath and slumped back into his chair. He admired Cole Tyler a great deal, and he hated to be on the opposite side of this issue from the marshal. But there were times when such things were inevitable, Michael supposed. All he could do now was run the story as planned. . . . and hope that Cole was wrong about it causing even more trouble.

The story of Medicine Creek had people talking in Wind River for two or three days, but then it was overshadowed by news of a bloody battle between the Sioux and some U.S. cavalry troops from Fort Laramie to the east. Billy Casebolt had to endure some good-natured ribbing from a few of the citizens about how the Shoshone treatment had proven that all he really needed to cure his ills was a good bath. Casebolt tolerated the gibes with his usual grin, and then people seemed to forget about the incident for the most part. Cole Tyler halfway decided that he had been worried about nothing.

Then an eastbound train came through from Rock Springs, and one of the passengers — a salesman of ladies' corsets named Hopper — got off the train long enough during the stopover to pick up a discarded copy of the *Sentinel* in the depot waiting room. He read it during the journey to Rawlins, where he got off again, this time to spend the night and call on the owners of a couple of general stores who were clients of his.

He left the newspaper on the train, folded and stuffed down beside the seat he had occupied. The train pulled out of the station a little later, bound for Cheyenne and points east.

10

Alexandra Fisk stepped out onto the porch of the big ranch house and looked up at the sky. The headquarters of the ranch were at the northern end of the valley, near where the mountains closed in, so large, snow-capped peaks rose up sharply around the house and blotted out some of the stars. The skies were clear this evening, and Alexandra could see moonlight sparkling on the snow that formed a near-permanent mantle on the mountains. She drew in a deep breath of the clean, pine-scented air.

Wyoming Territory was lovely in a rugged sort of way, that was undeniable, but there were times when Alexandra still missed Kentucky with its rolling hills and valleys carpeted in lush, blue-green grass. Her great-grandfather had been one of the men who came over the Wilderness Road with Daniel Boone to found Boonesborough, and there had been Fisks in Kentucky ever since. Alexandra's family and friends were still there, with the exception of her father and sister.

Her mother was still there, too, buried in a clearing not far from the house where Alexandra had grown up.

It was hard to believe that almost ten years had passed since her mother's death. Her passing had been so abrupt, so unexpected . . . a pleasant ride in the carriage on a sunny Sunday afternoon, a runaway team, a grinding crash as the carriage overturned . . . and just like that, with no warning, Eudora Fisk had been snatched away from her loving husband and two adolescent daughters, stolen away forever.

Austin Fisk had borne his loss well, or so everyone thought. No one except Alexandra had ever seen him sitting in his study in the middle of the night, the lamps all blown out, no sound except the low, wracking sobs that came from the shape huddled in a high-backed chair behind the desk. Her father would have been mortified if he knew that anyone else was aware of his pain, even his daughter, so Alexandra had always kept her knowledge to herself. She had been glad when, after almost a decade, he had decided to come west, to make a new start for the family here in Wyoming. She was sure it was what he needed.

But at times like this, Alexandra still missed her mother with an urgency that pierced her painfully. On a night like this, she could have used a mother's wise counsel.

Because even though a week had passed, she could still feel the hot pressure of Frenchy LeDoux's mouth against hers as he kissed her.

That . . . that ungentlemanly bastard! she thought, knowing that her mother would have scolded her for even thinking such language. Frenchy deserved it, though, Alexandra told herself. He had forced his company on her when they brought those cattle back through the pass, and then he had forced his kiss on her as well, a most unwelcome kiss.

She should have drawn her pistol and shot him herself, that was what she should have done. But she had been so shocked when he leaned over and pressed his lips to hers that the violent thought had never occurred to her. Not until later. At that moment, it was all she could do to gape at him and then watch, stunned, as he galloped off toward the pass. A few minutes later, she had still been staring after him when the group of her father's cowboys had gone racing past in hot pursuit of him. One of them had stopped and asked her if she was all right, and that had finally brought her out of her near-trance. She looked in alarm toward the pass, hearing the continued crash of six-guns.

But Frenchy had gotten away; she knew that now. The Latch Hook punchers hadn't found any sign of blood, which meant that he had probably escaped unscathed. In a way, Alexandra was glad of that. She wouldn't have wanted his death on her head.

But if he ever set foot on Latch Hook again . . . if he ever showed his face around here . . .

Well, he wouldn't, that was all. Even a . . . a *Texan* was too smart to push his luck that way.

A voice came from beside Alexandra, startling her. "What are you out here mooning about, Alex?"

Alexandra looked over and saw her sister. "I'm not mooning about anything, Catherine," she said sharply. "I'm just getting some fresh air after supper."

"Oh. Well, so am I." As usual, there was an undertone of mocking laughter in Catherine's voice, as if she found everything her sister said either unbelievable or vaguely ridiculous.

It would be difficult to find two sisters more unalike, their mother had been known to say when she was alive. Alexandra was quiet and withdrawn, her moodiness matching her dark good looks. Catherine, on the other hand, was as bright and open as the sun. Out of necessity, they had been friends and playmates as children, but Alexandra had always felt that there was more distance between them than there should have been. She wasn't sure how Catherine felt about the subject.

"It's a pretty night," Catherine said now, idly. She leaned on the railing around the porch and looked up at the stars. They shone brightly against the deep black sky.

"Yes, it is," Alexandra agreed. She pulled the shawl she wore a little tighter around her shoulders. "A bit chilly, though."

"I suppose." Catherine paused for a moment, then went on, "Thinking about your cowboy from the Diamond S?"

Anger and resentment flashed through Alexandra. "Stop it, Catherine," she snapped. "He's not my cowboy, and you know it. Frenchy LeDoux is an awful man, he's . . . he —"

Her breath hissed between her teeth as she searched for the right words to properly convey her loathing for Frenchy. Fervently, she wished that the men who had seen what happened over there by the pass had kept their blasted mouths shut about it.

She was afraid that Catherine would continue to tease her about the matter, but suddenly, faintly, out of the night came the sound of gunfire. The shots made thin popping noises, unthreatening on the surface but carrying an undertone of menace and dread.

"My God," Catherine breathed. "It sounds like a war! What's going on?"

"I don't know," Alexandra said as she turned quickly toward the door of the ranch house. "But I'm going to tell Father!"

Austin Fisk was at the door before Alexandra could reach it. He had a rifle in his hands, and he said, "Get in the house, girls! Something's going on out there, and it's nothing good."

Alexandra and Catherine did as they were told, hurrying into the house as Fisk stepped aside, out of the doorway. He strode across the porch to the railing and stood there holding the rifle, his stance as stiff and straight as one of the rails. Alexandra turned and looked back out at him as the gunfire continued, somewhere in the hills above the house.

"Sounds like it's coming from the northwest pasture," Alexandra heard her father mutter.

The shots continued for several minutes, then died away without coming any closer. Several of the hands had emerged from the bunkhouse, their attention drawn by the distant gunfire, and Fisk called them over.

"Wilt," the ranch owner said to his foreman, "we have some boys up in the northwest pasture, don't we?"

Paxton nodded, his face grim in the light that came from the house, and said, "There's a branding crew up there. They were supposed to finish up and come back in tomorrow."

"You'd better get some men together and ride up there."

Paxton nodded and started to turn away, but as he did so, he stopped abruptly and lifted his head. "Somebody's coming," he said.

Fisk came down off the porch. "I hear them, too."

So did Alexandra. She stepped through the doorway again, tightening the shawl even more around her shoulders, and said, "Father . . . ?"

Fisk's head snapped around. "Get in the house, I told you! You and Catherine go up to your rooms and stay there, Alexandra.

133

Do as I say."

The sound of hoofbeats that floated through the night air was louder now. The hands ran back to the bunkhouse to fetch their guns, and Fisk came up onto the porch again. Inside the house, Catherine plucked at her sister's arm and said, "Come on. Father won't be happy if we don't do as we're told."

"All right," Alexandra agreed grudgingly. If there was trouble on the way, she didn't like the idea of hiding out in her room.

As the sisters hurried toward the staircase that led to the second floor of the house, Alexandra made a quick stop in her father's study. There were several weapons there, and she took a Henry repeating rifle from a cabinet on the wall. The Henry was already loaded, but Alexandra took a box of cartridges from her father's desk anyway. Catherine stared at the rifle as Alexandra rejoined her on the stairs.

"You don't really think you'll need that, do you?"

"I hope not," Alexandra said. "But I want to be ready in case I do."

"Should . . . should I get a gun, too?"

Alexandra considered, then shook her head. "Come to my room with me. I'll protect both of us if I have to."

They hurried up the stairs and into Alexandra's bedroom. Alexandra went to the window that looked out at the front of the house and pushed the curtain back, then raised the glass that had been freighted out here at such great cost. She stood beside the window, the Henry held ready in her hands, while Catherine waited nervously on the other side of the room. Both of them could plainly hear the horses approaching the ranch.

Suddenly, the riders swept into view, vague shapes at first in the light from the moon and stars, then becoming more visible as they drew closer to the house. There were four of them, and they were riding hellbent-for-leather.

"Hold your fire!" Austin Fisk bellowed to his men.

Alexandra watched anxiously from the second-story window as her father hurried out into the open area between the house and the bunkhouse to greet the riders. All four men were hunched over their saddles as if in pain, and they had trouble bringing their horses to a stop. As they did, two of the men slipped from their saddles and sprawled on the ground. The Latch Hook punchers came running from the bunkhouse to reach up and help the other two men down from their mounts.

"Those are some of our men!" Alexandra exclaimed, startled by the realization. She turned away from the window and headed for the door of her room at a near-run.

"Alex!" Catherine said. "Where are you going?"

"Down there to see if I can help," Alexandra said over her shoulder. She didn't wait to see if Catherine was going to follow her.

By the time she reached the front porch again, the two men who had fallen from their horses were being carried off solemnly by some of the punchers. One of the other men was being supported in a sitting position by Wilt Paxton and another cowboy, while Austin Fisk knelt in front of him. The fourth and final man lay motionless on the ground nearby.

"You're the only one left alive, Hank," Fisk was saying, confirming Alexandra's fears. "The other boys made it this far, but that was all. What happened out there, son?"

"They . . . they hit the herd . . . we'd gathered for brandin'!" the cowboy called Hank gasped out. In the light that came from the house, Alexandra could see the dark, ugly stain on the front of his work shirt. "Didn't see 'em comin'. . . the sons o' bitches . . . they opened up on us . . . never had a chance to fight back. . . ."

"They stole the herd?" Fisk asked.

Hank managed a weak nod. "Ever' damn cow . . . sorry, boss . . . we should've . . . should've stopped 'em. . . ."

"Don't worry about it, Hank," Fisk said. "You did your best. The boys will take you in the bunkhouse now, and I'll send for a doctor —"

Fisk stopped as Hank's head lolled loosely to the side. The ranch owner reached out, put his fingers against Hank's neck, and held them there for a moment. Then Fisk sighed and said bitterly, "Damn it. He's gone, too."

Alexandra felt tears on her face and had to choke back a sob. Four men dead, just like that. No warning. Just cold-blooded murder in the night and a stolen herd of cattle.

Wilt Paxton asked quietly, "Who do you think would do such a thing, boss?"

Fisk stood up. "I don't know, but I intend to find out. It wouldn't surprise me a bit if that damned Texan and his men were behind this rustling!"

Alexandra opened her mouth to say something, then stopped the words before they could leave her mouth. She realized she had been about to defend Frenchy LeDoux for some unfathomable reason. True, he hadn't seemed to her like the kind of man who would murder from ambush, but she didn't really know him, couldn't be sure what he was capable of. Nor did she know anything about the rest of Sawyer's men, other than the fact that they all seemed to hate everyone connected with Latch Hook.

"We can't track that stolen stock in the dark," Fisk went on, "but I want men ready to ride at first light. We'll get to the bottom of this."

"We'll be ready, Mr. Fisk," Paxton promised. "And if the trail leads to the Diamond S?"

"Then we'll even the score," Fisk said bleakly. "With more blood, if need be."

11

"That was a mighty good lunch, Miss Rose," Lon Rogers told the proprietor of the Wind River Café as he pushed his plate across the counter. "Just like always."

Rose Foster smiled at the young cowboy. "Thank you, Lon," she said. "With Monty gone to visit his sister in Rawlins, I've been having to do all the cooking myself, so it hasn't been easy."

"No, ma'am, I expect not. But if anybody could do it, I reckon it'd be you."

Lon didn't want to pour the flattery on too thick. He had already learned that Rose Foster felt uncomfortable with a lot of fancy compliments. It was hard not to flatter her, though, considering the way he felt about her.

With her thick strawberry-blond hair, her peaches-and-cream complexion, and her large green eyes, Rose was the prettiest woman Lon had ever seen. The curves of her body in the bright calico dress were mighty impressive, too. She just about took Lon's breath away, and he was glad Mr. Sawyer had sent him into town today to wire a message to a cattle buyer in Cheyenne. The errand had given Lon a chance to have lunch here at the café and see Rose again.

He had already made it clear to her how he felt about her, and if she was still a mite standoffish, well, he could understand that. She was a successful businesswoman, after all, and he was just a forty-a-month-and-found cowpoke. He was a little younger than her, too, although he wasn't sure just how much. But he could be patient, and sooner or later Rose would come around. She had let him walk her home a time or two when he happened to be in town at the time she closed up the café in the evenings. That was progress, Lon told himself.

At the moment, much as he regretted leaving, he had to get back to the Diamond S. He had the cattle buyer's return telegram in his pocket, and Mr. Sawyer would be waiting for the reply. Lon dug out some coins and laid them on the counter next to his empty plate, then drained the last of the coffee in his cup and reached for his hat.

"I got to be going, Miss Rose, but I'll sure stop by to see you next time I'm in town."

"You do that, Lon," she said, and she smiled again. Lon's heart felt like it was fixing to pop as he put his hat on and headed for the door.

He stepped outside into a warm spring afternoon that was overcast, thick, gray clouds building over the mountains to the north. Might be a thunderstorm later, Lon thought, as he started toward the stable where he had left his horse. He hoped the rain would hold off until he got back to the ranch.

Suddenly, several men stepped out of a saloon as Lon passed, and they blocked his path. He veered to the edge of the board-walk to try to go around them, but the men moved as well. They were dressed in range clothes, and Lon recognized them as some of Austin Fisk's Latch Hook riders. Cold fingers began to tickle up and down his backbone.

"Excuse me, fellas," he muttered, hoping they would get out of his way and not force a confrontation. It was a futile hope, though, and he knew it even as he spoke.

"Thought I smelled a damned Texan," one of the men said. Paxton, that's who he was, Lon thought. Fisk's *segundo*. A dangerous man, according to Frenchy.

Lon suddenly wished that Frenchy was with him right now.

He was on his own, though, and he would just have to make the best of it. He drew a deep breath and said, "I'm not looking for any trouble."

"Well, maybe we are," Paxton shot back. "Four of our pards died last night, men who rode many a night herd with all of us, and you and the rest of that Diamond S outfit are to blame, mister."

Lon had to frown. "I don't know what in blazes you're talking about."

One of the other men stepped forward and prodded him roughly in the chest with a finger. "The hell you don't!"

Paxton said, "Somebody hit our herd last night and killed four of our men. Bush-whacked 'em, never even gave 'em a chance."

Lon shook his head. "Sorry to hear it, but I don't know a thing about it," he said. "You don't think that the Diamond S —"

"Never was a Texan who wasn't a rustler at heart," Paxton cut in. "We *know* you bastards are to blame, we just can't prove it. We followed the trail into the mountains between Latch Hook and the Diamond S, but it petered out in that rugged country."

142

"Doesn't matter," one of the other men said. "We still know who killed our boys." He put his hand on the butt of his gun. "And I say we start settlin' the score right now."

Lon felt a mixture of fear and anger coursing through his veins. He wanted to reach for his own gun, but he knew that if he did, the Latch Hook men would cut him down. They were three to his one, and they were obviously in the mood to kill somebody from the Diamond S.

"I don't know anything about any rustling or bushwhacking," he said quickly. "We didn't have anything to do with it. Except for a couple of nighthawks, our whole crew was in the bunkhouse last night."

Paxton laughed humorlessly and shook his head. "You don't expect us to believe you, do you, boy?"

"Let's ventilate the son of a bitch," one of his companions added.

"No," Paxton said firmly. "We're not going to kill him. We're going to let him take a message back to Sawyer for us."

With no more warning than that, Paxton's fist suddenly lashed out and slammed into Lon's jaw, driving him back on the boardwalk. One of the other Latch Hook men let out a whoop and swung a roundhouse blow of his own. Lon had no chance to block the punch, and when it crashed into his mouth, Lon felt himself sailing toward the edge of the walk. He hit the railing and went over it to land heavily in the street.

The three men were after Lon before he had a chance to recover. Booted feet smashed into him, the kicks jolting him and rolling him over a couple of times. He slapped desperately at his holster, but his gun wasn't there; it must have fallen out when he flipped over the railing, he realized.

He threw up his arms in an attempt to block some of the kicks, and his fingers scraped against somebody's boot. He grabbed hold of it as hard as he could and heaved. There was a wild, angry yell as Lon's unexpected move toppled one of the attackers. That gave Lon a little breathing room, and he was able to roll away from the other two and come up on one knee in a crouch.

He lifted his head just in time to get a fist in the face. The blow knocked him back onto his rump, and the other man — Paxton, Lon saw — tried to kick him again. Lon dove to the side, causing Paxton to miss and throwing the Latch Hook foreman off balance. Lon lunged at him, tackling him around the thighs and bringing him down.

A lot of people were shouting, Lon realized, and he heard running footsteps all around. A good fight always attracted plenty of attention. He jerked a punch into Paxton's stomach, but before he could follow up somebody else landed on top of him, then yet another heavy weight crashed down on him. All four men were rolling around frenziedly now in the dust of Grenville Avenue.

Suddenly, Lon caught a glimpse of a gun being lifted in an upraised hand. If it fell on him in a savage blow, as its wielder obviously intended, the barrel might well crush his skull. Lon tried desperately to squirm out of the way, but the other two men had hold of him and he couldn't throw them off. The gun barrel slashed toward his head.

A hand came out of nowhere, the fingers locking in an iron grip around the wrist of the man holding the revolver. Lon's rescuer gave the wrist a brutal twist, and then there was the sound of a fist cracking against bone. Part of the crushing weight left Lon.

"I'll shoot the next man who throws a punch or goes for a gun!" a familiar voice said angrily. "Now get the hell off that cowboy!"

The other two men let go of Lon and rolled away from him. A hand grasped Lon's arm and helped him to his feet. He found himself being supported by Billy Casebolt, Marshal Tyler's deputy.

Cole himself was standing a few feet away, .44 in his hand and trained on the Latch Hook men who were climbing unsteadily upright. It was Cole who had saved him, Lon realized, stopping the blow that had been about to fall and knocking the man off of him.

"What's going on here, Rogers?" the marshal demanded. Quite a few other people were standing around, too, the fight having caused a considerable commotion.

Lon took hold of his jaw and worked it back and forth for a moment, making sure it wasn't broken, then he said, "Paxton and those other Latch Hook men jumped me. Said Diamond S raided their ranch last night, rustled some of their stock, and killed four of their men."

"That's what happened, damn it!" Paxton blazed.

"You'd be Fisk's foreman, wouldn't you?" Cole said coolly. "You got any proof of those charges, Paxton?"

"We don't need proof —"

"The hell you don't," Cole cut in. "The way it looks to me, Rogers here could charge you boys with assault and attempted murder if he wants to. I imagine there are witnesses who saw the whole thing and can tell me for sure who threw the first punch. Besides, there are three of you and only one of him."

There was no love lost between Marshal Tyler and Mr. Sawyer, Lon knew. In fact, the marshal wasn't too fond of anybody from the Diamond S. But Cole was fair, and he wasn't going to let his dislike of the Texans blind him to the facts of what had happened here.

"I don't want to press charges, Marshal, not as long as you know I'm telling the truth," Lon said after a moment. "And I can promise you, we didn't have a thing to do with any raid on Latch Hook."

"You going to believe that lyin' Texan, Marshal?" one of the Latch Hook men asked hotly.

Cole nodded. "Until I see proof of something different, I am. Kermit Sawyer's an arrogant, stiff-necked old mossback, but he never struck me as a rustler. I want you Latch Hook riders to pick up your guns and get the hell out of Wind River."

Paxton glowered at him for a second, then said, "You haven't heard the last of this, Marshal."

"No, I reckon I probably haven't," Cole

replied with a sigh. "But there won't be any more trouble today."

Still grumbling, Paxton and the other two Latch Hook men retrieved their weapons from the street and went to their horses. Cole and Casebolt kept their guns drawn until the angry cowboys had ridden away and disappeared at the far end of the street.

Then Cole holstered his revolver and turned to Lon. "You all right, Rogers?" he asked.

"Just bunged up a little," Lon replied. "I've been hurt worse."

"What are you doing here in town?"

"Mr. Sawyer had me come in and send a wire for him, then wait for the reply."

"Have you got it?"

Lon nodded as he patted his shirt pocket and heard the rustle of paper. "Yep, right here. I was just about to start back out to the Diamond S when those fellas jumped me."

"All right. You're going back to the ranch — and I'm going with you. I want to have a talk with Sawyer about this trouble between him and Fisk. Besides, if you start back out there by yourself, Paxton and his friends might take it in their heads to do a little target practice — with you as the target."

Lon paled, knowing that Cole might be

right. He wouldn't put backshooting past Paxton and the other men.

"It's all Latch Hook's fault, Marshal —" Lon began.

Cole held up a hand to stop him. "I'll hash that out with Fisk. You feel up to riding?"

"Sure."

"I'll go saddle Ulysses while you get your horse from the stable."

Lon nodded, then looked around and found his gun lying in the street beside the boardwalk. He picked it up and shoved it back in its holster. Mr. Sawyer wasn't going to like it much when he showed up with the marshal, he knew, but somebody had to tell the owner of the Diamond S about the rustling that had taken place on the neighboring spread. If there was a gang of wide-loopers operating in this part of the territory, then every cattleman would have a stake in tracking them down.

Lon just hoped Marshal Tyler really believed that the Diamond S hadn't had anything to do with the raid on Latch Hook.

Cole and Lon Rogers rode out of Wind River a little later, the marshal leaving Billy Casebolt in charge of the office while he was gone. Casebolt stood on the boardwalk in front of the land development company building and hoped that Cole could get to the bottom of this trouble before it turned into a full-scale range war between the Diamond S and Latch Hook spreads. Casebolt had seen such bloody conflicts before and knew how they could draw everyone in an area into them, and then the innocent and the guilty alike suffered.

Casebolt sighed and leaned on the railing along the edge of the boardwalk. His muscles and joints were a little more stiff and sore today than they had been for the past week. He hoped his rheumatism wasn't coming back. It would be a shame if the waters of Medicine Creek proved to be only a temporary cure. He worried, too, about that mysterious fever returning, although so far there had been no signs of a relapse.

"You're frettin' about nothin', Billy," he muttered to himself. "Ever'thing's goin' to be just fine. . . ."

That was when he heard the commotion at the eastern end of the street.

12

Casebolt wasn't the only one to notice that something was going on. The sound of music and the happy, excited shouts of children drifted in through the open door of the newspaper office and caused Michael Hatfield to look up sharply from his desk. He was tired, having stayed up most of the night before to print the latest edition of the *Sentinel,* the one that had gone out on the streets today. But even tired, he sensed that the noises he was hearing meant a story.

Michael stood up and went to the door, looking east along Grenville Avenue. He saw two large wagons rolling along the street. The vehicles had brightly painted wooden sides and tops, instead of the usual canvas coverings. Garish red letters looped and swirled boldly against a vivid background of blue, yellow, and green. The writing on the side of the lead wagon proclaimed:

PROFESSOR NICODEMUS MUNROE'S TRAVELING MEDICINE SHOW AND REVIEW THRILLS AND ENTERTAINMENT!!!

WORLD-FAMOUS GENUINE CHIPPEWA MIRACLE TONIC!! CURES ALL ILLS!!

Michael watched, wide-eyed, as the wagon rolled past. A small man in a fancy suit and a top hat was handling the reins, and next to him was a solemn-faced Indian in buckskins and a large feathered headdress. The Indian's arms were folded across his chest, and he stared straight ahead, never looking to the side.

The tailgate at the rear of the wagon was down, and a young woman stood on it, waving to the crowd that was gathering. Thick masses of blond hair were piled on her head, and she wore a breathtaking red costume that was cut daringly low and clung to every curve of her body. The costume's skirt ended high on her thighs, revealing shapely legs in spangled tights like dancing girls in the best saloons wore. Michael had never seen anyone like her, and as she looked over at him and waved, his eyes met hers. The hair on the back of his neck stood up like the air was filled with the tingle of an impending lightning strike.

The blonde in the skimpy red outfit stunned him so that he almost didn't notice the occupants of the second wagon, which was as garishly painted as the first. But it was difficult not to notice a man who had to weigh at least three hundred pounds and who was so broad that he filled almost the entire wagon seat. Perched on the huge man's shoulders, also waving at the crowd, was a little girl in a costume similar to that of the blonde. No, Michael realized a moment later with a shock, she wasn't a little girl at all. She was a fully grown woman — who happened to be less than four feet tall.

Quite a few children were running alongside the wagons. The fat man driving the second wagon reached into a box on the seat beside him from time to time and brought out handfuls of hard candy. He tossed it to the children, which brought shouts of laughter and encouragement from them. The blonde standing on the lowered tailgate of the second wagon was eliciting whoops of approval from many of the men on the boardwalks as she waved and smiled at them. The man in the top hat tipped it to the ladies, most of whom sniffed and frowned in disapproval. Medicine shows appealed primarily to men and kids, Michael thought, as he watched.

"Lordy, did you ever see anything like it?" a voice asked from beside him.

Michael looked over and saw that Deputy Billy Casebolt had come along the boardwalk to join him in front of the newspaper office. Casebolt gaped at the wagons and their occupants as they moved on down the street.

"I've seen medicine shows before," Michael said. "There was one in Omaha when Delia and Gretchen and I were on our way out here from Cincinnati. We didn't stop to see it, though, so this is the closest I've actually been to one."

"Some of 'em can put on a humdinger of a show," Casebolt said. "Looks like they don't have but a few performers with this one, but if the folks are good at what they do, a medicine show don't need many."

"If the job of that, ah, blond young woman is to look lovely, she certainly handles that well," Michael said with a smile.

Casebolt grinned back at him. "That she does. Wonder what brings 'em to Wind River?"

"I imagine they're just traveling along the railroad, stopping in all the towns. That's what these itinerant shows usually do, I understand."

154

Down the street, the wagons came to a stop in front of the Wind River Land Development Company. Simone had emerged from the office and was standing on the boardwalk with her clerks. The man driving the first wagon leaped down agilely from the seat, swept his hat off, and spoke to Simone. She said something in return, then lifted her hand and pointed.

Michael realized with a shock that Simone was pointing at him.

No, not at him, but at Casebolt, Michael figured out a moment later. Casebolt muttered, "They must be lookin' for the marshal, but he's gone out to Sawyer's spread. Reckon I'd best go see what they want."

"I'm coming with you," Michael said immediately.

"Suit yourself." Casebolt started along the street toward the wagons. Michael trotted with him, hurrying to keep up with the deputy's long-legged strides.

As Casebolt and Michael came up, the man holding the top hat gave a little bow and said to Casebolt, "Good day to you, sir. I'm told that you represent the constabulary hereabouts?"

"I'm deputy marshal of Wind River," Casebolt admitted. "Name's Billy Casebolt. Marshal Tyler ain't in town right now, but he'll be back later today, I reckon."

The man stuck out his hand. "Allow me to introduce myself. Professor Nicodemus Munroe, at your service, Deputy Casebolt."

Munroe was several inches under medium height and slightly built, with graying blond hair. His face was lined, but the features had a gentle cast to them. He was around fifty, Michael judged.

Casebolt shook hands with the man and said, "What can I do for you, Professor?"

"I just wanted to make the local authorities aware of our presence in this lovely community," Munroe said. "I make a practice to follow that rule because, to be honest with you, Deputy, some so-called medicine shows are rather haphazard in their adherence to local laws and ordinances. Professor Nicodemus Munroe's Traveling Medicine Show and Review, on the other hand, is always honest and above-board and strictly legal."

"You're sayin' you ain't a bunch of crooks like some of them snake-oil shows."

Munroe beamed. "Precisely, Deputy! And if I could impose on you for a moment, perhaps you could tell me where a good spot would be for us to set up our wagons . . . ?"

Simone answered before Casebolt could.

156

"Down at the west end of town under the trees would be a likely place. There's a large open area, and we sometimes hold worship services there."

"We would *never* interfere with something like that," Munroe said quickly.

"I reckon it'd be all right," Casebolt said, "long as you ain't sellin' medicine whilst Jeremiah's tryin' to preach. I don't think he'd take kindly to that, and once you see him, you'll know why you don't want to get him riled."

"I assure you, Deputy, it's not our intention to upset anyone. If we're still here on the Sabbath, we'll be very circumspect."

"I figger it'll be all right for you to park these wagons down yonder, then."

Michael stepped closer and extended his hand to Munroe. "I'm Michael Hatfield, editor of the *Wind River Sentinel*, Professor Munroe."

"A gentleman of the press!" Munroe exclaimed as he grabbed Michael's hand and pumped it. "So very pleased to make your acquaintance, sir. Allow me to present the rest of my troupe." He turned and waved expansively at the wagons. "My bosom companion of the red-hued visage and solemn demeanor is Chief Laughing Fox of the Chippewa Nation."

157

The Indian was still sitting impassively on the wagon seat, and he made no acknowledgment of Munroe's introduction. The professor leaned closer to Michael and went on in a stage whisper, "You'll have to excuse the chief. Despite his name, he's a bit dour over the plight of his people. Always sends every bit of his part of the proceeds back to them, you know, to help them out in their time of need."

Michael nodded, not sure what exactly Munroe was talking about.

Nor did the professor take the time for any further explanation. He turned instead to the blonde in the red costume, beaming at her as he said, "And this is my lovely niece Deborah, who brightens all our days with her beauty and charm."

The young woman was still standing on the wagon's tailgate. She nodded and smiled and said, "Hello," in a throaty voice, and Michael felt that peculiar tingle go through him again.

"Wait until you hear her sing!" Munroe enthused. "You'll think you've died and gone to heaven and are listening to a chorus of angels, my friends."

Casebolt nodded to Deborah and tugged on the brim of his hat, saying, "Howdy, ma'am."

She barely glanced at the deputy. Most of her attention seemed to be focused on Michael, and he might have been a little uncomfortable about it . . . if he hadn't been enjoying it so much.

"And back there on our second wagon are Calvin Dumont and his lovely bride, Letitia," Munroe went on.

Michael tried to keep a look of surprise from appearing on his face. He wouldn't have guessed that the huge man and the diminutive woman were husband and wife.

Simone said, "We're pleased to meet all of you, Professor, and we hope you enjoy your stay in our town. Speaking of that, just what brings you here?"

Michael frowned a little. *He* should have been the one to ask that question, not Simone. After all, he was the editor of the local newspaper. He had been distracted, though, and she was doing his job for him. In the future he would have to be more careful, or she might decide to hire someone else to run the newspaper for her.

"Why, we're a traveling show, ma'am," Munroe said in answer to Simone's question. "Moving around from town to town is what we do. But I must confess, we do have a special reason for coming here to Wind River." He reached inside his fancy cutaway

159

coat and brought out a folded newspaper. Michael recognized the paper as Munroe unfolded it. Munroe went on, "We came because of this story about a place called . . . Medicine Creek."

13

Casebolt gaped in surprise at the professor, and he wasn't the only one. Michael was staring, too, and even Simone McKay seemed taken aback by Professor Munroe's statement.

" 'Scuse me for askin', Professor," Casebolt said, "but what's that creek got to do with you?"

"I'll be glad to explain, Deputy —" Munroe stopped short, lifted the newspaper, and looked at it for a couple of seconds before raising his eyes to Casebolt again. "Deputy Casebolt!" he exclaimed. "You're the one who was cured by the mystical, magical waters of Medicine Creek! I should have recognized your name from this newspaper story. My apologies, sir."

"Shoot, you don't need to 'pologize. Just tell me what you're doin' here, Professor."

"Well, you see, this is not my first visit to this part of the country. No, indeed! I first came here many years ago, when I was still nothing but a penniless wanderer." Munroe's voice had risen as he began his explanation, so that all of the townspeople who had gathered around the wagons could hear what he had to say. He continued, "I shudder to think what might have become of me had I not encountered something that would change my life forever! A miracle, that's what it was, nothing less than a miracle!" He began to pace back and forth on the boardwalk, making broad gestures with his arms as he got caught up in his own story. "I was sick, nigh on to dying, and then I stumbled on a small creek, miles from nowhere in the middle of what I thought was naught but a Godforsaken wilderness. I'd had no water for days, my friends, days! When I found that creek, I praised the Lord and fell on my knees beside it, plunged my head into the water, and drank deeply of it. No drink ever tasted so good or quenched such a thirst!"

"You're talkin' about Medicine Creek?" Casebolt asked with a frown. "I tasted it myself and thought it wasn't very good."

"You weren't dying of thirst at the time, were you, my friend?" Munroe shot back.

Casebolt had to shake his head.

"Well, there you are! Water tastes the

162

sweetest to a dying man. And I *was* dying, but not just of thirst. My stomach had ceased to function properly, my eyesight and my hearing were going rapidly, and certain other, ah, natural bodily functions were not operating as I would have wished. Even had I not gotten lost in the wilderness, I would have likely been dead within a month from the myriad host of other complaints that had beset me. But the stream you now call Medicine Creek changed all that!"

"You're saying it cured you like it did Billy here?" Michael asked.

"That is *exactly* what it did, Mr. Hatfield!"

Casebolt frowned and said, "Wait just a minute. I didn't drink the water from that creek. I sat down in a pool where the springs come out of a bluff. It was real hot, and I sat in it for a couple of hours."

"That's what I did once I had quenched my thirst," Munroe said without hesitation. "I was so happy to see the water that I bathed in it for an entire afternoon, and when I came out, I felt better than I had in years!"

Casebolt rubbed a thumbnail over the silvery stubble on his lean jaw. "Well, that sounds sort of like it was with me, all right."

"I knew I had accidentally discovered one of the wonders of the ages," Munroe went

163

on. "I had a couple of empty canteens with me, so I filled them with the water from the creek and went on my way. But I didn't drink that water, no, indeed! I found other creeks to slake my thirst, and I took the water from Medicine Creek with me. Eventually I wound up back east, and with my newly revitalized health, I was able to return to my first love — medical and scientific research! I analyzed the elements present in the water from Medicine Creek, and from that analysis I devised my now world-famous Chippewa Tonic, the most amazing concoction in the history of pharmacology!"

"But there ain't no Chippewa Indians out here in these parts," Casebolt protested with a frown. "The ones who took me to the creek was Shoshones."

"Yes, but it was Chief Laughing Fox who gave me the secret recipe for the Chippewa's own miracle herbal cure, which combined with the elements which are present in the waters of Medicine Creek, becomes doubly effective! So powerful, so potent, so effective that one small bottle of the famous Chippewa tonic — one small bottle that can be purchased for a mere one dollar American, my friends! — one small bottle will cure an entire family of whatever ails them!"

Simone said, "And you have an ample supply of this Chippewa tonic for sale, I trust, Professor?"

Munroe turned toward her and swept the hand holding his top hat in a grandiose gesture. "Of course I do, madam. But I won't allow a single one of the citizens of this lovely community to purchase my tonic . . . not until tonight, after you've all enjoyed the entertainment we intend to present for you." He clapped the hat back on his head. "Now, if you'll excuse us, we'll go find that camping place you so kindly told us about."

Immediately, several men and even more youngsters volunteered to lead them to the spot. Professor Munroe grinned and waved at them as he climbed up onto the wagon seat again. Once he was there, he opened a small door in the front of the wagon and reached inside to bring out three little bottles made of brown glass. He leaned over to give one apiece to Simone, Casebolt, and Michael.

"Samples for you and your families," Munroe said. "The best advertising is always word of mouth, my friends, so tell *your* friends about how Professor Nicodemus Munroe's Famous Chippewa Tonic ended all of your aches and pains permanently!"

With that, he took up the reins, slapped them against the backs of the horses pulling the wagon, and headed for the western edge of town. As the wagon moved past, followed closely by the second vehicle, Deborah Munroe waved and smiled again.

Simone said, "Well, what do you think about that?"

Casebolt shook his head. "You could've plumb knocked me over with a feather when I heard how somebody else'd been cured by sittin' in Medicine Creek."

Michael laughed. "You didn't believe him, did you, Billy?" he asked. "Munroe was making all of that up for some reason."

"You sure about that?" Casebolt asked with a frown.

"Why don't you try the tonic he gave you?" Simone suggested gently, lifting the bottle in her hand.

"Well . . . I reckon I could do that." There was a cork in the neck of the bottle. Casebolt got hold of it with his teeth and pulled it out, then spit it into the palm of his other hand. He held the now-open bottle under his nose and sniffed, making a face as he pulled his head back. "Stuff's got a smell to it."

Michael uncorked his bottle and smelled

the contents, too. His grimace mirrored Casebolt's. "What do you think, Billy? I'll try it if you will, but you've got to go first."

"Can't be any worsen some of the home-brewed rotgut I've had," Casebolt mused. He held the bottle to his lips. "Well, here goes."

He took a sip.

Michael and Simone watched curiously. Casebolt frowned, licked his lips, took another sip. Finally he nodded and said, "Not bad. Not bad at all. Goes down sort of warm and smooth."

Michael tilted his bottle up and took a healthy swallow. When he lowered the bottle, there was a look of pleasant surprise on his face. "You're right, Billy," he said. "That doesn't taste like medicine at all."

"Perhaps I should try it," Simone said. "If one of you gentlemen would be so kind as to take out this cork. . . ."

Michael uncorked the bottle for her, and she sampled the tonic. She smiled as she said, "That's very good. I don't know if it will really cure anything or not, but at least it's enjoyable."

"Well, if Professor Munroe's nothin' but a snake-oil peddler, at least he's got a good brand of the stuff to peddle," Casebolt said.

Michael was looking thoughtful. He said,

"And if the professor was telling the truth about using the ingredients he found in the waters of Medicine Creek, there might be a pretty good story here for the paper."

"Aw, now, Michael," Casebolt protested. "I already told you how the Shoshones won't want a bunch of folks messin' around that creek. It's a mighty special place to them. Bad enough that first story of yours attracted the attention of the professor. What if a bunch of other folks saw it, too?"

"I doubt if that happened," Michael said skeptically. "I'm not sure where Professor Munroe got hold of that copy of the *Sentinel,* but I don't see how the word could have spread very far."

Casebolt sounded dubious as he said, "Well, I sure hope you're right."

A locomotive whistle shrilled as a train pulled into the depot down the street. That would be the westbound, Casebolt knew. Either he or the marshal tried to be on hand every time a train came in, just to keep an eye on who was getting off, and since Cole wasn't in town at the moment, Casebolt figured he had better get down to the station.

He said as much as he put the cork back in his bottle of tonic. Michael had just about finished his, Casebolt noted, and Simone was still taking an occasional discreet, lady-like sip from hers. "See you folks later," Casebolt said as he slipped the bottle into his shirt pocket and ambled toward the Union Pacific depot.

Several passengers had already disembarked by the time he got there, but they were still on the platform, retrieving their valises and carpetbags from the baggage car. Casebolt looked them over and decided that none of them appeared to be the trouble-making sort. Far from it, in fact. He saw one gent on crutches, another with a twisted, withered arm, a gaunt, pale-faced man who had a wracking cough, and a fellow with such thick spectacles that his features were distorted grotesquely by the lenses. Even with the spectacles, the last man was stumbling around as if he could still barely see.

The man on crutches must have spotted the badge on Casebolt's shirt, because he suddenly said, "Hey, Deputy!"

Casebolt went over to him. "What can I do for you, mister?"

The man had a newspaper in his hand. It was a paper from Cheyenne, Casebolt saw as the man unfolded it. The man thrust the paper toward Casebolt, balancing awkwardly on his crutches as he did so, and poked a finger at a headline.

"Can you tell me where to find this place?" the man asked.

Casebolt looked at the headline and gulped, his eyes widening.

It read:

MIRACLE WATER CURES WIND RIVER MAN OF MYSTERY ILLNESS.

14

Cole was tired by the time he rode back into Wind River early that evening, and adding to his weariness was the undeniable feeling that in the long run he hadn't done a damned bit of good.

Kermit Sawyer had reacted predictably to the news that one of his hands had been jumped in town by some of Austin Fisk's Latch Hook riders. The Texan had been ready to strap on his six-shooter and start slinging lead. Sawyer had become even more incensed when Lon Rogers told him the men from Fisk's spread believed the Diamond S was responsible for the raid that had left four Latch Hook punchers dead and a sizable herd of cattle missing.

"Rustlers?" Sawyer had bellowed. "That son of a bitch Fisk thinks we're rustlers?"

It had taken some fast talking from Cole to persuade Sawyer not to saddle up and lead his men over to Latch Hook with guns

171

blazing. That would only make it look even more like the Diamond S had been responsible for the rustling.

"Fisk doesn't have a lick of proof against you," Cole had pointed out. "He and his men are just spewing out words to see where they land. If you can just keep your wits about you, Sawyer, nobody around here is going to believe Fisk when he makes those wild charges."

Finally, after a lot of arguing, Sawyer had agreed to wait and let things calm down a little. Cole's promise to investigate the situation had mollified him only slightly. But for now, Cole was willing to settle for that.

Sooner or later, though, this powder keg he was sitting on was going to explode. . . .

Something struck Cole as unusual as he rode Ulysses down Grenville Avenue toward the marshal's office. He reined the golden sorrel back to a slow walk and looked around. There was an uncommon number of people on the street, he decided. The boardwalks were busy with pedestrians, and the hitch racks were full. Wagons were parked in front of nearly every building. As Cole passed Hank Parker's Pronghorn Saloon, the noise coming from inside the place was even louder than it usually was.

Cole was accustomed to Wind River being

a busy place. Even though the railhead had moved on to Rock Springs, Union Pacific workers were coming through all the time, and more new settlers from back east arrived every day, anxious to make a fresh start with a farm or a ranch. However, Cole's instincts told him that the crowd in town tonight couldn't be explained that easily. Instead of dropping Ulysses off at the stable first, as he had intended, he rode straight to the marshal's office.

Casebolt must have been watching for him, because the deputy stepped out onto the boardwalk before Cole got there. The deputy's lanky figure was silhouetted by the yellow glow of lamplight from the window behind him. Casebolt came out to the edge of the boardwalk as Cole reined in and swung down from the saddle.

"Mighty glad to see you, Marshal," Casebolt greeted him as Cole looped the sorrel's reins over the hitch rail. "Things've been poppin' around here."

"I can see that," Cole said. He stepped up onto the boardwalk. "What's going on?"

"It started this afternoon when the westbound train pulled in. It was darned near full of people from Cheyenne and Laramie and Rawlins. Hell, some of 'em even come from as far away as Kansas and Nebrasky."

"People come here all the time," Cole said.

"Not like these folks," Casebolt said with a shake of his head. "They're all lookin' for Medicine Creek."

Cole stiffened. "What?"

"They found out about it somehow from that newspaper story Michael Hatfield wrote. Seems that some o' them reporter fellers in Cheyenne and other places wrote stories of their own 'bout what happened to me. It's all over this part of the country."

"Damn it!" Cole said fervently. "This is just what I was afraid would happen when Michael started spreading the news. I had started to hope I was wrong, but . . ." He glanced up and down the crowded street and shook his head. "It looks like I was right after all. I wish I hadn't been."

"What're you goin' to do?" Casebolt wanted to know.

Cole frowned for a moment, his rugged features bleak, then shrugged. "What *can* I do? No law against coming to Wind River, and so far that's all these folks have done. And that creek's not on private property, either. There's nothing to stop people from going out and looking for it."

" 'Cept maybe the Shoshone," Casebolt said.

"That's what I'm worried about. If a
174

bunch of fools start swarming over land that the Shoshones regard as their hunting ground, Two Ponies and his people won't like it. They'll be even more upset if anything happens to disturb that creek, and I can't say as I'd blame them for it, either. But my hands are pretty much tied as long as all these strangers behave themselves in town."

Casebolt sighed tiredly. "Might've been better if I'd just gone ahead and died when I was so puny. That way there wouldn't have been all this ruckus."

"I wouldn't go that far," Cole told him. "I'd rather have to deal with the ruckus and still have you around, Billy." He stretched weary muscles. "I'm going to go on over to the boardinghouse and see if Mrs. Paine still has supper on the table. I'll be back here at the office in a little while."

"All right, I'll keep on keepin' an eye on things. Oh, yeah, how'd things go with Sawyer?"

"He's mad as a badger after somebody's poked a stick down his hole," Cole said with a tired grin. "Just about what I expected. He says he and his men didn't have anything to do with raiding Fisk's ranch."

"You believe him?"

Cole nodded. "I do. Sawyer's no rustler,

no matter what his other faults are. I'll ride out to Fisk's place in a day or two and talk to him, try to keep a lid on this thing. Maybe I can get a line on who really raided his place."

"Hope those fellers don't get too proddy," Casebolt said. "We got enough on our plate right now. And speakin' of plates, I'd better let you get on to your supper. Didn't tell you about that medicine show yet, but it can wait."

"Medicine show? What —" Cole held up a hand. "No, you're right. It can wait. I'll see you later. Take care of Ulysses for me?"

"Sure."

Cole waved and started toward the boardinghouse where he had a room. Abigail Paine would probably still feed him, even if the other boarders had already eaten. She was pretty understanding of the unusual demands on a lawman's time.

And from the looks of things in Wind River tonight, Cole thought, it seemed that the demands were about to get even more unusual.

Frenchy slouched in his saddle as he rode along Wildcat Ridge. Overhead, stars glittered brightly in the night sky. There was still a definite hint of coolness in the breeze, which Frenchy suspected wasn't unusual here in this high country, even during springtime.

Sheer restlessness had brought him out here tonight. Like all the rest of the hands, he had been ready to charge over to Fisk's ranch when he heard about what had happened to Lon in Wind River. They could show those damned Latch Hook riders how a bunch of Texas boys raised hell and shoved a chunk under the corner!

But cooler heads — most notably Cole Tyler's — had prevailed, and Kermit Sawyer had promised to let things lie for the time being. Frenchy hoped that wasn't a mistake.

At the same time, *he* didn't want a shooting war with Latch Hook, either. Every time he thought about that, the image of Alexandra Fisk appeared in his mind, bringing with it memories of how sweet her lips had tasted and how soft they had been. Trouble between Diamond S and Latch Hook would wind up hurting Alexandra some way; Frenchy was sure of it.

And somehow, he couldn't stand the idea of anything hurting Alexandra. . . .

So he had come out here alone to ride and think and try to come up with some way of heading off the trouble between the two spreads. So far, he hadn't come up with a blessed thing. But he had enjoyed the moonlight and the smell of the pines and the cool evening breeze on his face.

Suddenly, that breeze brought a sound with it. The night was full of sounds, of course — the hoot of an owl, the far-off bugle of an elk, the sighing of the wind in the trees, the rustle of ground squirrels diving for their holes as the rider approached — but this was different.

Hoofbeats. Quite a few of them. But the rest of the Diamond S punchers were back at the bunkhouse tonight.

And that meant somebody was moving around on the ranch who had no business being here.

Frenchy reined in and listened intently. It was impossible to tell how many riders he was hearing, but he figured there had to be at least a dozen. They were still several hundred yards away, beyond the end of the ridge. But they were coming closer, and Frenchy knew it would be a good idea if he got out of sight.

He dropped down from his saddle and clenched the horse's reins tightly in his left hand. His right hand hovered over the butt of his gun. He led the horse toward a large stand of aspen that would offer some concealment.

A part of him wanted to challenge the men and demand to know what they were doing here. But if he did that and they were up to no good, they would probably open up on him as soon as he started to ask questions. That would be a quick way of getting killed. Better to lie low and find out just what the hell was going on.

Frenchy had been hidden in the aspens for only a few minutes when the mysterious horsemen swept out of the night and rode past his position. He couldn't tell much about them in the darkness, and he was able to make only a rough count of them. He numbered them at fourteen, pretty close to what he had estimated. They were headed north along the ridge.

He wasn't sure where they were going, but he couldn't help but remember how close the pass leading to the next valley was to the southern end of Wildcat Ridge. Some of Fisk's men could have easily come through there, even in the dark. Sawyer had never put a guard on that pass, but he might have to consider doing so in the future, Frenchy thought. That wouldn't help with the situation tonight, however.

When the strangers had moved on past, Frenchy mounted up again and eased out of the trees. He rode after them, following more by sound than by sight. After a few minutes, the group moved down off the ridge and into a wide, grassy meadow where more than a hundred of Kermit Sawyer's longhorns were grazing.

Frenchy's jaw tightened. It was pretty obvious what the men intended to do. They were spreading out, circling the cattle, gradually working them into a tighter, more manageable bunch.

They were rustling that stock, right in front of Frenchy's eyes!

The question was — what was he going to do about it?

He was sure none of the wideloopers had seen him. He could hang back, stay out of sight, and let them take the cattle. That might be the smartest thing to do, because then he could follow them and see where they were taking the stolen cows.

But if they gave him the slip somehow, Sawyer would lose a hundred head of prime longhorns. Regardless of what was most logical or most practical — or least dangerous — Frenchy knew he couldn't stand by and allow that to happen. He just couldn't.

The rustlers had the herd just about bunched up enough to drive without much trouble. Frenchy slipped his revolver from its holster and looped his thumb over the hammer. He lifted the gun, stood up in his stirrups, and shouted at the top of his lungs, "Hit 'em all at once, boys! *Now!*"

He loosed a couple of shots as he raked his mount with his spurs. The horse lunged forward and pounded down the slope toward the rustlers. Frenchy hauled it to the left, veering off to the side as he triggered the remaining three cartridges in his gun. Moving at an angle like that in the darkness, he might fool the cow thieves into thinking that there was more than one of him. He gave a high-pitched rebel yell as he guided the sure-footed pony with his knees and began to reload.

Return fire was coming from the rustlers by now, muzzle flashes bright in the night as guns crashed and boomed. When Frenchy's revolver was loaded again, he pulled his horse into a tight turn that sent him galloping back in the other direction. Again he began to fire, spacing his shots irregularly so that the rustlers couldn't detect a pattern in his attack.

There was no way he could outfight fourteen men; he knew that. But he was hoping that he could spook them and force them into fleeing. They were probably already a little nervous simply because of the dishonest errand that had brought them here to the Diamond S tonight. Frenchy wanted to play on that nervousness.

But if the rustlers *didn't* cut and run . . . if they didn't believe they were under attack by a large force of cowboys . . . then Frenchy was in trouble — bad trouble.

And in the next few moments, it quickly became obvious that was the case.

Several of the rustlers broke away from the others and charged toward him, guns blazing. Frenchy was no fool. He bit back a curse, jammed his gun in its holster, and wheeled his horse around. He used his spurs again and sent the animal leaping back toward Wildcat Ridge. If he could reach the top of the ridge, he could lose his pursuers in the heavy timber up there.

The rustlers' guns kept barking, and fingers of hot lead reached out in the night. One of them drew a fiery line of pain across Frenchy's upper right arm. He gasped, his lips drawing back from his teeth, but he kept riding and the horse underneath him didn't even break stride. He reached the ridge, started up the slope. Still the rustlers came after him, whooping and shouting. He wondered if Wilt Paxton was among them. Would Austin Fisk send some of his men over here to steal cattle in retaliation for the raid on Latch Hook? Frenchy thought that was more than possible.

Latch Hook had lost four men in that raid, and every man on the spread blamed the Diamond S for the deaths. Frenchy knew he could expect no mercy from the men chasing him, especially if they were some of Fisk's crew.

He rode hunched low in the saddle to make himself a smaller target, but that wasn't enough. A rustler's bullet suddenly clipped his left shoulder and went on to crease the neck of his mount. The impact of the slug drove Frenchy forward onto the neck of the horse even as it let out a shrill whinny of pain and leaped forward wildly. It was all Frenchy could do to hang on for dear life. The horse was out of control now. Frenchy felt blood trickling down his side from his wounded shoulder, and his head spun crazily.

Suddenly he realized he was among the trees again, as his mount reached the top of the ridge and darted into the thick stands of pine there. Darker shadows closed in around him. He had to trust the horse not to run headlong into one of the pines. The animal slowed slightly. Frenchy pushed himself straighter in the saddle and tightened his grip on the reins. He fought off the dizziness that threatened to overwhelm him.

The shots from the rustlers had slowed, and he knew they could no longer see him. He wondered if they would pursue him into the trees. To do so would be to expose themselves to an ambush if he turned and made a fight of it. He suspected they might abandon the chase and return to their companions. They had to know that all the shooting might have been heard at the ranch headquarters, even though it was several miles away. Loud noises earned a long way at night in this thin, dry air.

Frenchy became aware that no one was shooting anymore, and he knew his guess must have been right. The raiders had returned to the task that had brought them here to the Diamond S. They would push those cattle through the pass as quickly as they could and put the ranch behind them.

And there wasn't a damned thing he could do to stop them, not with the bullet crease in his shoulder still welling blood and pain jarring through him with every step of the horse. In fact, he was swaying in the saddle now, and he had to grab at the horn to keep from falling.

The next time a wave of dizziness hit him, he wasn't quite quick enough. He felt his fingers slide off the saddlehorn, and then he was falling. He had the presence of mind to kick his feet free of the stirrups, so that the horse couldn't drag him if it bolted. An instant later, he crashed to the ground, his fall cushioned only slightly by the carpet of pine needles that had fallen here under the trees.

The horse didn't bolt. Frenchy felt it nuzzling him curiously, and he tried to murmur a few words of reassurance. He didn't know if they came out of his mouth or not.

By that time, he didn't know anything.

15

It was his job to be here, Michael Hatfield told himself. The visit of the medicine show to Wind River was news, and news was his business, after all.

The fact that he was enjoying himself immensely didn't change the fact that he was actually working.

Those thoughts went through his head as he grinned and clapped along with the music coming from the squeeze box being played by Calvin Dumont. For such a huge man, Dumont had a delicate touch with the instrument and could coax a variety of tunes from it, ranging from melancholy dirges that brought tears to the eyes of his listeners to rollicking jigs such as the one he was playing now. His wife, Letitia, was dancing on the lowered tailgate of the wagon as Dumont played. The tiny woman moved with grace and dexterity, her legs and arms flashing as she darted about in time to the music in a different low-cut, spangled costume.

When the dance was over. Letitia took a bow as the audience applauded appreciatively. Dumont put the squeeze box aside and said in a high-pitched voice that was incongruous for his size, "Now, ladies and gentlemen, for your enjoyment, Chief Laughing Fox of the Chippewas will demonstrate his amazing skills with the tomahawk!"

Dumont waved an arm the size of a small tree trunk, and Chief Laughing Fox walked out from behind the wagon, pacing off some fifty feet and then turning to face the wagon. The audience shifted so that they could see better. A broad plank with the crude outline of a man on it had been set up against the side of the wagon. Laughing Fox was carrying six small tomahawks in his left hand. One by one, he took them in his right and threw them, the solemn expression on his face never varying as the weapons spun through the air and thudded into the target. He threw quickly, sending all six tomahawks into the target in less than a minute. When he was done, the tomahawks outlined the figure drawn on the plank. The men who had been watching broke into applause and whistles of admiration.

As stolid as ever, the Chippewa chieftain walked to the target and retrieved the tomahawks. The sharp heads of the weapons had sunk deeply into the wood, and he had to grunt a little as he wrenched some of them loose. Then he turned and walked back to his previous spot.

Michael wondered what Laughing Fox was going to do next. He didn't expect to see Deborah Munroe emerge from the wagon and walk over to the target, but that was exactly what happened. She had changed her costume, too, and was wearing a dark-blue outfit that was even more daring, revealing practically all of her lovely legs in dark-blue mesh stockings. With a smile on her face, she stood in front of the target and leaned back against it, spreading her arms and legs slightly so that she was lined up with the figure drawn on the plank. Michael's eyes widened as he realized what was about to happen.

He wanted to cry out for them to stop the act, but Laughing Fox already had one of the tomahawks in his hand and his arm was drawn back. If Michael shouted, it might throw off the Indian's concentration. All he could do was watch in hushed, shocked silence — like the rest of the men in the audience — as the Chippewa's arm flashed

188

forward and the tomahawk tumbled through the air toward Deborah.

The blade thumped into the wood about four inches from Deborah's right ear. The smile on her face never wavered, nor did she flinch. She stood there like a statue as the other five tomahawks struck the target around her, one on the other side of her head, two on either side of her torso, two flanking her lush hips.

Michael thought that was the end of the act, but Deborah didn't move. From a sheath on his belt, Laughing Fox produced a Bowie knife with a long, heavy blade, and he threw it with the same blinding speed and lack of emotion with which he had tossed the tomahawks. The tip of the Bowie's blade dug into the wood of the target between Deborah's slightly spread thighs, the handle quivering from the impact.

The spectators were silent for a couple of seconds, then thunderous applause burst from them, along with shouts and whistles. Deborah stepped away from the target, still smiling broadly, and took a bow. As Michael clapped, his eyes were drawn to the dark valley between her full breasts that was revealed as she leaned over. He felt a flush of embarrassment — but he kept looking anyway.

Professor Nicodemus Munroe came around the other side of the wagon, clapping just like everyone else. After a moment he held up his hands for silence, and the applause gradually died away. He took his niece's hand and led her to the tailgate of the wagon, where both of them climbed the portable steps that had been set up there. The professor said loudly, "Thank you, my friends, thank you. Another hand for Chief Laughing Fox of the Chippewas and his lovely assistant, my niece Deborah!"

There was another round of applause, and then Munroe continued, "Now, for your pleasure, Deborah will entertain you with a song."

Calvin Dumont began playing the squeeze box again, but more quietly this time so as not to overpower Deborah's voice. She sang an old ballad about lost loves and men going off to war, and more than one man in the audience was blinking rapidly and trying to surreptitiously brush away a tear when she was finished. Michael thought he had never heard a prettier song.

Nor seen a prettier singer. . . .

He was glad his wife, Delia, had chosen not to come with him tonight. She would have probably dug an elbow into his side when she saw how raptly he was watching

Deborah. Delia could be jealous at times, although Michael had never given her any reason to be, of course. He had always been faithful to his pretty, redheaded wife, the mother of his two small children. He intended to remain faithful to her.

But still, a man could look, couldn't he? Look, and maybe dream a little bit . . . even if it did get him a sharp elbow in the ribs every now and then.

Deborah launched into another song, and as she did her eyes met Michael's. He had the uncanny feeling that she was singing to him and him alone.

He liked that feeling. He liked it a lot.

And now he wasn't even thinking about Delia anymore.

Dr. Judson Kent was at the desk in his office, going over the notes he had made as he saw patients during the day and entering them into his permanent records. Most doctors were not so meticulous, but Kent had always found it helpful to be able to look up what he had done in the past.

The front door was unlocked, of course. Kent left it that way until he was ready to retire for the night. A doctor never knew when someone might have need of his services and come looking for him. So he wasn't surprised when he heard the door open and someone came into the foyer. Kent laid his pen aside and looked up.

A solidly built man of medium height stood there, a serious expression on his face. He had a short, ginger-colored beard, and wore a brown tweed suit and a derby. Kent had never seen him before.

"Dr. Kent?" the man asked.

"That's right," the physician replied. "What can I do for you, sir?"

The man came into the room and held out a hand. "Allow me to introduce myself. I'm Dr. Bramwell Carter."

Kent stood up and shook hands with Carter. "Another medical man, eh?"

"That's right," Carter said with a nod. "Harvard, class of '48."

"Oxford, '46," Kent said. He smiled. "I'm very glad to meet you, Dr. Carter. What brings you to Wind River? Have you come to establish a practice?"

Carter grinned. "No, I'm not after your patients, Doctor. I've plenty of my own back in Philadelphia. I'm just taking a bit of a sabbatical, if you will, in order to investigate something that interests me."

"And what would be . . . ?"

"The phenomenon that's being referred to in the newspapers as 'Medicine Creek.' "

Kent frowned in surprise. "You've heard about that all the way back in Philadelphia?"

"Such news often spreads quickly," Carter replied. "I read about how a man was cured of a mysterious illness by the waters of this creek. The papers played it up quite a bit. Surely you knew the story had made its way back east?"

"Not that far," Kent muttered. "I'm a bit surprised you put any credence in it, Doctor."

"Oh, I don't," Carter said. "But you see, that's a specialty of mine, revealing quackery and false cures for what they are — the refuge of the wicked and the last, often fatal hope of the desperate."

Kent took a deep breath. "Then you've come to the right place, Doctor, because quackery is in full force here. Wind River is full of people tonight who have come seeking some sort of miracle cure for whatever ails them, and there's even a so-called medicine show in town."

"I know," Carter said with another nod. "I heard about it over at the hotel. I came in on the train this afternoon, too, and I'm staying over at the Territorial House."

"The best hotel in town," Kent said.

"So I gathered. I inquired over there as to whether this community had a *real* physi-

193

cian, and I was directed here. Do I miss my guess, Doctor Kent, or have I found an ally in my quest?"

"Indeed you have, sir," Kent replied. "The whole territory seems to have gone mad because of this so-called Medicine Creek."

"Then it's up to men like us to restore some reason and sanity to the proceedings, eh?"

"It certainly is," Kent said as he reached for his coat. "Shall we start with that medicine show?"

"My thought exactly," Carter said.

The two men left Kent's office and walked west along Grenville Avenue, toward the trees on the edge of town where the medicine show wagons were parked. As they passed the marshal's office, Kent noticed that there was no light in the window. Cole Tyler and Billy Casebolt were probably out attending to law business somewhere. That was all right, Kent thought. He didn't need Cole backing him up on this.

He and the marshal hadn't really talked much since Cole and Casebolt had returned from the Shoshone village. Cole might not even be aware that despite his absence on the night of the dance, Simone McKay had not accompanied Kent to the social. That wouldn't have been fair to Cole, Simone had said.

Well, let the marshal think whatever he wanted to, Kent told himself. At the moment, there were more important things to be considered than . . . than romance!

He heard applause and shouts of approval as he and Carter approached the medicine show. "The entertainment portion of the evening must be going on," Kent commented.

"Just concluding, from the looks of things," Carter said. He gestured toward the man in the top hat who stood on the tailgate of one of the wagons, hands raised for quiet.

"That's Professor Nicodemus Munroe," Kent told his companion. "He was described to me earlier by someone who saw the wagons when they came into town this afternoon."

"Professor!" Carter snorted in contempt. "I'd be willing to wager that he conferred the title upon himself. No reputable institution of higher learning would dignify a man like that with such an honorific."

"I dare say you're correct."

The two men moved up to the edge of the crowd as Munroe said, "Now that you've been entertained, my friends — and entertained magnificently, I might add — we come to the real reason all of you are here tonight! I know you've come seeking relief from the torments of the mind and body that plague you! You have come seeking solace from your pain! And I will give you that relief! I will give you that solace! *Right here!*" He whipped one of the bottles of tonic from the pocket of his coat. "Right here is what you need, my friends! The world-famous Chippewa Tonic — made with the same ingredients as are found in your own well-known Medicine Creek, may I remind you — will cure your ills, will settle your stomach, will clear your mind, will restore every bit of your manly vigor! And what will this miracle cost you, you ask? Perhaps as much as . . . one hundred dollars?

"No, my friends! Not one hundred dollars, not fifty, not even twenty-five dollars! A bottle of this miraculous elixir will cost you only the paltry sum of one dollar American! One thin dollar to restore your health! That price is not too much to pay, is it, my friends?"

Several men in the crowd shouted out, "No!", and others began waving coins in the air.

"My lovely niece Deborah will move among you now with a supply of Chippewa

Tonic," Munroe went on. "An offer like this may never come along again, my friends. I beg of you, take advantage of it while you can."

Suddenly, Bramwell Carter bellowed, "The only one taking advantage here tonight is you, you damned faker!"

Kent stiffened beside the doctor from Philadelphia. He hadn't expected Carter to throw out such a blatant challenge. As a startled silence fell on the crowd and many of the men turned to see who had shouted, the massive Calvin Dumont started forward from his position by the wagon's tailgate, a scowl on his broad face and an angry growl issuing from his throat.

"Wait a moment, Mr. Dumont!" Professor Munroe said with a sharp motion of his hand. "I know you're upset, but I want to see the man who would make such a claim. Show yourself, sir!"

Carter strode forward, and Kent felt that he had no choice but to accompany the man. The curious crowd parted to let them through. Kent passed Michael Hatfield, and the young newspaperman asked him quietly, "What's going on, Doctor?"

"Just watch and learn, Michael," Kent advised him dryly.

Carter turned around to face the crowd

when he reached the rear of the wagon. He lifted his hands and said loudly, "Hold on a minute, folks! Let me speak, if you please! I'm here to tell you that this man is a faker, and that so-called tonic he's trying to peddle to you is nothing but flavored water and whiskey!"

"A lie, sir, a damnable lie!" Munroe thundered. Shouts of approval for Munroe and catcalls directed at Carter came from the crowd.

"I know you want to believe him," Carter called out over the racket, "but I'm a medical doctor, and I know he's the one who is lying here! My name is Dr. Bramwell Carter, and I've exposed many frauds just like this man here!"

One of the men in the crowd yelled, "Why don't you go back where you came from, mister? Professor Munroe's here to help us!"

"He's here to help himself to your money, that's what you mean!" Carter shot back. "Your own local doctor, Judson Kent, will tell you the same thing!"

Carter turned to look at Kent, who found himself compelled to go ahead with this, regardless of how uncomfortable the confrontation made him. He said, "I know you men, and you know me. I'm telling you no medicine can do everything that Professor

Munroe claims for his tonic."

That quieted the crowd a little. Kent was well respected in Wind River, and these men might listen to him more easily than they would a stranger like Bramwell Carter. Kent took a deep breath, ready to carry on, when Munroe interrupted him.

"I'm certain Dr. Kent is telling you what he believes, my friend, but allow me to remind you — Dr. Kent did not believe that the waters of Medicine Creek could cure Deputy Billy Casebolt. And yet there stands Deputy Casebolt now, living proof that miracles do happen!" The professor leveled a finger toward the edge of the crowd.

Everyone turned to look. Casebolt was indeed standing there, looking embarrassed, and Cole was at his side. The two lawmen must have come up after he and Carter had arrived, Kent thought.

Cole moved forward through the crowd. "What's all this ruckus?" he asked as he came up to the rear of the wagon.

"I was just conducting business as usual, Marshal, when these two men tried to interrupt and interfere with the sale of my Chippewa Tonic," Munroe said before Kent and Carter had a chance to explain.

Cole looked at Kent. "Is that true, Doctor?"

"We were simply trying to prevent these men from wasting their money on a fraudulent cure," Kent began.

"Nothing illegal about buying tonic, is there?"

"No, but —"

Carter interrupted Kent by pointing at Munroe and saying angrily, "This man is a quack! He's no professor!"

"I beg your pardon!" Munroe sniffed angrily. "I'm a scientist and researcher, and I've never been so insulted!"

"I don't care about that," Cole snapped. "Deputy Casebolt told me about this medicine show, so I thought I'd come down here and take a look. I don't see anything illegal going on."

"But, Cole, surely you won't allow this . . . this sham to proceed?" Kent said.

"I don't have any choice, Doctor. As long as Professor Munroe doesn't break any laws, he can sell whatever he damn well pleases. If anybody's doing anything illegal here, it appears to be you and this other fella."

Kent's eyes narrowed. Was Cole doing this only because of Simone? That was possible, he supposed, and yet in the relatively short time Cole Tyler had been the marshal, Kent knew he had tried to be fair and honest in the way he enforced the law.

"We have a right to be heard, too," Kent said.

Cole shrugged. "Yep. But do it someplace else. Anybody who wants to listen to what you have to say can go with you."

"That's the best you'll do, Marshal?" Carter asked.

"It's the only thing I can do."

"Very well. Come along, Dr. Kent." Carter addressed the crowd again. "Anyone who wants to hear the *truth* can come with us."

No one followed him as he strode off except Kent.

Behind them, Professor Munroe called out, "Now, don't crowd around, my friends. There's plenty of this miracle elixir for all of you. Step right up there . . . that'll be a dollar . . . step right up. . . ."

16

Michael was already mentally writing the story of what had happened tonight when Deborah Munroe came up to him. The crowd had dispersed, the men all heading home to try the tonic they had bought. Michael had purchased another bottle, since the small sample Munroe had given him that afternoon was already gone. The bottles the professor sold were larger, containing enough of the tonic to last quite a while, since Munroe had cautioned the audience not to drink too much of it at one time. It was too potent for that, he had said.

The weight of the bottle in Michael's right-hand coat pocket pulled the coat down on that side. He was trying to straighten it when he found himself looking at Deborah. She smiled at him in the light of the lanterns that were hung from the wagons.

"Hello," she said. "You're Mr. Hatfield,

aren't you? The editor of the local newspaper?"

"Ah . . . yes, I am." Michael blinked. This was the closest he had been to Deborah, and she was even more lovely than he had thought. A poet would have described her eyes as blue pools, he thought, and her skin was like cream. His eyes dropped for a second to the proud thrust of her full breasts against the silk of the daring costume. He jerked his gaze back up, hoping she hadn't noticed his impropriety.

She gave no sign that she had. She said, "A gentleman such as yourself must have seen a great many wonderful performers. Tell me, Mr. Hatfield, and please be honest — what did you think of my singing?"

"Why . . . why . . . I thought it was the best I've ever heard!"

"Really? I know you're only being kind —"

"Oh, no! Not at all! I mean it, you were really wonderful, Miss Munroe."

"You must call me Deborah."

"All right, and I'm Michael." He couldn't believe he was having this conversation. She was so lovely, and her perfume smelled so sweet. . . .

"Are you going to write about our little show in your newspaper?"

"I planned to." He looked more solemn as he went on, "I'm sorry about the disturbance. I know Dr. Kent quite well, and I didn't expect him to be quite so . . . so intolerant."

Deborah sighed and shook her head. "You'd be amazed how many people are so narrow-minded, Michael. They don't want to believe that my uncle's tonic can really help them. I hate to think about the poor souls who have turned away and gone back to their lives of misery, simply because they wouldn't believe!"

"Well, I certainly intend to be fair to your uncle in whatever I write for the *Sentinel,* if that's what you're worried about."

She laid a hand on his arm, and even through the sleeves of his coat and shirt, the warmth of her touch seemed to sear his skin. "I wasn't worried about that," she said softly. "I wasn't worried about that at all."

Michael swallowed hard, wishing that she could keep her hand on his arm all night.

"I have to get back to my uncle now," she said, and he tried not to let the disappointment he felt show on his face. "I will see you again, won't I?"

"You'll be here in town for a few days, won't you?" he asked.

"Of course."

"Then you'll see me again," Michael declared. "I'll be here for every performance. I want to hear you sing again."

"You're so sweet . . . Good night, Michael."

Then she was gone, leaving only a faint, delicious scent on the air and a spot on his arm that seemed to almost glow from the warmth of her touch.

Cole was in the Wind River Café the next morning with a plate of scrambled eggs, hash brown potatoes, and thick slices of ham in front of him on the counter. Steam rose from the cup of coffee at his elbow. To be honest, the food prepared by Rose Foster wasn't quite as good as the fare that her regular cook, old Monty Riordan, dished up, but Cole was still enjoying his meal.

Right up until the time the door of the café banged open behind him and a familiar voice said angrily, "Tyler! I been lookin' for you."

Cole's instincts cried out for him to spin around and grab the .44 on his hip, but he controlled the impulse with an effort. Instead he turned slowly on the stool where he sat and said, "Busting in on a man like that is a good way to get yourself shot, Sawyer."

Kermit Sawyer ignored the comment, just as he ignored the stares of the other diners. He stood with his big, knobby-knuckled hands half-clenched into fists and said, "I've got a man down at Kent's office bein' patched up, and that damned Fisk is to blame. His men made off with a hundred head of my stock last night, and shot my foreman to boot!"

"LeDoux's been shot?" Cole frowned. "Is he all right?"

"I reckon he will be. He's got a bullet hole in his shoulder and he lost some blood. Thought the slug just creased him, he said, but it went right through. I don't know what that sawbones'll say about it. I left Frenchy there with some of the boys and came lookin' for you. That old codger of a deputy told me you were down here."

Rose Foster came out of the café's kitchen. "I swear, Mr. Sawyer," she said, "you sound like an old bull bellowing out here. Could you be a little quieter? Folks are trying to eat breakfast."

Sawyer's face flushed under the scolding, and for a second Cole thought the Texan was going to explode. Rose was braver than most to talk to him like that. But despite his many flaws, Sawyer was a gentleman, and after a moment he reached up to tug at the brim of his black hat. "Sorry, ma'am," he said. "Didn't mean to upset you."

"That's all right," Rose said. "Why don't you sit down, and I'll pour you a cup of coffee?"

Sawyer looked like the last thing he wanted to do was sit down, but he did it anyway. Rose poured coffee for him, then offered him something to eat. Sawyer shook his head. "Much obliged anyway, ma'am. I ate a bite earlier, before I left the ranch."

After Rose had moved on down the counter, Cole said, "You'd better tell me what happened, Sawyer. Just try to hold it down."

The cattleman glowered at Cole and said, "I told you. A bunch of Latch Hook riders raided my spread last night. Frenchy caught 'em at it and got a bullet for his trouble. He's damned lucky they didn't kill him. He passed out from the bullet wound and didn't come to until nearly dawn. He was able to make it back to the ranch house, and we put him in a wagon and brought him right on to town. Like I said, he's down at Doc Kent's now."

"You said the thieves got a hundred head of your stock?"

"That's right."

"And LeDoux saw them, recognized them as Austin Fisk's men?"

Sawyer snorted. "Who else could they have been?"

"The same bunch that hit Latch Hook a few days ago?" Cole suggested.

"I'm not sure that raid ever happened," Sawyer said. "I think Fisk spread that story just so he'd have an excuse to come a'raidin'."

Cole shook his head. "Doesn't sound too likely to me. Could be the same gang of wideloopers hit both ranches, or there might have been two bunches. Plenty of hardcases and owlhoots drifting through these parts, Sawyer, you know that."

"I don't care who it was. What are you goin' to do about it, Tyler?"

"I'm going to finish my breakfast," Cole said. "Then I'll go down and talk to LeDoux. After I've done that, maybe I'll take a ride out to Fisk's place. I've been meaning to do that anyway."

Sawyer drained his coffee, dropped a coin on the counter, and stood up. "You'd better get to the bottom of this, that's all I've got to say. If you don't, me and my boys'll handle it ourselves."

"You stay away from Latch Hook," Cole warned.

Sawyer just gave him a hard stare and turned away. The rancher stalked out of the café, banging the door behind him again.

Rose drifted over and said, "Mr. Sawyer's not happy this morning."

Cole grunted. "Sawyer's never happy."

"Did he say something about one of his men getting shot?"

"Don't worry," Cole assured her. "It wasn't young Rogers."

"I wasn't worried. I was just . . . curious."

Cole looked down at his plate to hide a grin. Everybody in town knew that Lon Rogers was sweet on Rose.

It looked like maybe she was starting to return the feeling.

Cole had already noticed the hectic activity in Wind River this morning, and the town had grown even busier while he was eating breakfast, he saw as he headed for Dr. Judson Kent's office a few minutes later. The livery stables and wagon yards were doing a brisk business as the strangers who had begun flocking into the settlement rented saddle horses, buggies, and wagons. The scene reminded Cole of stories he had heard about San Francisco during the Gold Rush, only this time the seekers streaming out of Wind River to the southwest were searching for health, not wealth.

They were looking for Medicine Creek.

Cole shook his head and went on to Kent's office.

Frenchy LeDoux told him essentially the same story as Kermit Sawyer had. It had been pure happenstance that Frenchy had spotted the rustlers as they rode across the Diamond S, and he was indeed lucky to have survived his reckless attack on them. From the grim, angry looks on the faces of Sawyer and the men who had come into town with him, they were ready to settle this feud with Latch Hook once and for all, with guns and blood if necessary.

The only good news was that Frenchy would recover from his wound with a minimum of difficulty, in Kent's opinion. "The wound is a clean one," the doctor told Cole, "and the bullet did surprisingly little damage. Mr. LeDoux was very fortunate."

"Didn't feel lucky at the time," Frenchy said. "Figured I was a goner, in fact."

"Don't you worry, Frenchy," Sawyer assured him. "We'll settle the score."

"You won't do anything until I've had a talk with Fisk," Cole said. "I'll swing by your place later and let you know what he told me."

"I can tell you right now what he'll say. He'll deny knowin' anything about it, the lyin' son of a bitch."

Cole gave the rancher a hard look. "Just let me handle this, Sawyer."

"For now." Sawyer's face was bleak. "For now, Tyler."

17

Two Ponies sat his horse atop a ridge and watched the white men as they moved across the broad flat in front of him. They seemed to Two Ponies more numerous than grains of sand or the rocks that littered the plains. He knew that was wrong; in actuality there were probably not more than twenty or thirty of the strangers.

But they had no business here. This was the land where the Shoshones hunted and made their homes.

Two Ponies feared that he knew what the white men sought.

For the most part, the Shoshones had been friends with the whites who had come here to what they now called Wyoming Territory. Unlike the Sioux, who had fought savagely against the interlopers, the Shoshone had welcomed them, even when the white men had brought their steel rails and the thunder wagon which moved along them spouting smoke and fire like some sort of evil spirit. Like it or not, the white men were changing the face of this land. Two Ponies liked to think that the Shoshones were able to accept this because they were more intelligent and more courageous than the Sioux and the Cheyenne and the Pawnee.

But there were some things not even the Shoshones could accept. There were some things that were sacred, that must not be disturbed.

His strong features set in a grim mask, Two Ponies wheeled his horse and rode toward Wind River.

"You're not going to that medicine show again, are you?" Delia Hatfield asked her husband.

Michael didn't look at her. "What do you mean?"

"I mean you were there last night, so there's no reason for you to go again. You can write about it for the paper from what you already saw."

Delia sounded like she was just being logical, Michael thought, but there was an edge to her voice, an undertone that told him she was displeased. Faint though it was, it was a sound he had come to know intimately.

"I don't know yet," he said as he pushed his chair back and stood up from the kitchen table. He felt Delia's eyes on him as he went over to the counter and picked up the bottle of Chippewa Tonic he had purchased the night before. He got a spoon from a drawer and uncorked the bottle, then poured a dose of the tonic into the spoon.

"Should you be taking so much of that?" Delia asked from the table, where she was feeding some thin gruel to six-month-old Lincoln. Three-year-old Gretchen was at the other end of the table, spooning mush into her own mouth.

Michael lifted the spoon to his mouth and swallowed the tonic before answering. "Professor Munroe swears this concoction will cure just about anything," he said, and added to himself, *Except maybe an unhappy wife.*

"Well, you should be careful with it. You don't want to make yourself sick."

Michael didn't say anything, didn't point out that the whole idea of the tonic was to keep from being sick. His coat was on a hook beside the door. He picked it up and shrugged into it. "I'd better get down to the paper."

"Will you be home for lunch?"

"I don't know. Don't worry about me. Just

fix something for yourself and the kids."

With that he left the kitchen, going through the front room of the house and out to the side street which led to Grenville Avenue. A minute later, when he reached the main street, he started to turn east, toward the office of the *Sentinel.*

But then, for some reason, his steps took him west instead — toward the clearing under the big trees where the medicine show wagons were parked.

He wasn't sure if anyone would be out and about this early around the wagons, but he saw Deborah Munroe right away, his heart seeming to skip a beat as he spotted her in a calico dress, carrying some water to their horses. If she had looked rather worldly and sophisticated the night before in her daring costume, she appeared undeniably wholesome this morning — but no less beautiful for that. Michael practically sprang forward to help her.

"Here, let me take that," he said as he grasped the handle of the large wooden bucket.

"Oh, Mr. Hatfield — I mean Michael. You startled me." She relinquished the bucket.

"I'm sorry, I didn't mean to."

"No, that's quite all right. I'm glad to see you again."

"I wasn't sure what you do around a medicine show during the day," Michael said as he carried the water over to the hobbled horses and poured it into a wooden trough that had been put out for them. "You only put on performances at night, don't you?"

"Those performances take a lot of practice and rehearsal," Deborah said. "And Uncle Nicodemus is always looking for ways to improve his tonic, so he does a great deal of research."

"I'm sure he does. I'm not certain that tonic could be improved, though." Michael grinned.

"You've been taking it? I wouldn't think you'd need it. You seem to have plenty of manly vigor already."

Michael felt his face growing warm. "Well, there's something to be said for preventative medicine, don't you think?"

Deborah smiled at him and linked her arm with his. "I certainly do."

Once again he felt the warmth of her body as she walked closely beside him, and it was every bit as exciting as it had been the night before. His heart was pounding so loudly in his chest it seemed certain that she could hear it, too.

He wondered where the other members

of the medicine show were, but a moment later that question was answered as Professor Munroe and Chief Laughing Fox came out of the professor's wagon, followed by Calvin and Letitia Dumont. All of them were dressed in a less gaudy fashion today except the Chippewa chieftain; he still wore the same buckskin outfit.

"Ah, Mr. Hatfield, isn't it?" Munroe greeted Michael. "How nice to see you again. What can we do for you this morning?"

Michael was acutely aware that Deborah was still holding his arm. She didn't seem embarrassed by their closeness, though, so Michael saw no reason why he should be.

After all, these people probably didn't know that he was a married man. . . .

But he knew, and so did most of the other citizens of Wind River. So, in the interests of discretion, he gently disengaged his arm from Deborah and tried not to pay any attention to her faint frown of disappointment.

"I just stopped by to say hello," he told Munroe, "and to let you know that I've been taking your tonic and it's making me feel wonderful."

"What a generous testimonial! I may call on you to repeat it at tonight's performance,

Mr. Hatfield . . . if you're in attendance, that is."

Michael glanced at Deborah. "I sure intend to be there."

"Excellent! Would you care to watch my associates practice? Chief Laughing Fox might even be persuaded to let you assist him in his act."

The Chippewa looked at Michael, grunted, and nodded solemnly.

Michael swallowed hard. "You mean stand in front of that target? I . . . I don't think I'm quite up to that, Professor." He added quickly, "No offense, Chief."

"None taken, I assure you," Munroe said. "Perhaps another time — Blast it, what does *he* want now?"

The professor had glanced past Michael as he asked that question, and Michael turned to see Dr. Bramwell Carter striding purposefully toward the wagons. The Philadelphia physician's bearded features looked every bit as unfriendly today as they had the previous night.

Calvin Dumont moved to intercept Carter. He towered over the doctor and was twice as wide. "You're not wanted around here, mister," Dumont growled, sounding menacing despite his high-pitched voice.

"I came to speak to your employer," Carter snapped. "And you don't frighten me. Now get out of my way!"

Dumont bunched his ham-like hands into fists, and Michael tensed, afraid that he was about to witness a brutal beating. But Professor Munroe said quickly, "It's all right, Calvin. I'll speak with Dr. Carter."

"You sure, Professor?" Dumont asked over his shoulder.

"Of course. Welcome, Dr. Carter. What can we do for you?"

Carter stepped around the massive Calvin Dumont, who hadn't budged. Stiffly, Carter said, "Short of closing down this fraudulent business of yours, I don't know what you can do. But I came here this morning to serve notice on you — Professor." His voice dripped scorn as he added the title. Michael saw Munroe turn pale, but the professor didn't say anything. Carter went on, "I intend to prove once and for all that your claims about using the water from this so-called Medicine Creek to perfect the formula for your tonic are utterly false. I'm going out to the creek to get a sample of the water for analysis."

"Go ahead," Munroe said with a casual wave of his hand. "I don't mind."

For the first time, Michael saw a trace of confusion and uncertainty on Carter's face.

"You'll be proven to be a liar and a fake," Carter went on, but he didn't sound quite as sure of himself now.

"We'll see about that. I was thinking of returning to the creek myself to take further samples of the water. It's possible that I might be able to refine my tonic slightly and make it even more effective."

Carter snorted in disbelief.

Michael sensed a story here, and trying to keep the excitement out of his voice, he said, "Why don't the two of you go out there together to take your samples? I'll come along, too. I can help you find it since I know these parts fairly well."

That was stretching the truth a little. Michael had ridden over quite a bit of the territory to the north and east of Wind River when he accompanied Cole Tyler and a posse that had been chasing a band of outlaws the year before, but he had never traveled very far to the southwest, the area where the Shoshone village was located. He knew its approximate location from listening to Billy Casebolt talk about his visits there, however, and Michael was confident he could find the place.

Besides, from what he had seen as he walked along Grenville Avenue earlier, he and Munroe and Carter wouldn't be the only ones out looking for Medicine Creek. There was a virtual exodus of strangers heading in that direction.

"A fine idea," Munroe said to Michael. "We'd be glad to have your company, Mr. Hatfield."

"I'm going, too," Deborah said.

Michael was surprised — but pleased — by her decision to accompany them. That meant he would get to spend more time with her, yet there still wouldn't be anything improper about it since her uncle would be along for the trip, too. Excitedly, he said, "I'll get my horse and meet you back here in ten minutes."

"And I've already made arrangements to hire a buggy," Carter said. "I'm glad you're going along as well, Mr. Hatfield. That way an objective observer will be on hand when I expose this charlatan for the fraud that he is."

Calvin Dumont growled again and started toward Carter, but Munroe gestured to him and stopped him. "We shall see who is exposed as a fraud, Doctor. We'll leave in ten minutes, as Mr. Hatfield suggested."

"I'll be here," Carter promised, then hurried off toward one of the livery stables.

Michael said, "I'll be right back," and started toward the stable where he kept his saddle horse. Anticipation coursed through his veins. Not only was he going to witness what promised to be a good story for the *Sentinel,* but he was going to do it in the company of Deborah Munroe.

He couldn't have said which of those two things excited him more.

18

Billy Casebolt was in the general store picking up some spare cartridges for his revolver. The emporium's manager, Harvey Raymond, was standing on the other side of the counter making small talk. The skinny, horse-faced Raymond had a haunted look in his eyes, which seemed to have sunk farther into his skull than they had once been. Several months earlier, Raymond had lost his son when the infant had been stillborn. Raymond's wife, Estelle, had not survived the birth, either. Something like that was enough to give any man nightmares, Casebolt knew, so he had taken to keeping an eye on ol' Harvey. You never could tell when somebody who had suffered what this man had suffered would lose his mind.

Raymond seemed fairly cheerful today, though. He was saying, "— never so glad to see spring in my life. This was my first winter out here, you know, and I thought it would never be over."

"And this was a pretty tame winter for these parts," Casebolt commented. "Why, I recollect one time it was so cold up here you could go outside on a winter's day and yell at the top of your lungs and never hear a blessed thing. The sound froze quicker'n you could hear it, y'see. And then come spring, when things thawed out, you could be outside and you'd hear somebody let out a holler, but when you looked there wouldn't be nobody there. It was just them yells from back in the winter thawin'."

Raymond looked dubiously at him and began, "I never heard of anything like that —," but then he broke off his comment to stare past Casebolt, his eyes widening in alarm. Casebolt swung around hurriedly.

Through the open doors of the general store, he could see an Indian riding past on Grenville Avenue. Casebolt recognized him as Two Ponies, chief of the Shoshones.

"What in blazes is *he* doin' in town?" Casebolt muttered, more to himself than to Harvey Raymond. He started toward the store's entrance, moving quickly.

When he reached the porch, he saw that Two Ponies had already attracted a lot of attention. Quite a few kids and dogs were following behind the chief's horse, and several hard-faced townsmen were striding along the boardwalks, staying even with him. Two Ponies seemed to be paying no attention to them, but Casebolt was sure the Shoshone chief knew they were there. Two Ponies carried a lance in his left hand and had a bow and a quiver of arrows slung on his back. He was not painted for war, however, so Casebolt knew he hadn't come to town looking for trouble. Two Ponies wasn't the sort of man to do something like that, anyway.

Figuring that the chief might be looking for him, Casebolt hurried along the boardwalk and called out, "Two Ponies!"

The Shoshone reined in his horse and turned to face Casebolt. Although his face was grave, his dark eyes shone with pleasure at the sight of the deputy. As Casebolt caught up with him, Two Ponies asked, "How goes it with my friend Billy? The evil spirits that plagued you have not returned?"

"Reckon I'm fit as a fiddle," Casebolt declared. "My joints are a mite stiffer than when I first got out of that pool, but that's to be expected. I'm glad to see you, Two Ponies. What brings you to Wind River?"

"We must talk," Two Ponies replied gravely. "There will be trouble unless something is done."

"Well, come on down to the office, and we'll sure talk about whatever's botherin' you. Marshal Tyler ain't around right now, but I'll do anything I can to help."

A crowd was gathering around Two Ponies now, and one of the men called out, "Hey, Deputy, what's that damned Injun doin' in town?"

Casebolt swung angrily toward the man. "You can just shut your mouth right now, mister," he said. "Two Ponies is my friend, and he's comin' down to the marshal's office with me. You got any problem with that?"

The crowd had drawn back a little at the unexpected vehemence of Casebolt's reaction. The man who had spoken shook his head and said quickly, "No, sir, Deputy, I ain't got no problem."

"Good," Casebolt snapped. He turned back to Two Ponies. "Come on, Chief. These hombres won't bother us."

Two Ponies slid down from the back of his horse and led the animal as he walked alongside Casebolt. They reached the office after a minute, and Two Ponies tied the horse at the hitch rack. Casebolt called out to one of the boys on the boardwalk and motioned for him to come over.

"Listen here, Bert," Casebolt said as he dug in his pocket, found a nickel, and flipped it to the youngster. "I want you to keep an eye on the chief's horse. If anybody bothers it, you come and tell me, all right? There'll be another nickel in it for you if you do."

The boy nodded enthusiastically. "Sure, Deputy, I understand. You don't have to worry about that Injun's horse. I'll look after it."

Casebolt clapped him approvingly on the shoulder, then led Two Ponies inside. Bert was bigger and stronger than most of the other boys, and Casebolt knew they wouldn't try to bother the horse with him standing guard.

"Now," Casebolt said as he settled down behind the desk, "what brings you here, Two Ponies?" He was afraid he had a pretty good idea already, but it would be better to let the chief tell it in his own way.

"Too many of the white men come to our land," Two Ponies said with a sweeping gesture. "The Shoshone did not fight when the steel rails and the thunder wagon came, because the white men traveled across our land and did not stay to spoil it. Now they come on horses and in wagons, and my people fear that they will stay."

Casebolt nodded. "They're all lookin' for Medicine Creek, I reckon."

Two Ponies' expression became even more solemn. "This, too, is our fear. And it is something we cannot allow, Billy. Medicine Creek is a sacred place. It belongs to the Shoshones. If the white men come there uninvited . . . we will have no choice but to fight them."

Frowning, Casebolt said, "That'll lead to a whole mess of trouble. You see, Two Ponies, as far as the folks who are lookin' for Medicine Creek are concerned, the place don't belong to the Shoshones. It don't belong to anybody, because it's on what they consider open range. I understand what you're sayin', and I know the marshal would, too, but all them other folks don't."

Two Ponies took a deep breath. "Then there will be war."

Casebolt stood up hurriedly, shaking his head. "Nope, we can't let that happen. There's got to be some way to head this off."

"Already the white men are on Shoshone land," Two Ponies said emphatically. "It is too late. Soon they will find the creek. Some of my warriors have gone there to guard it, and when the white men arrive, they will fight."

"Damn it!" Casebolt exclaimed as he brought his fist down on the desk. "How could you let your warriors do something like that?"

"How could I stop them? Would you have me tell them that the white man must be allowed to do whatever he wishes, that the Shoshones have no right to stop them from ruining one of our most sacred places?"

Casebolt sighed. "No, I reckon you couldn't do that. But we better get out there while we still can. Maybe we can stop things from gettin' too bad."

And if they weren't in time, Casebolt thought as he hurried out of the office with Two Ponies . . .

Well, then, the waters of Medicine Creek might run red with blood before this day was over.

Cole followed the road that led to the Diamond S for several miles after leaving Wind River, then branched off on a smaller trail that angled to the northeast. This path would take him to Austin Fisk's Latch Hook spread, he knew. He rode easily, letting Ulysses stretch out and gallop part of the time. The long-legged golden sorrel didn't take kindly to being stabled, and he liked to work the kinks out every chance he got.

229

Cole wouldn't have minded working out some kinks himself. Thoughts of Simone McKay and Judson Kent, of medicine shows and rustlers and range wars, all made him wish that he could just put those things behind him and spend about a month in the high country hunting and fishing and not even seeing another human being. Until the past year, his had been a solitary life for the most part, with few close friends and long stretches when he was by himself. Did he really want to trade that for what he had found in Wind River?

He couldn't answer that question. All he knew for sure was that he wasn't ready to leave the settlement for good. If he had, he would have felt like he was running away from a job left unfinished. And that was one thing Cole Tyler had never done.

The trail wound into the foothills and then reached the valley where Fisk's ranch was located. The headquarters were all the way at the other end of the ten-mile-long valley, so Cole still had a ways to ride. As he did, he saw quite a few cattle, some of them still rather thin but most fattening up nicely on the good grazing to be had here. This valley wasn't as good as the one Kermit Sawyer had — Sawyer's place was as prime a piece of ranching land as could be found in the territory — but a man who was willing to work could make quite a success here. Cole barely knew Austin Fisk, but the Kentuckian struck him as a man who didn't mind hard work. The idea that he was behind the rustling on Sawyer's ranch seemed wrong to Cole, just as turning things around the other way did.

He hadn't yet come in sight of the ranch house when several men rode out of some nearby timber and galloped toward him. He noticed that they had their rifles across their saddles in front of them, ready to be used, and as he reined in he kept his hands in plain sight. No telling how trigger-happy these punchers might be, so he didn't want to do anything to spook them.

The riders reined in about twenty yards from Cole, except for one man who trotted his horse forward. "This is Latch Hook range, mister," he called out. "What are you doing here?"

Cole had already seen the brands on their horses and knew they were some of Fisk's men. He said, "I'm Marshal Tyler from Wind River. I came up here to talk to Austin Fisk."

"Marshal, eh?" The spokesman for the group, a well-built man with blond hair under the hat that was cuffed back on his head, rubbed his jaw in thought. "You got any proof of what you say?"

Cole jerked a thumb at the badge pinned to his buckskin shirt. "This badge and my word. That's always been good enough."

The man nodded. "I reckon it still is. I'm Wilt Paxton, Mr. Fisk's foreman, and I seem to recollect seeing you around the settlement before. Come on, we'll take you to the house."

The tension that had been in the air as the confrontation began relaxed as Cole fell in with the other riders. He said, "You boys out looking for strays?"

"Looking for rustlers is more like it," Paxton replied.

"You haven't had any more trouble, have you?"

Paxton shook his head. "Not since that raid where we lost four men. Four good men."

"I hear your boss blames Kermit Sawyer for that."

"Damn right. That Texan never has liked us over here on Latch Hook."

Cole asked, "Did you know rustlers hit Sawyer's spread last night? They got off with a hundred head of cattle and wounded his foreman."

"LeDoux got himself shot?" Paxton

sounded genuinely surprised. "He's not killed, is he?"

Cole shook his head. "Just a bullet hole in the shoulder. He'll be all right. You wouldn't know anything about that, would you, Paxton?"

The Latch Hook foreman snorted in disgust. "I wouldn't mind settling things with LeDoux, but when I do it'll be face to face, Marshal. And none of us take kindly to being accused of rustling."

"Neither do the boys who ride for Diamond S," Cole pointed out.

Paxton and the other Latch Hook punchers glared at him, but nothing more was said until they all reached the headquarters of the ranch. Austin Fisk must have seen them coming, because he strode out onto the porch to greet them.

"Hello, Marshal Tyler," he said with a curt nod to Cole. "What brings you out here?"

Before Cole could answer, Paxton said, "He's come to accuse us of rustling Sawyer's cattle and shooting his foreman, boss."

Fisk frowned darkly. "Is that true, Marshal?"

"Not exactly," Cole snapped. "You going to keep me sitting on my horse, Mr. Fisk?"

"Step down and come up here on the porch," Fisk said grudgingly. "I'll have something to drink brought out." He turned and called into the house. "Catherine! Bring us some lemonade, girl."

Cole climbed down from the saddle and stepped up onto the porch. Still with ill grace, Fisk motioned for him to sit down in one of the straight-backed rockers. As Cole did so, an attractive, young, blond woman brought a tray from the house with a pitcher of lemonade and several glasses on it. Cole recognized her as Catherine Fisk, the rancher's younger daughter. The older one, a cool-looking brunette whose name Cole couldn't recall at the moment, didn't seem to be around.

Fisk sat down as Catherine poured lemonade for both of them. The punchers, with the exception of Wilt Paxton, had headed for the bunkhouse. The foreman dismounted, and Catherine handed him a glass of lemonade as well. Cole thought her hand touched Paxton's for a little longer than was necessary as she did so, but that was none of his business.

"All right, Marshal," Fisk said curtly. "Explain what brings you here. What's this about rustlers hitting Sawyer's ranch?"

Quickly, Cole filled him in on what had happened on the Diamond S the night before. Cole concluded by saying, "Sawyer's convinced you're behind the rustling because you blame him for the raid on your ranch."

"Preposterous!" Fisk snorted. "None of my men would do such a thing, and I certainly wouldn't put them up to it. We abide by the law on Latch Hook, Marshal — unlike those wild Texans who think they're a law unto themselves."

"Sawyer and his men *do* act like that sometimes," Cole admitted. "But they're not rustlers, Mr. Fisk. I'm sure of that."

"Well, then, who *is* responsible for these depredations?"

"That's what I intend to find out," Cole declared. "The real reason I rode out here today is to ask your permission to do some poking around."

"What do you mean?"

"I'm pretty good at reading signs. I thought I'd look around the area where you lost those cattle and check out Sawyer's place, too. Maybe I can pick up a trail, find out where those wideloopers took that stock they stole."

Slowly, Fisk nodded. "I suppose that's a reasonable request. Somewhat out of your jurisdiction, though, isn't it? I was under the impression you were just the town marshal."

"Yep, that's true, but I'm also the only duly-appointed lawman in these parts, and if Latch Hook and Diamond S wind up at war with each other, it's bound to cause trouble in my town." Cole finished his lemonade, which was cool and sweet, and added flatly, "I don't want that."

"Neither do I," Fisk admitted. "Sawyer's a jackass, but I'd rather get along with him than have to shoot him, I suppose." The rancher nodded decisively. "You have my permission to ride wherever you like on my ranch, Marshal. Wilt, you spread the word among the men. Marshal Tyler has our co-operation."

"Sure, boss," Paxton said.

Cole stood up and handed his empty glass to Catherine, who had stood by silently during the conversation. "Thank you, ma'am," he said. "That was mighty good." To Fisk, he continued, "I'll start by taking a look around your spread."

"That's fine. Wilt can tell you exactly where the cattle were when we lost them."

Cole extended a hand to Fisk, who had been more reasonable about everything than he had expected. "Thanks. I'll let you know if I find out anything."

"And if you find that the trail of those stolen cattle leads to the Diamond S . . . ?"

Fisk asked as he shook Cole's hand.

"Then I'll handle it."

"See that you do. If not . . ." Fisk shrugged and left the rest unsaid, but his meaning was clear.

For the sake of this whole part of the territory, Cole hoped he was right and Fisk was wrong.

19

Not surprisingly, word had traveled quickly around town about the proposed visit to Medicine Creek by Professor Munroe and Dr. Carter, and quite a crowd of curiosity seekers and people desperate for a cure of some sort were following along behind as one of the professor's wagons and the buggy rented by Dr. Carter rolled out of Wind River. Michael rode alongside the medicine show wagon on his horse.

Munroe was handling the reins with Deborah sitting beside him. Michael rode on that side of the wagon so that he could see her better, and they kept up a conversation as they headed southwest out of town. It was fairly innocuous, of course, since Deborah's uncle was sitting right beside her, but Michael enjoyed it anyway. He enjoyed any time he was able to spend with Deborah, no matter what they were doing.

He wondered fleetingly if he should have

told Delia where he was going before he rode out of town. Then he dismissed that concern. The way she had felt about him lately, Delia wasn't likely to even care where he was, he told himself.

"Are you sure you can find this place, Mr. Hatfield?" Munroe asked when they had gone several miles.

"We're going in the right direction," Michael said. "We'll know it when we see it."

"I'm sure Michael is right," Deborah declared, and her support of him made a surge of warmth go through him.

Michael wished he was as confident as he sounded. He would look utterly foolish in Deborah's eyes if he took them off out here into the wilderness and got them lost. But he wasn't going to let that worry show on his face. He wore a smile instead as he continued to lead the procession.

He wasn't sure how far they had come when he spotted an Indian sitting on horseback on a rise about two hundred yards away. Michael took that as a good sign, even though it made him nervous. They had to be going the right direction if there was a Shoshone warrior keeping an eye on them.

"Does any of this look familiar to you, Professor?" Michael asked a little later.

"After all, you've been to Medicine Creek before."

"That was a long time ago, my boy. I'm afraid that even with the benefits of my own tonic, my memory isn't what it once was. But rest assured. As you say, I'll know the place when I see it."

There was a great deal of excited talk coming from the group trailing along behind. Some of them were townspeople from Wind River, while others were strangers who had been drawn to the community by the widespread newspaper reports about the miracle of Medicine Creek. Some of them were old and wanted relief from the infirmities of age; others were much younger and had been stricken by a variety of ailments. Some were lame and some were wracked by coughs. Others were blind or deaf or had withered limbs. Some were only children, and those were the most affecting of all. When Michael looked at them, he thought of Gretchen and Lincoln and how he would feel if some serious illness befell either of them, and at those moments he felt a hope far beyond the desire for another good story that he could print in the *Sentinel.* He hoped for the sake of those children that the waters of Medicine Creek really *did* contain a miracle or two.

A little later, from the top of a rise, Michael spotted the lodges of the Shoshone village clustered on the banks of a creek. He held up a hand to stop the others. Professor Munroe hauled back on the reins, bringing the wagon team to a halt, and said excitedly, "Is that it?"

"No, we have to go past the village a ways," Michael explained. "That's what Deputy Casebolt said. That creek is just the normal one they use for water."

"Well, as I said, my memory's not what it once was. Besides, things have changed since I've been in these parts."

That sounded reasonable enough to Michael. He thought about what Cole Tyler or Billy Casebolt would do if one of them were leading this little expedition, and he said, "We'd better swing wide around the village. We don't want to stir up the Shoshones."

"An excellent idea, young man," Bramwell Carter called dryly from the seat of his rented buggy.

Michael flushed and swung his arm, indicating to the others that they should turn to the south. That was the easiest way to skirt the Shoshone village. The terrain to the north was more rugged.

Of course, it was too late to keep the Shoshone from seeing them, Michael knew.

The Indians had probably known for a long time where they were and what their destination was. It was difficult to do anything in this part of the territory without the Shoshones knowing about it. But so far no one had challenged them, and Michael hoped that luck would continue to run in their favor.

Some twenty minutes later, he knew that was not going to be the case. The group from Wind River had topped another rise, and this time there was no mistaking the scene before them. The narrow creek that meandered through a shallow valley, the pool from which it sprang at the base of a bluff, the faint wisps of steam rising off the hot surface of the water. . . .

They had found Medicine Creek.

And sitting on horseback near the pool were about a dozen Shoshone warriors, each man holding either a lance or a bow. The warriors had stripped off their buckskin shirts and painted their torsos with various designs, including symbols to indicate bears, snakes, and buffalo. Their arms were marked with short vertical slashes of paint, and some of the men had their hands painted as well.

"Good Lord!" Munroe exclaimed. "They look as if . . . as if they're painted for war!"

"Is that true, Michael?" Deborah asked

242

anxiously.

Michael swallowed hard and hesitated before answering. Cole or Casebolt could have glanced at those warriors and known immediately what the painting meant, but he had to guess. He said, judging from the stiff attitude with which the warriors watched them, "I don't think they're happy to see us." His eyes searched among the warriors for Two Ponies, but he didn't see the chief anywhere.

Michael glanced back at the others. They had picked up even more stragglers during the journey out here, as people who were already looking for Medicine Creek joined the larger group. Now everyone was crowding the top of the rise, eager to get down there and find out for themselves if the waters of the creek were as miraculous as they'd heard. But if they rushed the creek, those Shoshone warriors might fire arrows into them, or charge with those war lances lowered. The bloodshed would be horrible, and it would only be the beginning.

And the worst of it, Michael realized, was that everyone here was looking to him to tell them what to do. How in blazes had he gotten himself into this?

"I'm not sure we should go down there —" he began tentatively.

"Nonsense!" That came from Dr. Bramwell Carter, who snapped the lines of his buggy against the back of the horse pulling it. The buggy rolled forward. "I came out here to prove once and for all that there are no magical cures to be found in either that creek water or this charlatan's so-called tonic! I intend to do just that. Get up there!"

He slapped the horse with the reins again, and the buggy started down the slope toward the creek. That was all it took to get the others moving again. They surged over the top of the rise and headed for the creek, some in wagons and buggies and buckboards, the others on horseback. Professor Munroe's wagon was among them, with Deborah looking back and calling urgently, "Come on, Michael!"

He had no choice but to go after them. He urged his horse into a trot, hurrying to catch up. On the banks of the creek, the Shoshone warriors were standing firm. The ones with lances lowered the sharp tips of the weapons so they pointed toward the oncoming whites, while the men holding bows drew arrows from their quivers and made ready to fire. Yells of anger rose from the people who had come looking for Medicine Creek. Several men riding on wagons lifted rifles to defend themselves and their

244

families. The two sides were only moments away from coming together in a bloody confrontation, and there didn't seem to be a damned thing Michael could do to stop it.

Suddenly, gunfire crashed behind him. Three shots rang out, and a voice bellowed, "Stop! Stop, you damned fools!" It was followed by another voice shouting something in Shoshone.

The shots and the angry voices stopped the charge toward the creek. Michael reined in and looked over his shoulder, seeing to his great relief that Billy Casebolt and Two Ponies were galloping down the slope. Casebolt still had his old Confederate revolver in his hand as he rode.

The two men picked their way through the ragged line of vehicles and riders and placed themselves between the Shoshone warriors and the people who had come here from Wind River. Casebolt wheeled his horse to address the whites while Two Ponies spoke sharply to his warriors.

"You folks might as well just turn around and head back to town," Casebolt said angrily. "This is a sacred place to the Shoshones, and you ain't welcome here!"

"They don't own this land!" a man shouted back. "It's open range. We got as much right here as any bunch of damned redskins!"

"We got *more* right!" another man added hotly. "This is government land and you know it, Deputy!"

"The Shoshones were around these parts a hell of a long time before any blasted government was!" Casebolt snapped. "I ain't here to argue law. I'm just tellin' you to back off, 'fore there's some bad trouble." He glanced over his shoulder. "I don't know how long Two Ponies can keep his warriors from tryin' to run you off."

One of the men said, "Let 'em try! We got sick folks here, and they need that magic water!" Mutters of agreement came from the others.

Michael rode up next to Professor Munroe's wagon, which was in the front ranks along with Dr. Carter's buggy. "I'm sure glad to see you, Billy," he said to the deputy.

Casebolt regarded him with narrowed eyes. "Was it your idea to lead this bunch out here, Michael?"

Michael grimaced sheepishly, but Munroe said, "I'm the one you should blame, Deputy, not Mr. Hatfield. He came to report the news, not to make it, as any journalist should. I want to take a sample of that water for further analysis."

"And so do I," Carter put in. "I'll prove conclusively that there's nothing to the claims this quack has been making."

Casebolt held up a hand as Munroe and Carter glowered at each other. "You two stop your argufyin'. We got bigger problems right now." Uneasily, he looked at the array of people facing him, none of whom wanted to turn around without getting what they had come here for.

An idea occurred to Michael, and he suggested, "Why don't you ask Two Ponies if Professor Munroe and Dr. Carter can each take a sample of the water, Billy? That wouldn't desecrate the place too much, would it?"

Casebolt rubbed his lean jaw and glanced at Two Ponies. "Well, I don't know. . . ."

Michael raised his voice so that everyone could hear him better. "Nobody wants to get hurt over something that might not even work — no offense to your people, Two Ponies. But if the professor and the doctor can take their samples, maybe they *can* prove one way or the other whether the creek can cure anything."

Carter said, "That's acceptable to me. I'll analyze the water and share my findings with anyone who is interested."

"As will I," Munroe said with complete

confidence. "I stand behind everything I've said concerning my tonic and the water on which I based it."

Casebolt looked over at the Shoshone chief, who sat beside him on horseback, still facing the other direction. "What do you think, Two Ponies?"

For a long moment, Two Ponies considered the proposal. Then he nodded and said, "This can be done." He spoke to his warriors in their own tongue, obviously ordering them to allow Munroe and Carter to approach the stream. The warriors moved aside reluctantly.

"Get your samples, and do it damned quick," Casebolt snapped to the professor and the doctor.

Both men hopped down from their vehicles and went to the edge of the stream. Carter took several glass vials from the pocket of his coat and bent to fill them, afterward replacing the cork stoppers, while Munroe dipped a couple of silver-coated flasks into the creek. All the while, the Shoshones watched with dark expressions on their faces.

When the two men were done and had returned to the medicine show wagon and the buggy, Casebolt said, "All right, turn around and get back to town." He raised his voice. "Everybody, just go on back to Wind River! The doc and the professor will let you know what they found."

One of the men, who was sitting on a wagon seat with his wife beside him, the woman holding a sick child in her arms, said, "If that creek can do my Bobby any good, mister, then we'll be back out here in no time. And then there ain't nobody going to stop us from getting what we need!"

Shouts of anger and agreement came from the others.

"We'll have to hash that out later," Casebolt said. "For now, all of you git while you still got the chance!"

Slowly, the pilgrims who had come seeking what they all saw as some sort of holy grail turned their horses and vehicles and started back toward Wind River. The last ones to depart were Professor Munroe, Deborah, and Dr. Carter. Michael watched the medicine show wagon and the buggy roll away, then turned to Casebolt and said, "That was mighty close, Billy. I'm glad you and Two Ponies showed up when you did."

"I reckon we was all pretty lucky," Casebolt said. "Next time it might not work out so good."

"Are you coming back to Wind River?"

"Not just yet," Casebolt replied. "Reckon

I'll stay around out here for a while, just in case some of them folks try to slip back. If you see the marshal in town, tell him where I am, will you?"

Michael nodded. "Sure." He started after the others.

"Michael."

He stopped and turned around in the saddle as Casebolt called his name.

"You be careful," Casebolt warned. "You might not know what you're gettin' into."

"You mean the trouble between the Shoshones and the people who want the water from the creek?"

"I mean you best just think about whatever you're doin' before you do it. Now get movin'."

Michael rode quickly after the medicine show wagon, still unsure exactly what Casebolt was talking about.

But he wasn't going to worry about it. Now that this crisis was over, he was anxious to catch up to Professor Munroe . . . and Deborah.

20

Following the directions Milt Paxton had given him, Cole had no trouble finding the area of the Latch Hook spread where the rustlers had struck the first time. More than a week had passed since that night, however, so Cole expected the trail to be cold. He was right. Although it hadn't rained since then, there had been plenty of wind to wipe out any sign. Fortunately, that many cattle left quite a few tracks when they were moved in a hurry.

The trail led generally toward the pass in the mountains, on the other side of which was Sawyer's Diamond S. That didn't look too good, Cole thought with a frown. He kept riding with his eyes on the ground, watching intently for the telltale signs of the stolen herd being pushed along.

From time to time, he lost the trail, but only briefly. He was always able to pick it up again by riding back and forth, quartering across the area where the tracks had vanished. Each time the trail still led toward the pass.

But it never got there, Cole discovered to his bafflement. The tracks veered to the north instead, toward the seemingly solid wall of mountains, then stopped abruptly, petering out on a wide stretch of rocky, boulder-littered ground. Cole rode to the far side of the rocks, Ulysses's shoes ringing loudly against stone as he did so. He sent the golden sorrel back and forth along the area where the tracks had vanished, but they didn't reappear as they had every time in the past. Cole looked to the west, along the line of rocky terrain. It ended in a sheer bluff about half a mile away.

He reined in, leaned forward in the saddle, and frowned in thought. Cattle couldn't disappear into thin air, whether they were stolen or not. That Latch Hook stock had gone somewhere.

But where?

After a few minutes, Cole sighed. He couldn't figure it out from what he had seen so far, but this wasn't the only piece of the puzzle, either. He turned Ulysses south again, angling toward the pass that would lead him to the Diamond S.

He recalled from his questioning of

Frenchy LeDoux that the foreman had run across the rustlers not far from the pass, along the rugged high ground they called Wildcat Ridge. After he had followed the twisting path through the pass, Cole headed for that ridge. He hadn't gotten permission from Sawyer to be out here looking around, but he didn't think any of the Diamond S hands would take a potshot at him without first making sure of who he was.

On the other hand, with all the tension between the two ranches, anything was possible, including shooting first and asking questions later. Cole told himself to keep his eyes and ears open. He wanted to spot any Diamond S riders before they spotted him.

It didn't take him long to reach the location where the raid on Sawyer's spread had taken place. He recognized the meadow from Frenchy's description. The grass was trampled where the longhorns had been bunched and then driven off — toward the pass again.

In both raids, the stolen stock had been driven toward the pass. On Fisk's side of the mountains, the cattle had been turned before they ever got there. Cole wondered if the same thing was going to hold true on this side.

The next hour told him that his guess was correct, but it was also frustrating. Once again, the cattle had been turned north before ever reaching the pass. Only the keenest of observers would have noticed that, however, because almost immediately, the trail disappeared on ground that was covered by a layer of rock. Most people following the tracks would have assumed that they continued straight on toward the pass.

Maybe that was what the rustlers wanted folks to think, Cole mused as he reined Ulysses to a halt and turned over in his mind what he had discovered this afternoon.

Fisk blamed Sawyer for the rustling. Sawyer blamed Fisk. Could be that was exactly what somebody wanted the two ranchers to think. Fisk and Sawyer would be too busy trying to settle the score with each other to find out who was really behind the widelooping.

That theory made sense, Cole decided. But there was still the question of where the stolen cattle were going.

On this side of the mountains, the band of rocky ground ran almost all the way to the point where the heavily timbered peaks jutted steeply up from the floor of the valley. Cole crossed it anyway and began riding along the base of the mountains, his eyes alert for tracks or any other sign of a good-sized herd moving through here. He didn't find anything, but his frown deepened as he reined in and studied the heights looming over him.

He thought about the way both sets of tracks had turned, and he tried to orient himself in relation to them. All the tracks had wound up pointing at roughly the same area of the mountains, he realized. Almost as if they were bound for the same place, just coming from different directions.

Well, that made sense if there was really one gang behind the raids on both ranches, he told himself. They were getting those cattle into the mountains some way and holing up with them there, maybe moving them on to the north and out onto the plains again once they were well away from both ranches. The rustlers could take the cows and loop well to the north, avoiding everybody until they swung south again toward Laramie or Cheyenne, where there were always cattle buyers who would make an offer on a herd without asking too many questions about where it came from. A phony, scrawled bill of sale putting the stolen cattle in the names of the rustlers would be enough to satisfy some of the buyers.

Cole's hand clenched into a fist, and he

struck the saddlehorn, making Ulysses jump a little. That had to be it, he told himself. He had figured out what was really going on around here. Rustling by one gang of outlaws, pure and simple, only the wide-loopers were muddying the waters behind them by playing Fisk and Sawyer against each other.

All Cole had to do now was prove it.

Whatever route the rustlers were using on this side of the mountains to drive the stolen cattle into hiding, Cole doubted that he could find it. But he had been thinking about the layout in the other valley and the way the tracks of Fisk's cows had disappeared. There was something over there he should have taken a closer look at. He turned his horse and rode back along the slab-shouldered heights toward the pass.

It was late afternoon by the time he reached Latch Hook range again. He knew he ought to be starting back to Wind River by now, but he wanted to follow up on this idea while it was fresh in his mind. Besides, he doubted if anything could be going on back in town that was as important as stopping a range war before it got started.

When he reached the rocky area where the tracks had vanished, Cole turned Ulysses toward the distant bluff where the boulder-strewn band of ground ended abruptly. He rode straight toward the jutting upthrust of granite. Above and behind the bluff rose a snow-capped peak.

Cole was about two hundred yards from the bluff when he spotted a sudden spurt of smoke, seemingly from the face of the cliff. That was just enough warning to give him time to sway sharply to the side. The crack of a rifle and the flat *whap!* of a bullet passing close beside his ear sounded almost simultaneously.

"Son of a bitch!" he exclaimed as he drove his heels into the golden sorrel's flanks and sent Ulysses leaping toward the nearby cover of some boulders.

More bullets whined through the air around him. From the sound of the shots, he knew more than one man was firing at him. He was lucky he hadn't been blown out of the saddle with the first volley.

Luck could only carry him so far, though. He would have to fight back if he was going to get out of this spot alive.

When he reached the rocks, he jerked his Sharps from its boot and rolled out of the saddle, landing on his feet and running forward a few steps before throwing himself down. Ulysses, as though by cunning, ran behind some of the larger boulders and stopped there, safe from the bullets of the bushwhackers. The horse tossed his head and neighed angrily.

"I'm not very happy with 'em, either, fella," Cole called to Ulysses. "Let's see what we can do about this."

The Sharps was loaded. All he had to do was ear back the hammer, set the trigger, raise up quickly, and aim toward the place on the bluff where he had seen the gun-smoke that had warned him. A mere touch of the second trigger was enough to make the Sharps buck heavily against his shoulder and send its lead ball whipping toward the bluff with a roar of exploding powder. He ducked back down without taking the time to see if his shot had done any harm or not. If it hadn't, kneeling there and gawking would be a good way of getting a bullet through his fool head.

At least the ambushers knew he still had some fangs, though. That was all he had intended to accomplish with his first shot.

Cole thought furiously as he crouched behind the boulder and reloaded the Sharps. There had to be some sort of path leading up the bluff, a trail too narrow to be seen from any distance, more than likely. And obviously there were guards posted up there with orders to shoot anybody who came too close. But what were they guarding?

Another way out of this valley, maybe?

That could be the answer he had been looking for all along without really being aware of it.

How could there be some sort of passage out of the valley and off of Latch Hook range without Austin Fisk being aware of it, though? Cole found himself wondering if Fisk really *had* been behind the raid on Sawyer's ranch. The story about the rustling of Latch Hook stock could have been a phony. Fisk's own men could have driven those cattle out of the valley and lied about four of their number being killed, just to make it look good when rustlers hit Sawyer's place later on.

Cole gave a little shake of his head. His brain was running around in circles now. Unless he concentrated on his present predicament, there was a good chance he would never have the opportunity to figure out the twists and turns of whatever plot had brought him here. He would be too dead to care about them by then.

The Sharps boomed once more as he popped up and fired toward the bluff. He thought he had hit pretty close both times to the spot where the bushwhackers were hiding. They might be getting a little nervous by now. Cole wished he had his Winchester instead of the Sharps. The buffalo gun packed a lot more punch, but he could have really peppered the bluff with his repeater and spooked those bastards up there into running. At least he thought so.

He would just have to make do with what he had. He loaded the big carbine one more time.

Before he could lift himself to fire it, however, a slug whined past him to splatter itself in a splash of lead against the boulder behind which he crouched. At first Cole thought one of the bushwhackers had managed to sneak around behind him, but then, as more bullets spanked the air around him, he realized to his dismay that the gunmen had gotten smart. They had lifted their aim a little and were sending their shots into the cluster of big rocks behind him. Those slugs dancing around him were ricochets. Not all of them came his direction, of course, but enough of them did to make things hot in a hurry. One of the rebounding slugs burned across the back of his left hand, and another tugged at the side of his shirt.

He had to get out of there. It was only a matter of time before one of the crazily bouncing slugs cut him down.

His legs driving fiercely, he leaped out

from behind the boulder and ran toward the rocks where Ulysses waited. It galled him to cut and run, but that was all he could do.

Suddenly something slammed into the outside of his left thigh and sent him spinning off his feet. One of the ambushers had clipped him with a slug, he knew. He landed hard and rolled over a couple of times but managed to hang onto the Sharps. It was still loaded, so he brought it to his shoulder as he came up into a sitting position and fired toward the haze of smoke floating in front of the bluff. That might buy him a second or two.

He used that time to push himself to his feet, propping himself up with the now-empty Sharps as his left leg tried to fold up underneath him. As he hobbled toward the horse, Ulysses bolted out from behind the rocks, racing toward him. Cole knew he would have only one chance. More slugs kicked up dust around his feet as he dropped the Sharps. He hated to lose it, but that was better than getting himself killed. As Ulysses loomed up next to him, he reached out with both hands, grabbed the saddlehorn with his left and the sorrel's mane with his right. He leaped, stabbing his foot toward the dangling stirrup. His fingers locked onto their grips like iron. If he got his foot in the stirrup and then lost his handholds, he would likely be dragged to his death on this rocky ground before Ulysses could stop.

Then he was swinging up, pulling himself onto the sorrel's neck while his useless left leg dangled, dripping blood. The pain from the wound was starting to grow, but Cole forced it out of his mind. He heard more bullets coming close to him, then he managed to get his left leg over the horse's back and settled down better into the saddle. He leaned forward, grasping Ulysses's neck and hanging on tightly. Cole didn't have the reins, but it didn't matter. He was in no condition to guide Ulysses. Better to trust to the horse's judgment. Cole had done it before and lived to tell about it. He ventured a glance behind him at the bluff that was rapidly fading into the distance as the sorrel's long-legged stride ate up the ground.

That was when something crashed into Cole's head and drove him forward, almost knocking him out of the saddle. Blackness swept up to engulf him, and his last conscious thought was that he had to hang on. If he could stay on Ulysses, he still had a chance, even wounded. But if he fell off, unconscious, there was no doubt about it.

He would die, likely before the lowering sun even touched the western horizon. . . .

21

Michael tried not to smile as he slapped bay rum on his freshly shaven cheeks. It was difficult to keep a grin off his face, however. He was looking forward to the medicine show this evening, looking forward to it very much.

Professor Munroe had promised to reveal the results of his analysis of the water sample from Medicine Creek at the evening's performance. Michael was anxious to hear what the professor had found. It was all part of the story he would write for the newspaper, he told himself, the fact that he would soon be seeing Deborah again had nothing to do with the way he felt. But it did, and deep down he knew it.

He gave a little shake of his head as he reached for his suit coat and shrugged into it. He was adjusting the string tie around his neck when his wife came into the room and said, "I suppose you're going to that medicine show again."

Michael hesitated, trying to read the tone of Delia's voice before he answered. "As long as those people stay in town, it's news," he finally said.

"I suppose so. Why don't you take Gretchen with you? I'm sure she'd enjoy it."

Michael blinked in surprise. He had never considered taking Gretchen with him. Every time he had pictured himself at the show again, he had been by himself. Well, not by himself exactly . . . He had pictured himself with Deborah Munroe.

"Ah, I don't think that would be a good idea, Delia."

"Why not?"

"She might be frightened. I mean, there's an Indian in the show, and he throws tomahawks and knives."

"Gretchen isn't scared of Indians."

"How do we know that?" Michael asked. "She's never really seen any up close, has she? And this Chief Laughing Fox can look really fierce."

"If you don't want to take her because she'd be a bother, just say so," Delia snapped. "After all, I'm here with her all day long. I know how annoying she can be."

Michael felt frustration welling up inside him. "I never said Gretchen was annoying!"

"Ssshh! Keep your voice down, Michael. You don't want her to hear you."

"But I said she wasn't —" Michael stopped short and rolled his eyes. He realized this was one argument he stood absolutely no chance of winning. "All right, I'll take her. I'd be *glad* to take her. But if she gets scared or stays up too late, it's not my fault."

Delia looked at him, her features tight. "I never said you *had* to take her. It was just a suggestion. She can stay home with me and the baby."

It was all too much for Michael. He threw his hands up in the air and said, "Damn it, Deb—"

He stopped short, swallowing hard as a look of horror washed over his face. Delia's eyes widened as she stared at him in a mixture of surprise and rage. He swallowed again and said, "I meant —"

"I know what you meant," Delia cut in, her voice as cold as the eternal snow on the peaks of the Wind River range to the north. "You just go on to your little medicine show, Michael Hatfield. Gretchen is staying here with me. I wouldn't send her with you if you were going to a . . . to a dogfight!"

Michael didn't know what the hell that meant, but obviously Delia wasn't thinking too straight right now. He took a step toward her and lifted his hands, reaching out to her, intending to take hold of her shoulders. She moved back quickly, putting herself out of his reach.

"Go on," she said hollowly. "Don't let me keep you here."

He felt some anger of his own, then. She was being unreasonable. There was no need for her to be so mad over a simple, innocent slip of the tongue. Sure, he thought, Deborah Munroe was on his mind a lot these days, but so were the other members of the medicine show. Their visit to Wind River was news, for God's sake!

"You're sure you want me to go?" he asked quietly.

"Please," Delia said, her voice little more than a whisper.

"Then that's just what I'll do." Michael was trying to sound defiant. He turned and walked out of the bedroom, heading for the front door of the house. He just wished he could have carried it off a little better.

And he wished he hadn't heard the strangled little sob that came from behind him. . . .

By the time he reached the clearing on the western edge of town where the two wagons were parked, Michael's guilt had faded and been replaced by anger. He had never given her any reason to doubt his faithfulness. Since their marriage five years earlier, he had hardly even glanced at another woman. And he had agreed to bring Gretchen tonight, even though he hadn't thought it was a good idea. So it had been completely unfair for Delia to be so angry with him, he decided.

There was already a good crowd on hand when Michael got there, even though the evening's performance had not yet begun. Everyone in Wind River had doubtless heard about Professor Munroe and Dr. Carter visiting Medicine Creek earlier in the day, along with the story of the confrontation with the Shoshones. That would have only increased what had already promised to be a large audience.

As Michael came up to the edge of the crowd, he saw an elderly man trying to make his way through the press of people. The man was having trouble because he was walking with the aid of two crutches. Both of his legs were unusually short and twisted grotesquely. He was saying in a quavery voice, "Please let me through. Have pity on a crippled old man and let me through."

No one seemed to be paying any attention

to him, however. Michael was struck by the man's plight and moved to his side, reaching out to grasp one of the man's arms.

"I'll give you a hand, old-timer," he said.

The man looked up at Michael with an expression of gratitude on his weathered, beard-stubbled face. "Thank you kindly, young fella," he said. "I heard about this here professor bein' in town, and I want to see if maybe he can help me with that tonic of his'n."

Michael led the old man through the growing audience, taking advantage of every gap in the crowd and elbowing his way through when he had to. He smiled and muttered apologies to the people who turned angrily toward him, and they always subsided when they saw that Michael was just assisting an elderly, crippled man. When they finally reached the front row, near the wagons, Michael heaved a sigh of relief.

"Can't tell you how much I appreciate this, son," the old man said. He balanced on the crutches and stuck out his right hand to Michael. "Name's Otis Stokes."

"Glad to meet you, Mr. Stokes," Michael replied as he shook hands with the man. "You're not from around here, are you?"

"Nope. Reckon you'd call me a drifter. Do a few odd jobs, whatever I can to get by." He looked down at his twisted legs with disgust. "Ain't much I *can* do, if you get my meanin'."

"Sorry," Michael murmured.

"Aw, hell, don't be. I was born like this, so I reckon I ought to be used to it by now. Anyway, maybe my luck's about to change. I was over in Rawlins when I heard about this Professor Munroe fella and that miracle water he makes his tonic out of. Figure maybe it'll fix me right up. I took all the money I'd scraped up and bought a train ticket to come over here."

Michael tried not to frown. He hadn't completely made up his mind about the efficacy of Professor Munroe's tonic or the so-called magic in the waters of Medicine Creek. But he couldn't see how the tonic or the water could help a problem like the one Otis Stokes had.

Still, he didn't want to destroy what might be the old man's last hope, so he just smiled and nodded and said, "Maybe so." Then, before he could say anything else, he spied Deborah Munroe at the corner of the wagon. She seemed to be looking for someone, and as she caught his eye, she motioned for him to come to her.

Michael frowned, pointed at himself, and mouthed the word *Me?* Deborah nodded.

He wasn't going to keep a lady waiting, especially one who looked like Deborah. He said, "Maybe I'll see you later, Mr. Stokes," then left the old-timer in the front ranks of the waiting audience. When he reached the corner of the wagon, Deborah reached out to grasp his arm and tug him along with her — as if he wouldn't have gone willingly wherever she wanted to lead him.

"I'm so excited, Michael," she said. "Uncle Nicodemus has finished his analysis of that water sample, and he says he's going to be able to use it to make his tonic better than ever!"

Michael heard what she was saying, but much of his attention was focused on the way she was dressed. Tonight she was wearing a bright-red gown that was cut low in the front, as usual, to reveal the creamy swell of her breasts. It had a bustle in the back and a train that swept around to the sides and trailed behind her, exposing her legs clad in mesh stockings. Her beauty had a powerful, visceral impact on Michael, almost as if he had been struck by a physical blow. She took his breath away, that was what she did. She just simply took his breath away. . . .

Professor Munroe was waiting on the other side of the wagons, an excited expression on his face in the light of a lantern hanging from a peg on the side of one wagon. Calvin and Letitia Dumont and Chief Laughing Fox were with him. Munroe smiled when he saw Michael and said, "Ah, there you are! I was hoping you'd be here tonight, Michael."

"Wouldn't miss it," Michael assured him. He pointed to a bottle that Munroe was holding. "What's that?"

"That's the reason I'm glad you're here," the professor replied as he lifted the bottle. It was full of a thick, noxious-looking pink liquid. "This is the miracle of the age, Michael! And you're here tonight to witness its debut!"

"Is that . . . a new tonic?" Michael guessed.

"Indeed it is, my boy." Munroe turned to the Dumonts and the Chippewa. "Go on with the show, my friends, while I explain things to our young journalist friend."

"Sure, Professor," Calvin Dumont said. Holding his wife's tiny hand, he led her and Laughing Fox around the wagons.

Michael took a pad of paper and a pencil from his coat pocket. The paper and pencil went with him nearly everywhere, because as an editor and reporter, he never knew when he might run across something newsworthy. He said, "What did you find when you analyzed the water from Medicine Creek, Professor?"

"Exactly what I expected to find, Michael, exactly what I expected to find . . . only more. The elements which give the water its curative powers are present in even higher concentrations than before. My theory is that the springs which feed the creek are themselves fed by an underground river, and that river is constantly cutting its channel lower and lower into the earth. It must have struck a level in which the elements in question are even more prevalent."

"And what elements would those be, exactly?"

Munroe smiled tolerantly. "The scientific world must have its little secrets, Michael. And so must a businessman. I'm sure you understand why I have to keep the ingredients of my tonic confidential."

Michael frowned and said, "I'm sure the readers of the *Sentinel* would like to know —"

"And so would every other proprietor of a medicine show," Munroe cut in, his voice gentle but firm. "I'm not trying to be uncooperative, Michael, I'm really not."

"I suppose I understand," Michael said,

nodding. "You have to protect your liveli-hood."

"Not only that, but there are some people who would not be as meticulous as I am in the preparation of the tonic. If they were not careful, a concoction might result that could harm someone. No, I'm afraid I have to keep some things to myself."

Seeing that he wasn't going to get any farther with this line of questioning, Michael switched tacks by asking, "What will this new tonic do?"

"I'm not sure yet," Munroe admitted. "It should cure everything that the old tonic did, plus some other ailments. I only know one way to find out for certain, and that's by trying it."

Michael thought of Otis Stokes and said, "There's an old man in the audience tonight — a really pathetic sort. His legs are crip-pled and always have been. Do you think the tonic might help someone like him?"

Munroe said slowly, "I'm not sure. I deal in what seems like miracles or magic, true, but in actuality it's only science and medi-cine, and they have limits, as much as we might like to believe otherwise. But if this gentleman is in attendance tonight, we could certainly try the tonic on him and see what happens."

Michael nodded in excitement. "Sounds like a good idea to me, and I know Mr. Stokes will be happy to give it a try."

Straightening his top hat, Munroe said, "Well, I believe I should join the others. Are you coming, my dear?"

Deborah shook her head. "I'll be there in a moment, Uncle Nicodemus. I want to talk to Michael first."

"Oh." Munroe smiled. "I see. Well, I'll leave you two alone." He started toward the front of the wagons.

Michael was startled by what Deborah had said, and he didn't much like the knowing smile that had appeared on Munroe's face. It was true that he hadn't gone out of his way to let them know that he was a married man, but surely they were aware of it.

"Michael," Deborah said as she laid a hand on his arm, "I can't tell you how much it's meant to us to have a friend like you here in Wind River. So many places where we go, people assume that since we have a medicine show, we're nothing more than fakes and thieves. You've had an open mind right from the start, and you've been very fair to us."

He shrugged. "Well, a journalist is supposed to be fair."

"Yes, but so many of them aren't." Sud-

275

denly, she leaned closer to him, coming up on her toes to brush her lips across his cheek in a quick kiss. "That's for being fair."

Michael could still feel the kiss like a brand burning on his skin. His throat was choked and he couldn't seem to breathe properly. His heart was pounding. He managed to croak, "Deborah . . ."

"Yes, Michael?" she whispered, her face only inches from his.

He kissed her.

This was the first time he had kissed anyone other than Delia in years, and the feel of her, the taste of her, the smell of her, all were incredibly exciting to him. His arms went around her, tightening, pulling her to him, and she came willingly, eagerly. He felt the soft thrust of her breasts against his chest. Her body molded brazenly to his. He found himself reacting more strongly than he had in a long time with Delia.

The thought of his wife went through him suddenly, and he broke the kiss and stepped back. Deborah made a little noise of disappointment. "What's wrong, Michael?" she asked. "That was . . . nice. Very nice."

"I . . . I can't do this," he stammered. "I'm married!"

"I know," Deborah said softly. "But I don't care. I've wanted you ever since the first time I saw you."

Her statement struck him like a hammer blow. He felt the same way. From the first instant he had set eyes on Deborah Munroe, he had desired her. More than that, he had felt a connection, an attraction, stronger than anything he had ever known. He was thrilled to discover that she returned the feeling. She was more worldly, more sophisticated than anyone he had ever encountered, and yet *she* wanted *him,* too! It was unbelievable.

But at the same time as the flood of passion was sweeping through him, a strong undertow of dismay tugged at him. He was married, he had a wife and children whom he loved, he had no business dallying here behind a medicine show wagon with a beautiful temptress in a bright-red dress —

He was eternally grateful that he didn't have to decide what to do next. The loud, angry shouts coming from the other side of the wagons did that for him.

22

Billy Casebolt was in the marshal's office, trying to decide if it was too early to start on the evening's rounds, when the haggard, bloody figure of Cole Tyler appeared in the doorway.

Casebolt sprang up from the chair behind the desk and ran over to grasp Cole's arm as the marshal limped into the room. "Tarnation!" Casebolt exclaimed. "What happened to you, Marshal?"

"Got winged by some bushwhackers," Cole grunted as Casebolt helped him ease down onto the chair in front of the desk. There was an ugly-looking gash on the side of his head with a fan of dried blood underneath it, and the left leg of his denim pants was black with bloodstains as well.

"I was gettin' a mite worried about you, since you'd been gone so long after ridin' out to Fisk's place. Him and his boys do this to you?"

Cole shook his head, grimacing at the pain the movement caused him. "I don't rightly know who did it," he said. "Don't think it was anybody from Latch Hook, though."

"Well, you just sit right there. I'll run fetch Doc Kent to take a look at you."

Casebolt pounded out of the office, but he was back a moment later. Anxiously, he said, "There's some sort of commotion goin' on down at the west end of town, Marshal. Folks're yellin' like there's a big fight. You reckon I ought to . . . ?"

Cole pushed himself wearily to his feet. "Law business comes first. I'm not hurt that bad, just worn out more than anything. I'll go with you."

"I can handle whatever it is —"

"Come on, Billy," Cole said as he limped past the deputy. "Let's go see what's going on, and then Judson can patch up these creases."

That was all the wounds were, Cole knew. They hurt like blazes, and the one on his left thigh, especially, had bled quite a bit, but he had been able to hang on to Ulysses and remain conscious as he fled from whoever had ambushed him out on Austin Fisk's ranch. It had taken him quite a while to make it back to town since he'd been forced to hold Ulysses to a walk once he had ridden out of range of the hidden gunmen's rifles. Every step the big golden sorrel took sent a jolt of agony through Cole's head, and he hadn't been able to stand a gallop or even a trot.

He explained that to Casebolt as they made their way along Grenville Avenue toward the western edge of town, leaving out what he had theorized concerning the rustling on Latch Hook and the Diamond S. That was all too complicated to go into now. On the way, they passed Dr. Kent's office, and the building was dark. The medico wasn't there, obviously, which meant Cole was going to have to wait to have his wounds tended to, anyway. Might as well see what all the commotion was about while he was waiting, he thought.

As he had halfway expected, the disturbance was coming from the medicine show. Cole heaved a sigh. With the rustling that was going on, he didn't need the added distraction of this squabbling. As he and Casebolt moved up to the edge of the crowd, he saw Professor Munroe and Dr. Bramwell Carter confronting each other again. Carter was trying to say something, but the crowd kept shouting him down. Judson Kent stood with him, appearing uncomfortable and angry at the same time.

The big fellow, Dumont, was behind Munroe, and it looked like the professor was having to almost hold him back to keep him from attacking Carter. Dumont's diminutive wife was perched on the lowered tailgate of the nearest wagon, and off to one side were standing the stoic Chippewa, the professor's pretty blond niece — and Michael Hatfield.

Cole didn't waste time wondering what Michael was doing with Deborah Munroe. Instead, ignoring the pain in his head, he lifted his voice and shouted, "Hey! Settle down, damn it!" When the noise from the crowd subsided a little, he went on, "What's going on here?"

Bramwell Carter swung toward Cole and said, "You have to listen to me now, Marshal! I have proof! I analyzed that water sample from Medicine Creek —"

Cole held up a hand to stop him, then glanced over at Casebolt. "What the hell's he talking about?"

"It's a long story, Marshal, and I ain't had a chance to tell you about it yet."

Cole shook his head. "Never mind, I'll figure it out as I go along. Go ahead, Doctor, and the rest of you people, shut up!"

Carter took a deep breath and said, "I took a sample of water from Medicine

Creek this afternoon, Marshal, and with the assistance of Dr. Kent here, I've analyzed it and found out just what's in it. Of course, a complete analysis was difficult, since our facilities here are limited —"

"What did you find?" Cole broke in.

"Plain water," Carter said triumphantly. "Nothing but plain water."

"That's a lie!" Professor Munroe burst out, and more shouts came from the crowd despite Cole's earlier warning. The professor went on, "The mineral content of that water is exceedingly high, just as I always claimed. It makes the perfect basis for my elixir. With certain ingredients provided by my friend the chief added to the mixture, that water forms perhaps the most effective medicinal tonic the world has ever seen!"

Cole looked at Kent. "What do you think, Doctor?"

"I'm not certain," Kent said slowly, stroking his short beard. "It's true the water does have a high mineral content, but there's nothing unusual about that. I don't see how it could have any sort of special powers —"

"Let's put it to the test," Munroe said suddenly. "I'm willing to stand behind everything I've said, and not only that, I'll prove it! I'll prove that this new batch of tonic is the most powerful one of all!" He held up a bottle filled with thick, pink liquid.

"I don't know how you're going to prove that, Professor," Cole said with a shake of his head.

"Mr. Hatfield, the editor of your own local paper, told me there was a man here tonight with a crippling, lifelong condition — You, sir! Would you be that man?" Munroe pointed suddenly to an old man in the front row of the audience who was balanced on a pair of crutches. His legs were bent and twisted beneath him, but his lined face lit up like the sunrise as Munroe turned toward him.

"Can you help me, Professor?" he said desperately. "I ain't never been able to walk right, and I'll do anything, give you all the money I got —"

"No need for payment, my friend," Munroe told him gently. "You'll be helping me as much as I am helping you. What's your name?"

"Otis Stokes, Professor. I'll drink your tonic. I'll try anything that might help!"

Munroe cast a scornful glance toward Carter and Kent. "You see? You would deny hope to a poor wretch like this, gentlemen? I think not!" He uncorked the bottle in his hand and extended it toward Otis Stokes.

"Don't let him do this!" Carter exclaimed.

283

"That stuff might be poisonous!"

Cole limped forward and said, "Hold on a minute."

Judson Kent caught hold of his arm. "My God, Marshal, you're wounded!"

"Nothing that won't wait," Cole said. "Mr. Stokes, are you sure you want to try this stuff?"

Stokes's head bobbed up and down eagerly. "I sure do, Marshal."

Cole looked at Munroe. "All right, go ahead."

Carter tried one more time as Munroe held the bottle to the old man's mouth and tipped it up. The doctor began, "I must protest —" before the roar of the crowd drowned him out as they shouted encouragement to Otis Stokes.

Stokes swallowed about half the liquid in the bottle, then Munroe took it away from his mouth. "We don't want to give you too much, my friend," the professor said. "How does that feel?"

"Can't tell no difference so far," Stokes said. "That tonic sure does go down smooth — Oh, Lord!"

He stiffened, and the spectators gasped. A series of shudders went through Stokes's body, and Munroe had to catch his arm to keep him from falling. "Mr. Stokes! Mr.

Stokes!" Munroe said anxiously. "Are you all right?"

"I told you!" Carter crowded. "I told you it was dangerous to let that quack give him the tonic!"

Otis Stokes was still shuddering. He dropped his crutches and clung frantically to Munroe, who was the only one holding him up. Several men started forward to help, but Munroe called, "Stay back! I've got him!"

Suddenly, Stokes stiffened again, and he seemed to be standing taller than before. Casebolt pointed and cried out, "Lordy! Look there!"

Before the amazed eyes of the crowd, Stokes's right leg seemed to straighten and lengthen. The old man's face was pale as milk, and there were audible popping and crackling sounds. His pants seemed to be shrinking, as more and more of his ankle appeared beneath the end of the trouser leg, but everyone in the crowd realized that his leg was really getting longer. After a moment, he rested his weight on that leg and let out a moan as the same thing began to happen to the other leg.

"Glory be," Casebolt breathed beside Cole. "I never seen nothin' like it."

Obviously, neither had anyone else in the

crowd. Cole forget about his own injuries as he watched in amazement and hushed awe, just like everyone else. After a couple of minutes, the formerly bent and withered Otis Stokes was standing upright on legs that had been useless — until now. Stokes looked down at his own legs, an expression of astounded disbelief on his face. "I never . . . I never really dreamed. . . ."

"It's a miracle!" someone in the crowd cried raggedly. Others took up the shout. Stokes shuffled back and forth, trying out his legs, and suddenly broke into a little jig as he let out a whoop of joy.

Cole looked around at everybody else. Michael Hatfield was watching with an expression of stunned amazement on his face, while beside him Deborah Munroe was beaming with pride. Calvin Dumont swept his wife, Letitia, up in his arms as both of them grinned broadly, and even the Chippewa, Laughing Fox, looked vaguely pleased. As for Bramwell Carter and Judson Kent, both of them appeared surprised and not a little upset.

As Otis Stokes continued to caper around, Professor Munroe turned to Carter and said in a voice dripping with scorn, "Well, Doctor? What do you think of my new and improved Chippewa Tonic now?"

"I . . . I don't know what to make of it," Carter said miserably. "I was so sure it wouldn't work . . ."

"Well, it did!" Munroe said triumphantly. He turned to the crowd. "You saw it with your own eyes, my friends! You saw what my tonic did for this poor man! It can do the same and more for you!"

Casebolt tugged at the sleeve of Cole's buckskin shirt and said, "Uh, Marshal, with you bein' hurt and all . . . I figger we better get out of the way."

Cole knew he was right. They barely moved to the side in time to avoid the rush as the crowd mobbed Professor Munroe, waving greenbacks and coins in their hands. Cole and Casebolt worked their way around the press of frantic people in front of the wagons and soon found themselves at the rear of the crowd. They were joined there by a crestfallen Bramwell Carter and a clearly baffled Judson Kent.

"What do you think, Doctor?" Cole asked Carter.

"I . . . I don't know what to think. If I hadn't seen that with my own eyes . . ." He shook his head.

Cole turned to Kent. "Judson?"

"It appears that Professor Munroe's tonic may have some medicinal value after all,"

Kent said. "But I'm going to reserve judgment on that until after I've had a look at those wounds of yours. You've neglected them much too long as it is, Marshal. Come on down to the office with me right now."

"Won't argue with you," Cole said with a nod. "They do hurt like blazes. Billy, stay here and keep an eye on this . . . this fandango for me."

The deputy nodded. "Sure will, Marshal. Say, Doc, maybe you ought to get some of the professor's tonic to put on them bullet wounds. Might heal 'em right up."

"I think I shall trust to established medical procedures instead, Deputy," Kent said stiffly. He looked at Cole. "That is, unless the marshal would prefer —"

"I'm in your hands, Judson," Cole said. "And right now, I want to get off my feet for a while. I'll see you later, Billy."

He limped down the street with Kent while Dr. Carter started back toward the Territorial House. Carter was shaking his head and was obviously quite upset by what he had witnessed.

Cole was a little surprised by it all himself. Now, in addition to a mysterious gang of wideloopers, he had on his hands what would undoubtedly be an even bigger uproar here in town, once word got around of how Professor Munroe's tonic had cured the old man's crippled legs. And that word would spread quickly, Cole knew.

It all made him wonder — and worry — about what in blazes was going to happen next.

23

For a couple of days, nothing much happened in Wind River except that Professor Nicodemus Munroe and his medicine show made money hand over fist.

Once Cole had heard the whole story from Billy Casebolt of the confrontation at Medicine Creek between the Shoshones and the pilgrims who had come in search of the miracle water, Cole feared the trouble would become even worse. By the next morning, everyone in town knew how Munroe's new and improved tonic had cured Otis Stokes. That was liable to prompt an even worse rush on Medicine Creek and lead directly to fighting with the Indians.

Luckily, it didn't work out that way. Professor Munroe announced that he would be able to produce the new tonic without using the actual waters of Medicine Creek, now that he knew which elements the stream contained, and in what concentrations. He set to work immediately making up a new batch of the stuff, and no one waited until the show that night to buy the elixir. They lined up at the medicine show wagons all day, forking over their hard-earned cash for bottles of the tonic. By that night, Munroe was running low on his supply of bottles and asked the members of the audience to return their empties, promising them a nickel's discount on the next bottle they purchased if they did so.

The next day was more of the same, and as Cole and Casebolt strolled down to the clearing where the wagons were parked and looked at the line of people waiting to buy the tonic, Cole had to shake his head in wonderment.

"Doesn't look like this run on the professor's elixir is going to end any time soon," he commented.

"Folks're feelin' healthier than they have in a long time," Casebolt said. "I, uh, bought another couple o' bottles for myself, and it sure has helped my rheumatism again. Why, I hardly feel these old bones achin' anymore."

"I'm glad to hear it."

Casebolt gestured at the bandage on the side of Cole's head. "You ought to give it a try, Marshal, if your skull's still a-poundin' from where that slug kissed you. It'll fix you right up."

Cole smiled. "No, thanks, Billy. I don't mind Munroe selling the stuff, and I'm not going to argue about whether or not it works, but I think I'll steer clear of it."

"Suit yourself," Casebolt shrugged. "Me, I'm startin' to swear by it."

"That Dr. Carter must be swearing *at* it. Reckon he's pretty much a laughingstock around here now, after what happened the other night. Judson Kent tells me Carter's leaving on the next eastbound."

"Good riddance," Casebolt snorted. "Fella was too uppity for me."

The medicine show performers were too busy selling tonic and assisting Munroe in the preparation of it to do any practicing during the day, and as Cole watched Deborah Munroe making change for the customers, he frowned a little. "Billy, have you noticed how much Michael Hatfield has been hanging around that gal?"

"Which gal? That yellow-haired one?" Casebolt's frown matched the marshal's. "Yeah, I seen him around here a lot. Reckon he's not here right now because the newspaper's comin' out tomorrow and he's got to get ready for that. Come to think of it, I believe I saw a light in the newspaper office

292

late last night, like there was somebody stayin' there." Casebolt rubbed his lean jaw as his frown deepened. "Aw, hell, Marshal, you don't reckon that young feller's been moonin' so much over that medicine show gal that he's gone and left that pretty little redheaded wife of his, do you?"

"Or gotten booted out of their house by her, maybe," Cole said with a sigh. "I'd hate to think so, Billy, but you can't ever tell what'll happen when a man gets some fool notion in his head about a pretty woman."

"Want me to have a talk with that younker?"

Cole shook his head. "Not yet. Likely that medicine show will move on sooner or later, and then Michael will come to his senses. With any luck, it won't be too late for him and Delia by then."

The two lawmen walked back down Grenville Avenue, Cole limping only slightly. His wounded leg was still quite sore, but he was able to ignore the pain for the most part and the injury was healing well, according to Dr. Judson Kent. The doctor had been concerned that the bullet crease on Cole's head might have caused a concussion, but there had been no sign of one and the shallow gash itself was also healing cleanly. Cole's active, outdoor life had given him good recuperative powers, Kent had said. The way Cole saw it, a man who had things to do just didn't have the time to be laid up for very long while injuries healed.

He had things to do, that was certain. There was still the matter of that rustling to deal with. He hadn't been back out to either the Diamond S or Latch Hook, but he thought his leg would be well enough for him to ride again in another day or two.

Then he would continue his investigation and get to the bottom of this. He had laid out his theory for Casebolt, and the deputy had agreed it was possible a gang of owl-hoots had deliberately made it look as if Sawyer and Fisk were responsible for the raids on each other's ranch, while all the time the real cow thieves were hiding the stolen stock somewhere in the mountains before driving it on to market.

"Sure you don't want me to ride out to Sawyer's place and have a talk with him?" Casebolt asked now, as if reading the marshal's mind. "I could tell that fella Fisk what you think about their problem, too."

Cole shook his head. "I don't completely trust Fisk. He could still be tied up in it somehow. I ought to be able to ride tomorrow. I'll go out there then."

Cole glanced across the street and saw

that they were passing the office of the *Wind River Sentinel.* Through the big plate-glass windows in the front of the building, Cole could see Michael Hatfield moving around the big press in the back of the room, assisted by his two printer's devils. It was late afternoon, and the press would be turning soon, printing newspapers that would be distributed early the next morning.

At least Michael wasn't neglecting his job too much, Cole thought. Michael was devoted to newspaper work.

But Cole had believed that Michael was devoted to his wife, Delia, too, and from what he had seen the past couple of days, that looked like it was no longer true.

It was a damned shame, Cole thought as he walked on. A pure, damned shame.

He couldn't put it off any longer, Michael thought as he checked the lines of type set in the forms that would go in the printing press. He had to make a decision. It was torturing him to draw things out like this, unable to make up his mind what to do.

Of course, he'd had a lot of time to think the past two nights, since he had come home to find that Delia had thrown all of his clothes onto the front porch, along with some bedding. Michael had gathered it all up in a hurry and made his way to the newspaper office using back alleys, not wanting anyone to see him and realize that he had been kicked out of his own house. There was a cot in the back room, and he had been sleeping there at night ever since.

Once before, he and Delia had separated briefly, back before Lincoln was born, but that time *she* had moved out, taking a room in the hotel with Gretchen. That had led to plenty of trouble, too, and Michael had been utterly relieved when they had reconciled.

But it appeared the reconciliation had not been as complete as he might have hoped, and he had to admit that most of that was his fault.

He just hadn't counted on falling in love with another woman.

The time he had spent with Deborah Munroe the past two days had been wonderful. They were seldom alone, since the medicine show was doing such a booming business, but they had been able to steal a few private moments. Michael had kissed Deborah again, several times, and each kiss had left him shaken and faint with wanting her. And Deborah had made it plain that she wanted him, too, that she was more than

296

willing to take their relationship a step farther.

She wanted to make love with him.

If that happened, he would be crossing a
line, taking a step from which there was no
retreating. He would never be able to go
back to Delia. Not that Delia even wanted
him anymore, he thought glumly as he
added ink to the reservoir on the printer.

But eventually, the medicine show would
leave Wind River, and Deborah would go
with it. The logical part of Michael's mind
knew that. He couldn't ask her to stay here
with him, and even if he did, he was certain
she would refuse. Any passion he might
share with Deborah, no matter how thrill-
ing and exciting, would be temporary. And
then, when she was gone, he would be left
alone, his wife and children beyond a bar-
rier that he could never breach. Would it be
worth it to give in to the desire he felt?

But if he didn't, would he ever be able to
live with not knowing what he might have
had, even if it was fleeting?

The answer to that, he knew with sudden,
crystal clarity, was no. He was not a man to
whom such opportunities came often — or
even *ever,* he thought bitterly — and for the
first time in his life, he had to take a chance.
What was the old Latin phrase? *Carpe diem,*

that was it. *Seize the day.*

Or in this case, the night — tomorrow night. . . .

Alexandra Fisk reined in her horse atop a wooded knoll and looked across the valley toward the mountains that formed the boundary between her father's Latch Hook spread and the Diamond S. Somewhere on the other side of those mountains was Frenchy LeDoux, she thought. A frown appeared on her face. Why in the world was she even thinking about Kermit Sawyer's foreman? True, Frenchy had a certain rough charm about him, and he was handsome in a rugged sort of way, but she had known men back in Kentucky who were much more charming and handsome, and they hadn't been as arrogant and reckless as LeDoux.

But still she found her mind straying back to the man, and although she had been trying for a couple of weeks now, she couldn't banish him entirely from her thoughts.

Night was falling with the suddenness that was common to the high country. Alexandra had ridden out here onto the range after supper in an attempt to clear her head, not telling anyone where she was going because she knew her father did not like her riding around the ranch after dark. So far she wasn't having much luck.

She spotted movement down in the valley and leaned forward in her saddle. It was difficult to make out any details through the gathering shadows, but she thought she saw about a dozen men on horseback moving through one of the pastures. The frown on Alexandra's face deepened, but for a different reason this time. The mystery of what she was seeing had finally succeeded in driving thoughts of Frenchy LeDoux out of her head.

She had just come from the ranch headquarters, and she knew that most of the men were there at the moment. Only a handful of the crew were out on the range.

Which meant that these men she was watching couldn't be Latch Hook punchers. They had no right to be here.

The strangers were riding northeast, toward the area of the ranch where most of the stock was gathered. That thought gave even more weight to the idea that had sprung into Alexandra's mind as soon as she saw them.

The rustlers who had hit Latch Hook before had returned.

Without thinking, she put her hand on the stock of the Winchester that was sticking up from its saddleboot under her left leg. She drew the rifle with a quick jerk and worked the lever, jacking a shell into the chamber. She wasn't going to sit by and do nothing but quiver in fear while those men raided the ranch; that would be more like what Catherine might do. But she was smart enough to know that she couldn't fight all of them, either. They had her outnumbered too badly.

But maybe she could throw a scare into them and then light a shuck for the ranch house, where she could alert her father, Wilt Paxton, and the rest of the men.

She brought the Winchester to her shoulder, lined it on the horsebackers moving through the valley, and squeezed the trigger.

The rifle bucked heavily against her shoulder as it cracked wickedly. She was used to the recoil, though, and fought the barrel back down as she levered the Winchester again. She squeezed the trigger a second time and sent another shot toward the distant riders.

Alexandra didn't know if she had hit anything or not, didn't really care if she had. All she wanted to do was spook the rustlers and delay them in the errand that had brought them to Latch Hook. She wheeled her horse and kicked it into a run through the timber. Her last glance at the riders showed her that they were milling around in surprise at the shots. She saw a couple of winks of orange flame and knew they were throwing lead back at her. They weren't likely to hit her at this range. An instant later the trees closed in thickly around her and she knew she was safe. There was no way the men could catch up to her.

Now all she had to do was get back to the ranch house and let her father know the wideloopers had returned to Latch Hook.

24

Cole started out of the marshal's office into the foyer of the building and almost ran into Simone McKay. He stopped short and said, "Sorry, Simone. Guess I wasn't looking where I was going."

"That's all right," she smiled. She had been on her way into the building, no doubt heading for the offices of the land development company down the hall.

Cole hadn't seen much of her the past few days, between his duties as marshal and all the things she had to attend to as a business-woman and leading citizen of the town. He supposed she had been spending most of her time either at the hotel or the house her late husband had built for her on Sweet-water Street, on the western edge of town. Not far from that medicine show, in fact, Cole realized, and he wondered if the com-motion from there had been disturbing her.

He was about to say something about that,

but she spoke first. "I think there's going to be another dance soon," she said. "I was wondering, since we weren't able to go to the first one . . ."

Cole couldn't believe his good luck. He grinned and said, "Sounds like a mighty fine idea to me. I never have forgiven Billy Casebolt for getting sick when he did and causing me to miss that dance. I thought about you while we were out there at that Shoshone village."

Simone began to blush prettily. "You shouldn't hold that against Billy. I'm sure he didn't mean to — Oh, I understand now. You're just . . . joshing me. Isn't that the word?"

"It'll do," Cole admitted. It was easier to talk to Simone now. He had always felt there was a wall of sorts separating them, a wall constructed of the differences between his station in life and hers. Not that he thought she was too good for him. She was just accustomed to a totally different way of living.

She seemed to have adjusted quite well to the frontier, though, and that gave Cole a reason to hope that maybe someday . . .

Maybe what he really needed to do, he thought suddenly, was to stop waiting for some vague time in the future when he could tell Simone how he really felt about

303

her. Life was just too damned uncertain for that. An emotion that was honest ought to be expressed, because folks never knew when, without warning, it might be too late.

"Simone?" he said, acting before he could stop to think about what he was doing.

"Yes, Cole?" she replied softly.

"There you are, by God!"

The loud, angry voice didn't come from Cole. The words issued from the mouth of Austin Fisk, who strode through the door from the boardwalk. He glared at Cole, who swung around in surprise. "I want to talk to you, Marshal," Fisk went on.

Cole bit back the curse that sprang to his lips. The moment between him and Simone, the moment that might have turned out to be very special, was gone. Cole said tightly, "What in blazes is this all about, Fisk?"

"Those damned rustlers hit my place again last night." Fisk looked at Simone and added, "Beg your pardon, ma'am, but I'm upset."

"And you seem to have every right to be, Mr. Fisk," Simone said. "Was anyone hurt?"

"Not this time, thank the Lord. It was my daughter Alexandra who spotted them and brought word to the house." Fisk turned and gestured to someone who was still outside on the boardwalk. "Come in here

304

and tell the marshal about it, Alexandra."

The tall, slender brunette came into the foyer. She was wearing denim pants and a jacket today, along with a flat-crowned hat dangling behind her neck from its chin strap. She nodded to Cole and said, "Hello, Marshal."

"Miss Fisk. What happened out there on Latch Hook?"

"I was out for a ride last night after supper," Alexandra explained. "I saw about a dozen men moving across our spread, and I knew they couldn't be any of our punchers. I took a couple of shots at them to slow them down, then headed back to the ranch house as quickly as I could."

Cole frowned. "If they didn't see you, you should've just headed for home without letting them know you were there, miss. You put yourself in danger by taking potshots at them."

Anger flared in Alexandra's eyes as she said, "I didn't want them to think they could get away with riding onto our land and doing as they pleased."

Cole nodded. The young woman came by her fiery nature honestly, he supposed. Her father probably would have been even more foolhardy if he had run across those rustlers. Cole could imagine Austin Fisk charging right into them, even though he would have been outnumbered.

"What happened then?" Cole asked.

"I took my men and went out looking for those thieves, of course," Fisk snapped. "We didn't catch up to them in time, unfortunately. They hit my herd again and chased off the men I had standing guard. Luckily they only got about fifty head. I suppose they were hurrying because they were afraid Alexandra had alerted us to their presence."

"You *were* lucky, you and your daughter both," Cole said slowly. "Were you able to track the stolen cattle?"

"That's what we did first thing this morning. The tracks disappeared before they got to the mountains." Fisk's voice was bitter.

Cole had a hunch he knew on which stretch of ground the tracks of the stolen cattle had vanished. There was something else on his mind, though, so he said, "I haven't heard you blame Kermit Sawyer for this raid yet."

"Well, I still think he might've had something to do with it," Fisk said stubbornly. "I'm trying to abide by the law, though. That's why I came into town to tell you about it. What are you going to do, Marshal?"

Cole hesitated, then said, "I'm not sure

yet. I've got a couple of ideas where those cattle could be going. . . ."

"Well, for God's sake, tell us!" Fisk exclaimed.

Cole shook his head. "Not yet. Not until I do some more checking around first. Last time, the gang hit your place, Fisk, then turned around and raided the Diamond S. Could be they'll follow the same pattern this time. Think I'll ride out and have a talk with Sawyer."

"That's all?" Fisk sounded disbelieving and angry.

"Like I said, I'll be looking into it," Cole told him, letting an edge creep into his voice. His instincts told him he still didn't have the whole story, and he didn't want to start explaining any of his theories until he had the proof to back them up.

"I've been damned patient, Marshal," Fisk said, and this time he didn't apologize to Simone for his language. "But if you don't put a stop to this — and soon! — I'll take whatever actions are necessary to do it myself." He jerked his head toward the door. "Come on, Alexandra."

The young woman followed him out, and when Cole and Simone were alone again, Simone said, "I hate to see trouble like this."

"So do I," Cole agreed. "I'd better find

Billy, and we'll take a ride out to the Diamond S. I want to keep an eye on that spread tonight, just in case the rustlers strike again there like they did last time. I'll talk to Jeremiah before we leave. Maybe he won't mind holding down the fort again here in town."

As he started to turn away, Simone said, "Cole . . . you were about to say something else before Mr. Fisk came in."

He had been hoping that she'd forgotten about that. Now just wasn't the time to go into what he had been feeling. "Nothing that can't wait," he said. "I'd better get moving."

He nodded to her and left the building, heading down to the café in search of Billy Casebolt. The deputy had mentioned earlier that he had a hankering for a piece of Rose Foster's apple pie, so he might still be there. As he strode down the street, there was more on Cole's mind than the rustlers who had struck again on Latch Hook.

Had that been a trace of disappointment he had seen in Simone's eyes?

Kermit Sawyer met the lawmen in the big main room of the log ranch house, and he didn't look happy about it.

"If you've ridden out here to accuse me of

something again, Marshal, I ain't goin' to be happy about it," Sawyer said. "In fact, I'm gettin' damned tired of it!"

"It's true Fisk's spread was hit by rustlers again last night," Cole told the Texan, "but I know you didn't have anything to do with it, Sawyer."

That declaration brought a frown of surprise to Sawyer's weathered features. "You know who's behind all the trouble around here?"

Cole shook his head and said, "I don't know who's heading up the gang, but I'm convinced there's only one bunch of wide-loopers and they don't come from either the Diamond S or Latch Hook. Somebody's been playing you and Fisk against each other."

"You sure Fisk ain't just bein' sneaky?"

"I'm convinced he's telling the truth," Cole said. "Which means there's a good chance those cow thieves will hit your spread again, Sawyer."

The cattleman snorted. "We'll give 'em a hot reception if they do!"

"No," Cole said, "that's exactly what you won't do."

Sawyer stared at him. "What in blazes are you talkin' about, Tyler?"

"Billy and I are going to keep an eye on

your herd tonight, tomorrow night, however long it takes. If the rustlers hit, let them take the cows. Your men can put up a little fight to make it look good, but not enough to drive off those wideloopers. Then Billy and I will follow them and find out how they're getting those stolen cows into the mountains."

"That's the craziest damn thing I ever heard!" Sawyer protested. "You're askin' me to *let* those sons o' bitches steal my stock?"

Cole nodded. "That's what I'm asking, all right. I want to find their hideout, and the best way to do that is to have them lead me right to it."

"Yeah, well, what if they give you the slip? Then I lose those cows!"

"It's a risk, all right," Cole admitted. "But if you want to put a stop to these raids, I think this is the way to do it."

Sawyer's eyes narrowed menacingly as he said, "You'd better be right. If I let you go through with this damnfool plan of yours and wind up losing the rest of my herd because of it, I'll be settlin' up with *you,* Tyler."

"That's a chance *I'll* take," Cole snapped. "You'd better tell your men what the plan is, so they'll know what to do."

"I'll tell 'em, all right. And I'll tell Frenchy

to keep an eye on you two, special-like. Because to tell you the truth, mister . . . I don't particularly trust *you*. Maybe you're in with them rustlers."

Cole took a step forward, a red haze creeping in from the corners of his eyes. He had been accused of being a lot of things in his life, but never a cow thief. His hands bunched into fists, and he might have taken a swing at Sawyer if Billy Casebolt hadn't caught hold of his arm.

"Come on, Marshal," the deputy urged. "We got to find us a good spot to lay low and keep an eye on them longhorns."

Cole took a deep breath and nodded, but he continued to glower at Sawyer. "You're right, Billy. Besides, the air in here's starting to bother me."

With that, he shook off Casebolt's hand, turned, and stalked out of the ranch house, leaving the tense, angry Texan behind him. Casebolt followed.

Cole hoped his plan worked. If for no other reason, he wanted to see the expression on Kermit Sawyer's ugly face when he came back with the stolen cattle and those rustlers face down over their saddles.

25

Michael thought Deborah had never been more lovely than she was that night, and her singing was beautiful, moving him deeply with its poignancy. The crowd had roared its approval when she finished, and Michael had been one of them, cheering and applauding wildly. As he looked around at the other men, however, he felt a special thrill.

None of them knew it — and how they would envy him if they did! — but before this night was over, he would be holding Deborah Munroe in his arms and kissing her and feeling her soft flesh pressed excitingly to his body. A shudder of desire went through him as those thoughts danced in his head. All he had to do now was wait until the show was over and everyone else had gone home. He hadn't told Deborah what he was planning, but he was sure she would welcome him. She had made it plain that she wanted him. They could go back to the newspaper office, which would be deserted tonight since the latest edition had already been distributed.

The wait for the show to be over was maddening. As he stood on the edge of the crowd and watched Professor Munroe extol the benefits of the world-famous and newly improved Chippewa Tonic, Michael tried not to think about Delia . . . and Gretchen . . . and little Lincoln. He wasn't doing anything to hurt his children, he told himself. He still loved them, loved them dearly. It might not have ever come to this if Delia hadn't been so . . . so cold to him. If she hadn't lost her temper and thrown him out of the house —

Michael's jaw tightened. There was no point in fooling himself. What was going to happen tonight would take place because he *wanted* it to happen. To believe anything else would just be lying to himself.

But that *might* make it easier, he thought.

Finally, the show was over, after an interminable period in which people had lined up to purchase more bottles of the potent elixir. The crowd drifted away, and Michael stood under the trees, cloaked in the thick shadows, as they left. He would give Deborah, the professor, and the other members of the troupe a few minutes to relax, then he would knock on the door of the wagon that Deborah and her uncle shared. He would invite Deborah to go for a walk with him, and then they would go back to the newspaper office and —

Suddenly, he felt cold all over and began to shiver. If he hadn't known better, he would have said that he had caught a chill. However, no illness could strike so suddenly. Although he wanted desperately to push the knowledge out of his head, the reason for this feeling crowded relentlessly into his brain.

It was guilt, pure and simple. He was about to do something he would regret for the rest of his life, and he knew it. He was going to give in to his own selfish lust and ruin forever any chance of lasting happiness with his family.

Because Delia would *know* what had happened. God, even if he never said anything, she would *know.*

Michael leaned against a tree, grimaced, and pounded his fist against the rough bark of the trunk for a long moment. Guilt, love for his family, desire, frustration, anger . . . they all warred violently inside him. Damn, how he envied people who could just *do* things, rather than thinking them to death first!

But he was the way he was, and there was nothing he could do about it. Nothing except give up the foolish idea that had brought him here tonight, go home, and beg Delia's forgiveness. A wave of relief washed through him as he made his decision. He took a deep breath and started to step away from the tree.

That was when he saw the shadowy figures slipping up toward the medicine show wagons.

There were two of them, and something about them made Michael tense in the deep gloom underneath the trees. Their furtive movements were suspicious, to say the least.

Professor Munroe had taken in a great deal of money during the past few days, Michael knew, probably over a thousand dollars, perhaps even more. The two men sneaking up on the wagons could be thieves intending to rob the professor. Michael had seen Marshal Cole Tyler and Billy Casebolt riding out of Wind River earlier in the day, and he didn't know if they were back yet, nor where they had been going. But Jeremiah Newton looked after things in town when the two lawmen were gone, and it would take Michael only a few minutes to run over to the blacksmith shop and fetch Jeremiah. The massive smith had his living quarters in back of the shop.

But to do that, Michael would have to leave the concealment of the shadows, and if the two skulkers saw him, they might abandon their plan and run off to try again some other time. Worse yet, they might even take a shot at him.

Once again, indecision paralyzed Michael. He wished he had a gun. If he had been armed, he could have stepped out from the trees, called out to the men to stop, and covered them while someone else fetched Jeremiah.

He had to do *something* soon. The two men had reached the rear of the professor's wagon. One of them reached up stealthily —

And knocked on the door on the side of the wagon.

Michael heard the faint, surreptitious rapping, and he stood frozen in surprise as the door quickly opened. The gap was there only for an instant, because the two late-night visitors stepped inside the vehicle quickly, but during that instant, lantern light spilled out of the wagon and washed over the faces of the two men climbing inside. Michael recognized both of them.

The formerly crippled old drifter called Otis Stokes — and Dr. Bramwell Carter, noted physician from Philadelphia.

What the devil were *they* doing here?

Michael could understand why Otis Stokes might have come to the professor's wagon. After all, Munroe's tonic had healed the old man's legs. Stokes could have come to express his gratitude once more. But Carter and Munroe were bitter enemies. There was no reason for Carter to be here, and there was certainly no reason for the two men to have been skulking around together like thieves in the night.

Unless, Michael thought suddenly, that was exactly what they were.

He gave a little shake of his head. He didn't want to believe that. But he was a newspaperman, a journalist, and he knew he had to find out the truth. He took a step, then another, moving quickly but silently across the clearing toward the wagons.

When he reached the one where Carter and Stokes had gone, he stepped up onto the narrow platform built underneath the door into the wagon. There were a few cracks around the door, and by leaning his head against one of them, he could make out some of what was being said inside. He heard Professor Munroe saying, "— nobody following you?"

"Don't worry, Nicodemus, I'm sure. Everyone has left, and no one is around outside."

That voice belonged to Dr. Carter, Michael realized. And it certainly sounded friendly, too, not at all as if Munroe was the bane of the physician's existence.

The words faded again as Munroe replied, but then Michael caught, "— cleaned up in this town . . . more than two thousand . . ."

Somebody laughed. "Most of it on account o' me." That was Otis Stokes. "You sure were right, Perfessor. The way them joints o' mine slip in an' out makes it mighty easy to pretend I'm all crippled up!"

"And it's always good for even more when I watch Otis being cured and then look so flabbergasted," Carter added with a chuckle of his own. "Well, Nicodemus, what do you say? Are we about ready to move on?"

"Just about," Munroe replied.

As he eavesdropped, Michael's heart thudded heavily in his chest. He could barely believe what he was hearing. The whole thing had been some sort of swindle. Carter and Stokes were partners with the professor. The Chippewa Tonic was probably completely worthless, no matter how smoothly it went down. They were thieves, the whole lot of them!

Even . . . even *Deborah*? Michael asked himself.

He didn't get the chance to try to figure it out. Suddenly, strong arms went around him from behind and tightened in a vise-like grip. Michael tried to jerk free, and he opened his mouth to let out a howl for help. Before he could make any noise, however, something wet and sickly sweet-smelling was clapped across his face, covering his nose and mouth. He tried to draw a breath, but the stuff made him gag. He writhed and twisted to no avail against the arms holding him. The smell that filled his senses was familiar somehow, and abruptly he realized what it was. *Ether!* Someone was holding a cloth soaked with ether over his face.

That thought did him no good, because it was the last one he had before darkness swept up, washed over him, and carried him away.

The first thing he knew when he regained consciousness was that he was sick, sicker than he had ever been in his life. He had read that ether could do that to a person, and as his head began to clear and sensation returned to him, he knew what he was feeling came from the ether.

Some of it, anyway.

The rest of the sickness inside him came from the knowledge that he was nothing but a damned fool.

Memories of what he had overheard before he was knocked out came flooding back in on him. Of course, Deborah had been a part of the scheme from the first; he knew how close she and her uncle were. All of them, all the members of the medicine show, were crooks, as well as Dr. Carter and Otis Stokes. Michael wondered if Carter was even really a doctor. It was doubtful, he decided; nobody had even thought to check the man's credentials. Everyone had just accepted him for who he claimed to be. He was just another thief with a smattering of medical knowledge, like the professor. Both of them knew just enough to sound like they knew what they were talking about.

Those thoughts flashed through Michael's head in a matter of instants as his eyes flickered open. Bright light struck them like a blow, and he winced. That made his head spin even more, and he let out a groan.

"Our young friend seems to be awake," a voice said. "Keep an eye on him, Chief."

Michael became aware that he was lying on his back, on something soft. A bunk of some sort, he decided. And there was a lantern hanging over the bunk and that was what was blinding him. He blinked rapidly until his eyes began to adjust to the light.

Something blocked it off abruptly, and he focused blearily on the object. It was a face, the face of someone leaning over him. . . .

"Hello, Michael," Deborah said. "I'm glad to see you're awake. Sometimes ether can be dangerous."

Michael moaned again. It was bad enough to have figured out what was really going on here; to have it confirmed so blithely by Deborah was doubly painful.

He tried to move but found that he couldn't. He was tied up, bound hand and foot. Deborah moved a little so that the light struck him in the face again. She put her hand against his cheek. Her fingers were cool and soft.

"Please don't struggle, Michael. You'll only make things worse for yourself."

He licked dry lips and tried to ignore the pain in his head and the roiling ball of nausea in his stomach. "What . . . what are you going to . . . do to me?" he managed to rasp out. His throat hurt from breathing the ether.

A different voice answered him, a voice he recognized as Bramwell Carter's. "We're going to have to kill you, of course."

"No!" Deborah cried. "Uncle Nicodemus —"

"I'm afraid Bramwell is correct, my dear," Munroe said. Michael's vision was still a little fuzzy, but he could see the professor now, along with Carter, Stokes, the Dumonts, and Chief Laughing Fox. All of them were crowded into the wagon. Munroe went on, "Michael knows the truth about us now, and he can't be allowed to spread that information. We're ready to move on from Wind River and begin again somewhere else, and we can't very well do that with a mob on our heels howling for our blood, now can we?"

"I suppose not," Deborah said gloomily. "But I wish there was some other way. . . ."

Michael swallowed and said, "How . . . how did you know —"

"That you were outside eavesdropping on us?" Munroe smiled. "I heard the platform creak and felt the shift in weight when you stepped up on it, so I knew that someone might be sneaking around out there. I sent the chief and Deborah out through the front of the wagon to check on things and deal with the intruder, if there was one. Deborah can be quite light on her feet, as you know, and the chief . . . well, he's an Indian. What more do I need to say?"

Michael closed his eyes. A bitter taste filled his mouth, and it had little or nothing to do with the drug that had knocked him out. He said, "It was all a fake from the start, wasn't it?"

"If you mean the Chippewa Tonic, I suppose it might have some slight medicinal value. It makes people believe they feel better, whether they really do or not."

"Why did you come to Wind River?"

"It was a natural," Munroe said as he leaned over the bunk. "When I read that newspaper story in Cheyenne about the miraculous healing of Deputy Casebolt's ailment, I knew your little community was ripe for us to visit."

"You were never here before, were you?" Michael accused. "That story about finding Medicine Creek years ago and being inspired by it to create your tonic —"

"Was just a story," Munroe finished. "But an effective one, you'll have to admit. Of course, we all knew things would be even better once Bramwell arrived and we went through with our little performance. No one makes a better witness on one's behalf than a converted enemy. And with the aid of Otis, we were able to convert the eminent Dr. Carter."

Michael looked over at the old drifter.

"You weren't ever crippled at all!"

Stokes cackled. "It's all in the joints, kid, all in the joints."

"Otis used to be a member of a traveling carnival before I persuaded him to join us," Munroe said. "He doesn't have to work nearly as hard, and the pay is ever so much better."

Calvin Dumont grunted. "There's been too much talk already. Let's kill him and get it over with."

"You're right, Calvin," Bramwell Carter said. "Deborah, get some more of that ether. That'll be the quietest way to get rid of him."

"No!" Deborah said firmly. "I won't let you kill him."

"My dear," Munroe said, his voice growing impatient, "we've been all through this —"

"You don't have to kill him to stop him from being a threat. Let's take him with us. We were leaving anyway. We can turn him loose when we have a big enough lead so that no one can come after us."

Carter and Dumont both started to shake their heads, but Munroe frowned and said, "I suppose that might work. But you'll be responsible for seeing that he doesn't cause any trouble, Deborah."

She nodded eagerly in agreement. "Of course."

"I don't like it," Carter said. "It's much more certain if we just go ahead and —"

"I said we would do it the way Deborah suggested," Munroe snapped, and there was no doubt he was in charge here, despite his mild appearance. "As long as Michael cooperates, I don't mind giving him a chance for life." Munroe came a step closer to the bed. "What about it, Michael? Do you want to die now — or would you rather live?"

Michael took a deep breath and fought down the sickness again. "I want to live," he said.

"Now you're being smart." Munroe turned to the others. "Let's get ready to pull out, shall we?"

They filed out of the wagon while Deborah held her hand over Michael's mouth, just in case he decided to cry out. She leaned over closer to him and smiled. "I'm almost glad things worked out this way," she said in a whisper. "Now we'll get the chance to have some fun after all."

Michael's eyes widened.

26

Alexandra Fisk patted the smooth wooden stock of the Winchester that was snugged in the saddleboot under her leg and felt better about being out here in the darkness.

Her father would have pitched a fit if he had known where she was. Despite the fact that Austin Fisk was growing more convinced the men from the Diamond S didn't have anything to do with the rustling, he still hated Kermit Sawyer. He wouldn't want either of his daughters anywhere near Sawyer's ranch, especially after dark like this. Of course, Alexandra told herself, she wasn't on the Diamond S. She was just near the entrance to the pass that led through the mountains to Sawyer's spread.

When she got back to the ranch, she would tell her father that she had been out for a ride. He would be angry enough about that, but he knew his eldest daughter's restless nature. Alexandra had never been one to allow herself to be penned up. Besides, it would probably be safe enough. The rustlers had struck only the night before, so they wouldn't push their luck by trying something again so soon. And if they ran true to form, they would raid the Diamond S next, anyway.

But if the thieves *were* out and about tonight, they might use this pass, and if that was the case, Alexandra intended to trail them this time and find out where they went.

She was sitting on horseback in a thick stand of pines, using their shadows to hide herself. The night was alive with noises, as it usually was, but suddenly she heard something out of place. It was the clink of a steel-shod hoof against rock, she decided after a moment, and as she listened intently, it came again several times. Someone was riding not far from here.

Alexandra slipped down from her horse and moved silently on foot to the edge of the trees. She peered through the darkness in the direction of the sounds and after a moment spotted a couple of moving shapes. Riders, she realized with a mingled thrill of anticipation and fear rippling through her. And they were headed in her direction.

The two figures on horseback veered to

the side before they reached the pines, however. They rode toward a towering bluff north of the pass, but they stopped when they had gone a short distance. One of the riders reached over and grasped the reins of the other's horse, jerking the animal to a halt. They were several hundred yards away, but Alexandra's keen eyes could make out that much. She frowned. What was going on?

The two people stayed where they were, evidently deep in conversation. Alexandra took a chance and darted back to where she had left her horse. There were a pair of army field glasses in the saddlebags, a legacy of the Late Unpleasantness in which her father had served as an officer in the Confederate Army. When she had the glasses, she ran back to the edge of the trees, not worrying as much now about being quiet.

There was a bright moon tonight, another reason to suspect that rustlers would not be abroad. Alexandra lifted the field glasses to her eyes and tried to locate the two riders through them. It took her a moment, but suddenly she saw them, her eyes drawn by the moonlight shining on long, fair hair.

Catherine! One of the riders was her sister, Catherine!

And unless Alexandra missed her guess,

the other was her father's foreman, Wilt Paxton. It was difficult to make out many details in the poor light, but she thought she recognized the shape of his high-crowned hat.

Without warning, Paxton reached over and grasped Catherine's arm. Alexandra gasped as she watched through the glasses. Paxton moved the horses closer together, pulled Catherine to him, and kissed her.

Kissed her, for God's sake!

Alexandra didn't know whether to gasp again or laugh out loud. Flighty little Catherine, who had never met a man she couldn't flirt with, seemed to have met her match. Her arms went around Paxton's neck as they kissed. Alexandra felt her own face growing warm.

She had no right to spy on them like this, she told herself. Obviously, they had come out here to get away from the eyes of Austin Fisk. Alexandra knew her father probably wouldn't like it if he was aware that his younger daughter was carrying on so shamelessly with his foreman.

Alexandra lowered the glasses and chuckled. "You should be ashamed of yourself, Alexandra Fisk," she told herself aloud. "How would you like it if you were —"

She stopped that sentence before she

could complete it, but the thought was there in her head. How would she like it, she had started to ask herself, if she had been kissing Frenchy LeDoux and Catherine had been spying on her?

Well, *that* would never happen. Not in a million years. Alexandra shook her head and started to turn away, intending to go back to her horse.

The sound of more hoofbeats, ringing abruptly through the night air, stopped her.

She turned back and lifted the field glasses again. When she found Catherine and Paxton through the lenses, she saw that both of them were looking toward the big bluff to the west. Alexandra swung the glasses in that direction, and this time she did gasp as she spotted the large group of riders galloping toward her sister and Paxton.

The raiders were back! Alexandra had no idea where they had come from, but she knew they hadn't used the pass. She was close enough to the opening in the mountains that she would have heard them sooner if they had. But how they had gotten here didn't really matter. What was important was that they were sweeping right at Catherine and Paxton.

Alexandra jerked the glasses back to the two of them. Why didn't they run? she asked herself. They had a head start on the rustlers; they might be able to outdistance them. But they were just sitting on their horses, watching the night riders coming closer. Paxton was probably afraid that if they turned and ran, the rustlers would open fire.

As Alexandra watched in horror, she saw the raiders close in around Catherine and Paxton. Moonlight winked on drawn guns. It was too late to save them now. There was so much confusion that Alexandra couldn't tell exactly what was going on. The gang of rustlers surrounded her sister and Paxton so that she couldn't even see them anymore. After a few moments, they broke into a gallop again, heading across the valley.

At least there hadn't been any shooting, Alexandra thought as she lowered the glasses shakily. Catherine and Paxton might have been taken prisoner, but at least they were still alive. The rustlers probably planned to use them as hostages, just in case any pursuit caught up to them.

Alexandra turned and ran back to her horse, shoving the glasses in the saddlebags and swinging up hurriedly into the saddle. She didn't worry about trying to be quiet. She jammed the heels of her boots into the animal's flanks and shouted encouragement to it as the horse lunged into a gallop that carried them out of the trees. Alexandra didn't try to follow the rustlers and their prisoners. Instead she pointed her mount toward the ranch house.

The only real chance Catherine and Paxton had was if Alexandra could alert her father and the rest of the men in time. She leaned forward over the neck of her horse, knowing all too well that she might be in a race for her sister's life.

By the time Alexandra reached the ranch house, she heard the distant popping of gunfire to the north. Her heart fell. That was where most of her father's herd was being kept, and it was obvious the rustlers had struck again, crossing everyone up by raiding Latch Hook two nights in a row. As Alexandra's horse pounded up and slid to a halt in front of the house, Austin Fisk was already running onto the porch, a rifle in his hands. Some of the punchers were tumbling out of the bunkhouse, shouting questions.

"It's Alexandra, Pa!" she called to her father. "The rustlers are back! They've got Catherine and Wilt Paxton!"

Fisk stared at her in shock. "What? What are you saying, Alex?"

"I saw them," she said breathlessly without bothering to dismount. She clung to the saddlehorn to steady herself. "Catherine was with Wilt Paxton . . . they were kissing — and then those rustlers rode up and captured them!"

"Damn it, you're not making any sense, girl!" Fisk bit out. "Catherine and Paxton . . . ?"

"I suppose they're in love," Alexandra said impatiently. "That doesn't matter. What's important is that those rustlers have them!"

Fisk jerked his head in a curt nod. "You're right, of course." He turned to the Latch Hook riders who had gathered around the porch. "Saddle up, men! We've got to get to the herd and stop them!"

The punchers ran for the corral to get their horses. Fisk turned back to Alexandra and went on, "You saw the rustlers, you say?"

"That's right."

"Did they come through the pass from the Diamond S?"

Alexandra shook her head. "I don't know where they came from, but they didn't use the pass. I'm sure of that."

Fisk took a deep breath. "I seem to have misjudged those damned Texans. We may need help, Alexandra. I want you to ride over there and alert Sawyer to what's going on. Can you do that?"

She nodded without any hesitation. "Of course I can. You're going after the rustlers?"

"With every man I've got," Fisk said fervently. "How many of them were there?"

"More than I saw last night. Twenty, I'd say, maybe a few more."

"We're liable to need help, then. I hate to send you out like this at night —"

Alexandra wheeled her horse. "Just go after them, Pa. You've got to save Catherine!"

Without waiting for any more talk, she heeled her horse into a run again, this time heading for the pass that would take her to the Diamond S.

Cole sat with his back against a tree trunk while not far away, Ulysses cropped contentedly on Kermit Sawyer's grass. Casebolt was sitting beside another tree, his hat tilted down over his face. Soft snores came from him.

Frenchy LeDoux and Lon Rogers both hunkered on their heels nearby. All four men waited in the shadows of the trees on this hillside. Not far off was the spot where Cole had lost the tracks of the stolen cattle. If the rustlers came back tonight, Cole figured they would use this route.

"Hope you don't mind us waitin' out here with you, Marshal," Frenchy said softly. "It's Mr. Sawyer's orders, you know."

"I know," Cole said. "That boss of yours doesn't trust us. I reckon he knows Billy and I aren't mixed up with those rustlers, but he just doesn't like anybody else poking around on his land."

"That's about the size of it," Frenchy said with a nod. "You think those thievin' sons o' bitches will be back tonight?"

"Could be," Cole said with a shrug. He sat up suddenly as a faint noise came to his ears. "Listen! You hear that?"

Casebolt snorted and lifted his head. The other three men stood up and moved to the edge of the trees, listening intently.

"Hoofbeats," Lon said after a moment. "And moving fast, too."

"Somebody's in a hurry," Frenchy agreed. "Sounds like it's gettin' louder."

Casebolt joined them. "Who's that ridin' hell for leather in the middle of the night?"

Cole shook his head. "Don't know, but I reckon we ought to find out." He started toward Ulysses.

The others followed suit, catching the reins of their horses and mounting. Frenchy said, "Sounds to me like it might be comin' from that pass over to Latch Hook."

"Can we get there in time to head off whoever it is?" Cole asked.

"We can damn sure try," the *segundo* said. He put his heels to his horse.

The four men galloped down off the hill and turned to the south, following the line of mountains toward the pass. By the time they reached it a few minutes later, the lone rider they had heard had already emerged and was racing across the valley toward the headquarters of the Diamond S. Cole spotted the horsebacker in the moonlight and pointed. "There!"

The urgency with which the man rode told them there was some sort of trouble afoot. Cole and his companions galloped after the rider, whose horse seemed to be tiring. Within minutes, they had closed the gap, and Cole shouted, "Hold on there! This is Marshal Tyler from Wind River!"

The rider reined in, and as Cole, Casebolt, Frenchy, and Lon trotted up, they all saw that she was a woman, not a man. Long, dark hair framed the pale face she turned toward them.

"Marshal Tyler!" she exclaimed. "I'm Alexandra Fisk, from Latch Hook."

Frenchy had already recognized her, and he couldn't stop himself from saying, "Alexandra! What are you doin' here?"

"The rustlers," she said, having trouble catching her breath. "They . . . they came back to Latch Hook. Took my sister Catherine and our foreman Wilt Paxton prisoner. They're hitting our herd again."

"Damn!" Cole burst out. The wideloopers had fooled everybody, had done the one thing it had seemed least likely they would do. And now Catherine Fisk and Wilt Paxton might pay with their lives for Cole's mistake in judgment.

"My father sent me over here to ask Mr. Sawyer for help," Alexandra went on. "He and our cowboys were going after the rustlers."

Cole thought rapidly. "LeDoux, you and Rogers take Miss Fisk on to Sawyer's house. Tell your boss what happened and see if he'll send some men over to Latch Hook. Billy and I will head there right now."

"Nope," Frenchy said. "Lon can take Alexandra to see Mr. Sawyer. I'm goin' with you and the deputy."

There wasn't time to argue. Cole nodded curtly and heeled Ulysses into a run, pointing the sorrel toward the pass. Casebolt and Frenchy followed.

Alexandra would have gone with them if Lon hadn't reached out and caught the reins of her horse. "I want to go with them!" she protested. "You can take the message to Sawyer, cowboy!"

"No, ma'am," Lon told her. "That horse of yours is just about played out. There's no way you can keep up with Frenchy and those two lawmen." He paused, then added, "But you can get a fresh horse from our corrals, I reckon."

Impatiently, Alexandra jerked the reins out of his hands and turned her mount toward the headquarters of the Diamond S. "Come on, then," she said.

She wished she could have gone with Frenchy, but she knew the young cowhand they had left with her was right. Her horse couldn't go much farther. She just hoped Frenchy, Marshal Tyler, and Deputy Casebolt got to Latch Hook in time to help.

And she prayed that Catherine and Paxton were still alive, that death hadn't already struck in the night. . . .

27

Michael was as miserable as he had ever been in his life. The sickness in his belly had subsided and the pain in his head was only a dull ache now, but he still felt like a fool. And that was the worst feeling of all.

He had lain there on the bunk inside the wagon and listened to the others making preparations to leave Wind River. Deborah had left him for a while, after using a strip of cloth to gag him so that he couldn't call for help, but now she was back. She leaned over the bunk and untied the gag. "I'm sorry I had to do that, Michael," she told him. "But I couldn't take any chances. It was hard enough to convince the others we ought to keep you alive. Bramwell and Calvin still want to kill you, you know."

He swallowed and nodded. "They probably will, once we get away from town," he said. "They're just playing along now to keep you from causing trouble."

She shook her head. "Uncle Nicodemus won't let them hurt you. He agreed with me that we should let you live."

Michael didn't believe that for a minute. Professor Munroe was just placating her, too. He was convinced that his hours were numbered. Before the sun came up the next morning, he would be dead.

And he would never see Delia or Gretchen or Lincoln again, would never again hold his son or hear his daughter's laugh or feel the touch of his wife's hand. . . .

He had to swallow hard once more to keep a sob from welling up his throat. He concentrated on his anger instead of what he was about to lose and said to Deborah, "It was all an act, wasn't it? You never really cared for me."

"How can you say that?" she protested as she sat down beside him on the edge of the bunk. "Of course I liked you, Michael. You're so sweet and handsome. But I have to admit it came in handy to have you helping us, even when you didn't know you were doing it. You even spotted Otis and pointed him out to Uncle Nicodemus, so he didn't have to do it himself. That looked even more convincing."

He turned his head away, unable to look at her anymore.

Deborah put her hand on his chin and turned his face back toward her. She leaned over and kissed him, pressing her mouth hard against his, letting her breasts prod his side. Her hand moved down over his belly to his groin. She took her lips away from his and whispered, "As soon as we've gotten started, I'll untie your legs so that we can have some fun."

Michael suppressed a groan of despair. A hundred times in the past few days — no, a thousand! — he had dreamed of Deborah caressing him like this, saying soft words of love and passion. Now her touch shriveled him and made him want to flinch away from her, and her voice was like the hiss of a demon.

How could he have been so stupid?

But maybe, he suddenly thought, just maybe he didn't have to die after all. There might be the slightest chance he could get out of this. . . .

A moment later, Munroe poked his head in the side door of the wagon and told Deborah, "We're ready to roll. You stay in here with our young friend."

"That's exactly what I intended," she said with a smile.

Munroe closed the door, and a few seconds later, Michael felt the wagon shift a little as the professor climbed onto the seat. He was joined there by someone else, Michael could tell, probably Chief Laughing Fox. That would leave the Dumonts to handle the other wagon. Carter had probably slipped back to the hotel, and Stokes would go back to wherever he had been staying, since it wouldn't do for anyone to see them leaving with the medicine show. Doubtless they would rendezvous somewhere outside of town.

As the wagon lurched into motion, Michael took a deep breath and said, "Deborah?"

She came to the bunk and sat down beside him again. "Yes, Michael?"

"Thank you for . . . for everything you've done for me," he forced himself to say. "I realize I owe my life to you."

She leaned over him, smiling. "You're welcome. And if you want to repay me, well, I can think of a way."

He pasted a smile of his own onto his face and said, "Anytime you're ready."

She leaned over and kissed him again, probing at his lips with the wet tip of her tongue until he opened them. Despite everything, he felt himself becoming excited. That was all right, he thought. It would just make the act more convincing. Deborah had

342

pulled the wool over his eyes; now it was his turn to fool her.

Her breath was coming faster and harder as she pulled away from him and reached down to his bound ankles. Several deft tugs loosened the ropes, and she pulled them away from his feet. "There, now you can move around a little," she said. She stood up and reached for the buttons of her dress.

"I wish I could put my arms around you," Michael said, hoping he wasn't overplaying his hand.

"I'm sorry, Michael," she said, sounding as if she meant it, "but you know I can't let you loose. Not yet. Maybe when we're out of town. . . ."

He would just have to make do, he thought. Deborah had her dress unbuttoned, and she slipped it off her shoulders and pushed it down around her hips. She wore a chemise under the dress, and Michael had to admit she was beautiful as she came toward him, hips swaying.

He twisted on the bunk, rolling onto his side as if he was eager for her, and she smiled seductively. She leaned toward him once more, her tongue coming out to lick over her lips.

Michael pulled his knees up, straightened his legs suddenly, and kicked her in the stomach as hard as he could.

Deborah didn't even have time to cry out. She flew backward across the wagon and slammed into the wall. She crumpled to the floor, curling up around herself, gagging and gasping for breath. Michael rolled off the bunk and landed on his knees. Pain shot through them, but he ignored it. He got a foot under him, then surged to his feet.

The inside of the wagon was fitted up as living quarters for the professor and Deborah, including a wardrobe and a dressing table. Michael spotted a pair of scissors lying on the table and lunged backward toward them, fumbling for them behind his back with his fingers. He felt the wagon coming to a halt and heard Professor Munroe call, "Deborah! Deborah, are you all right back there?"

Munroe must have heard the thump when Deborah hit the wall, Michael knew. His fingers closed around the scissors, and he brought them up and began using them to saw awkwardly at the cords around his wrists.

The smaller door that led to the seat of the wagon flew open, and Michael saw the face of Chief Laughing Fox peering in at him. For once, the Chippewa's features weren't devoid of any expression. Laughing

Fox glared angrily at him, and Michael saw a glint of lantern light on steel as the chief's arm raised.

Michael threw himself to the side as a tomahawk flashed through the air at him. As he fell, he felt the scissors slicing into his arm. Luck was with him, though, and the ropes around his wrists parted at the same instant. He jerked his arms around in front of him, wincing at the pain that shot through stiff muscles, then rolled desperately out of the way of a second tomahawk that hit the floorboards of the wagon and stuck there. Michael came up on his hands and knees and lunged toward the door where the chief crouched.

Terror gave him enough speed to beat the Chippewa's third throw. Michael crashed into Laughing Fox's midsection in a diving tackle, and both of them went sprawling on the wagon seat next to Professor Munroe. The professor cursed angrily as Michael slammed a couple of punches into the Indian's belly. He fumbled a small pistol from under his coat and slashed at Michael's head with the barrel.

Out of the corner of his eye, Michael saw the blow coming and jerked out of the way. Munroe cried out in frustration as the pistol missed Michael and caught Laughing Fox in the nose. The Chippewa sank back, stunned by the impact, blood gushing from his nose.

Michael drove his left elbow back into Munroe's side, then twisted and sledged a fist into the professor's face. Michael had never been much of a brawler, but he was fighting for his life now and that gave him unexpected strength and speed.

Munroe sagged against the body of the wagon. Michael got his hands on the pistol and twisted it out of the professor's hands. A grunt warned him that Laughing Fox was back in the fight. Michael turned on the crowded seat to see the Indian looming over him, face bloody, another tomahawk poised to fall in a blow that would cleave Michael's skull.

Without thinking about it, Michael thumbed back the hammer of the pistol and pulled the trigger. The gun cracked spitefully, and Laughing Fox staggered back, the tomahawk slipping from his fingers. He fell, landing on the backs of the horses hitched to the wagon.

That was more than enough to startle the already spooked animals into flight. They bolted, pulling the wagon behind them.

The sudden start threw Michael back against the seat. He felt a heavy bump and knew with a sickening certainty that it had been the wheels of the wagon passing over the body of Chief Laughing Fox. Michael grabbed the edge of the seat and hung on tightly. He wondered what had happened to the reins.

Fingers grabbed his throat, and Munroe cursed luridly as he tried to choke the life out of Michael. Michael's eyes widened. Munroe had caught him without any air in his lungs, and in a matter of seconds the world was swimming crazily around Michael. He brought the gun up and struck out with it, aiming by instinct. It thudded against the side of Munroe's head and the professor fell back again, this time out cold.

Michael pushed himself upright on the swaying seat. He didn't know what had happened to the other wagon or to Calvin and Letitia Dumont, and at the moment, he didn't care. He spotted the reins of the team lying on the floor of the driver's box and dropped the gun to lunge for them, grabbing them just as they were about to slip off.

The horses were running wild, and as Michael glanced around he saw that they were on Grenville Avenue, heading east instead of west, the direction the professor had no doubt intended to go when leaving Wind

River. The crazed horses didn't care about that, though. They just wanted to run.

Michael hauled back on the reins as hard as he could and shouted for them to stop, but the horses ignored him. His gaze fell on the brake lever, sticking up to the left of the seat, and he let go of the reins to reach across Munroe's body and grab the lever. He threw all of his weight against it as he pulled it back.

He realized at the last instant that probably wasn't a very smart thing to do.

The wheels locked and skidded on the hard-packed dirt of the street, and the wagon listed suddenly to the right, the rear end beginning to swing around. Michael let out a startled yell as the wheels on the left side of the vehicle lifted from the ground. He pushed himself up and off the seat as the wagon went over.

Something slammed into him as he tumbled through the air, and then an instant later he hit the ground with bone-jarring and tooth-rattling force. He rolled over and over as the rending, grinding sound of the wagon crashing filled his ears. A horse gave a shrill whinny of pain. Michael heard yelling and then shooting.

He came to a stop lying on his stomach, his mouth and nose and eyes filled with dust and grit. He coughed and shook his head, then pawed at his eyes in an attempt to clear his vision. Several yards away, what was left of the wagon was lying on its side. Kindling-like debris was scattered around it. One of the horses was down, but the others seemed to be all right as they stood in their traces, trembling with fear.

"Michael!" a familiar, bull-like voice bellowed. "Is that you? Are you all right, brother?"

Michael pushed himself onto his hands and knees and looked over to see Jeremiah Newton striding quickly toward him. Tucked under Jeremiah's arm, struggling fiercely but futilely against his grip, was Letitia Dumont. Michael glanced past the blacksmith and saw the second wagon, which had been brought to a stop nearby. A huge shape lying next to it could only be Calvin Dumont.

Michael got to his feet as Jeremiah reached him. All his limbs seemed to work, so he said, "I'm all right, Jeremiah. What happened?"

"Seems like I ought to be the one asking that," the blacksmith rumbled. "I heard a shot, and when I looked out I saw these wagons careening past my shop. I thought I saw you on the first one, but I told myself

I'd lost my mind. But then you came flying off of there and the wagon turned over, and then that big fellow chasing you in the other wagon —" He jerked a thumb at Calvin Dumont. "— stopped it and started shooting at you. He didn't pay any attention when I told him to stop, so I had to hit him, even though it pained me to do so."

Michael would have liked to have seen that. Any hand-to-hand battle between Jeremiah and Dumont would have been worth watching.

Letitia was still punching and cursing, and Jeremiah went on, "Please settle down, sister, and don't talk like that. It's an affront to the Lord."

"I'll affront you, you big, damned ape!" Letitia howled. "Let me go! What have you done to Calvin?"

More citizens were running up, drawn by the commotion, and Michael knew he was going to have to explain what had happened. First, though, he had to find out if Deborah and the professor were all right.

Munroe was lying in the street, in what appeared to be a puddle of Chippewa Tonic that was leaking from the wrecked wagon. Every bottle of the elixir in the vehicle must have shattered when it overturned, Michael thought. Munroe didn't appear to be injured too badly; he was moving around and moaning as he regained consciousness.

"Keep an eye on him," Michael said to Jeremiah, then trotted over to the wagon itself. The side with the door in it was facing upward. Michael clambered onto the wreckage, grasped the latch of the door, and wrenched it open. One of the curtains from the window was on fire, set ablaze by the overturned lantern. The light from the fire showed him Deborah, lying unconscious amidst a welter of broken glass and a pool of spilled tonic. A stink that reminded Michael somehow of a saloon assaulted his nostrils.

Michael let himself down through the door and dropped lightly beside Deborah. He bent and got his arms around her, lifting her clear of the pool of tonic and keeping her away from the burning curtain.

"I say, do you need a hand, Michael?"

He looked up to see Dr. Judson Kent looking down through the open door. "Help me get her out of here, Doctor," Michael said.

With Kent pulling and Michael pushing, they hoisted Deborah's dead weight out through the door, and Michael scrambled after her. He knew she was still alive, because he had already felt her pulse beat-

351

ing strongly as he lifted her. Kent took her shoulders and Michael took her feet as they carried her away from the wrecked wagon toward the boardwalk.

Just in time, too, because the next moment, a huge ball of flame erupted inside the overturned vehicle, completely engulfing it. The heat staggered Michael. He heard a scream and looked around to see that the flames had shot out of the wreckage, following the trail of leaking tonic, and Professor Munroe was ablaze, too, although it seemed that only his tonic-soaked coat was burning at the moment. Several of the townsmen grabbed him, threw him down, and rolled him in the dirt of the street to smother the flames. When the fire was out, Munroe lay huddled on the ground, sobbing.

"Good Lord preserve us," Jeremiah said fervently as he looked at the blazing wagon. "What were they carrying in there? Hellfire and brimstone?"

"Just about," Dr. Kent said crisply. "I did some analyzing of my own on that so-called tonic. It's more than half alcohol, you know." The doctor looked at Michael. "You seem to know what's going on here. Why don't you tell the rest of us?"

Michael glanced past him at the body of Deborah Munroe, who was lying on the

352

boardwalk where he and Kent had put her. She was starting to move around now.

"I'll tell you," Michael said hollowly. "I'll explain everything."

28

Cole reined in and motioned for Casebolt to do likewise. Beside them, Frenchy LeDoux brought his horse to a stop as well. Once all three men had halted, the sound of hoofbeats came clearly to their ears.

And those hoofbeats were drawing closer by the second.

"Better get your rifles ready," Cole warned the other two men. "We don't know who this is coming toward us."

They were on Latch Hook range now, having ridden through the pass between the two ranches. They hadn't heard any shooting, but that didn't mean anything. The rustlers could have struck already and been on their way out of the valley.

As soon as they were through the pass, Cole had led his companions toward the big bluff to the north without explaining why. He was certain there was some sort of passage there that was not easy to find without some searching. That was how the rustlers had gotten the stolen cattle out of the valley, by following the strip of rocky ground to the bluff and then hazing the animals through a hidden cleft or a tunnel or some such. Had to be the answer, Cole thought.

He just hoped they weren't too late already.

From the sound of the approaching hoofbeats, he was afraid they were. There were no cattle noises to go with the horse sound, no lowing, no clashing of horns. Just riders. That would mean the wideloopers had already made their escape through here or had gone some other way entirely.

He spotted figures moving in the darkness and lifted his Winchester, pointing the muzzle toward the sky. He fired three times, as fast as he could work the rifle's lever. The oncoming riders swung directly toward Cole, Casebolt, and Frenchy.

"Fisk!" Cole shouted, knowing he was asking for trouble if he had guessed wrong and these were really the raiders galloping toward them. "Fisk, is that you?"

A shout came back. "Who's that?" Cole recognized the voice as Austin Fisk's.

"Marshal Tyler from Wind River!" he called. "Hold your fire!" He urged Ulysses forward, riding out to meet the other men.

A few moments later, the two groups, small and large, came together. Fisk was accompanied by about a dozen men, probably all of his crew except for the cook and the wrangler, who would have been left back at Latch Hook headquarters. As Fisk reined in and faced Cole, he asked, "What are you doing out here, Marshal? And who's that with you?"

"Heard that rustlers hit your spread again," Cole replied. "This is Deputy Casebolt and Frenchy LeDoux, from the Diamond S."

"I know LeDoux," Fisk said. His voice was anxious as he went on, "Did my daughter Alexandra find you?"

"We ran into her on the other side of the pass," Cole said. "I sent her on to Sawyer's place for more help while Billy and Frenchy and I came right on. What happened?"

"They have my daughter and my foreman," Fisk answered bitterly. "And damned near all that was left of my herd. They killed two more of my nighthawks and came in this direction. You didn't see them?"

Cole shook his head. "They must've beaten us to the back door they're using to get out of here."

"Back door?" Fisk repeated. "What the

devil are you talking about, Marshal?"

Cole swung Ulysses toward the bluff. "Come on. I'll show you."

He hoped his hunch was right. Otherwise, he was going to look mighty foolish, and more importantly, the outlaws who had captured Catherine Fisk and Wilt Paxton would have an even larger lead on the pursuit.

Cole's theory was correct, however, as they discovered a quarter of an hour later when they reached the bluff. Cole had a couple of men make some torches and light them, and a few minutes of searching revealed the narrow, slanting passage through what appeared, even from as short a distance as fifty yards, to be solid rock.

"I didn't know that was there," Fisk said in amazement as he stared at the narrow canyon that was concealed by a jutting shoulder of the bluff.

"I reckon not many people did," Cole told him. "But those rustlers did, and they put it to good use — after starting the stolen stock toward the pass leading to the Diamond S, just so you'd be more likely to blame Sawyer for your troubles."

"And I fell right into their trap," Fisk said. "I was an idiot, a complete fool." His voice was filled with self-loathing.

Casebolt leaned over and spat. "Don't much reckon feelin' sorry for yourself's goin' to do much good right now," he said to Fisk. "What we'd better do is get after them sorry skunks."

Cole was about to nod in agreement when he heard more horses moving somewhere in the night. The sounds didn't come from inside the hidden passage, however, but from down the valley toward the pass.

"Let's hold up a spell," he said, raising a hand to forestall Fisk's protest at any further delay. "Sounds to me like we're about to get some reinforcements."

Sure enough, a sizable force of men led by Kermit Sawyer swept up a few minutes later. Cole rode out to meet them. "It's Cole Tyler, Sawyer!" he called. "Tell your men not to get itchy trigger fingers! The rustlers are gone."

Sawyer reined in, his black hat and clothes making him almost invisible in the darkness. He said, "What's goin' on here, Tyler? Has the whole damn country gone crazy?"

"No, we just got outsmarted by those owlhoots. They hit Latch Hook again tonight."

One of the riders among the newcomers pushed forward. "I told Mr. Sawyer and his men all about it," Alexandra Fisk said.

"Alexandra!" her father exclaimed. "What

358

are you doing here? I want you to go on back to the ranch house right now."

"I won't do it," she said stubbornly. "Catherine's my sister, and I'm going to help find her."

Frenchy edged his horse forward. "You can't do that," he said sharply.

"Oh? And why not, Mr. LeDoux?" Alexandra's voice was cool.

"Because it's dangerous, that's why! You might get hurt."

"And why should you care about my safety?"

Fisk growled, "I don't think I want to hear the answer to that, LeDoux. Bad enough I had to ask a bunch of Texans for help."

"You want your daughter back, don't you?" Sawyer snapped.

"Of course I do!"

"And them rustlers dealt with?"

"Naturally," Fisk said. "I want to see justice done."

"Then you came to the right folks." Sawyer hipped around in his saddle and called to the punchers he had brought with him, "Come on, boys. We got some rustlers to chase down!"

The Diamond S hands whooped in anticipation.

Cole took a deep breath. Tracking down

the rustlers was going to be difficult enough without having to deal with budding romances and hard feelings between the two ranch crews. But that was the hand he'd been dealt, and he had no choice but to play it out.

"Let's get one thing straight here," he said to Sawyer and Fisk. "I'm in charge of this posse."

"The hell you say!" Sawyer exclaimed, and Fisk added, "That's my daughter — and my cows — those bastards have stolen!"

"That's right, but we've got to have some sort of command or we're never going to catch up to them. I figure since Deputy Casebolt and I are the only duly authorized lawmen in the bunch — and since both of you dislike me about the same — that I ought to be the one giving the orders. If you don't like it —" Cole started Ulysses into the dark, forbidding passage through the bluff. "— you can go on home. I'm done talking."

Casebolt fell in behind him, and as the two lawmen disappeared into the cleft, Sawyer and Fisk looked at each other in the moonlight. After a couple of seconds, Sawyer muttered, "Oh, hell. Come on, Fisk."

"All right," the Kentuckian said. "Alexandra . . ."

"Don't waste your breath, Pa," she told him. "I'm coming along."

"Well, for God's sake, be careful. I don't want to lose both of my daughters."

Cole overheard that and thought that with any luck, Fisk wouldn't have to lose either of his daughters.

But it was going to take luck, all right. A lot of it.

Dawn came late to the little valley hidden in the mountains, shadowed as it was by towering peaks all around. The posse reached it about the same time as the first slanting rays of light from the sun edging over the mountains to the east. Cole reined in, knowing they had found the rustlers' hideout.

Unfortunately, it appeared that the place was deserted.

It had taken them several hours to work their way through the twisting passage that led from the bluff. Cole would have thought that during that time they would have caught up to the men driving the stolen cattle, but obviously the rustlers had enough experience at escaping through this cleft that they were able to push the rustled stock pretty fast. At one point the posse had come

361

across another narrow canyon joining the one they were in from the west, and although some of the men had wanted to explore it, Cole had decided against that idea.

"This is likely the way they brought the stolen stock from the Diamond S. If we follow this canyon, we'll just come out somewhere over there in Sawyer's valley."

"You can't know that," Fisk had protested.

Cole had pointed north. "That's the way they went," he said. "I'd stake my life on it."

"It's my daughter's life you're risking, not yours," Fisk had reminded him grimly.

Cole's decision had prevailed, however, and the posse had moved on, finally emerging from the canyon onto a winding trail that eventually brought them here to this isolated valley. In the dawn light, Cole saw a couple of crudely constructed cabins and some large pole corrals, all of which were now empty.

"They've been holding the stock here," he said. "But now they've cleared out. I guess they decided they had gotten away with all they were going to get."

"We can trail them," Fisk said. "We have to."

Cole nodded. "That's exactly what we're

going to do. But I reckon I already know where they're going. They'll probably swing east once they're out of the mountains, then cut back down to Cheyenne to get rid of the herd. If they keep going north, there's nothing in that direction until you get to those gold camps in Montana Territory, and there's a lot of rugged ground in between."

"They could get a mighty nice price for them cows in those gold camps," Casebolt pointed out. "Them miners are hungry for beef, from what I hear."

"Yes, but they can get almost as much by taking the herd to Cheyenne, and the drive would be a lot faster and easier." Cole shrugged. "That many cattle leave a trail that's easy to follow. We'll be dogging them whether they go north or south."

There was a spring-fed pool in the center of the little valley. The posse stopped there for half an hour to water their horses and let the animals rest. That gave the men a chance for a cold breakfast, too. The cook from Fisk's ranch had sent a bag of biscuits with the Latch Hook riders, and the Diamond S men had brought along some jerky. When the food was combined, there was enough for everybody.

Cole knew that Ulysses had plenty of strength left, so after only a few minutes of rest, he swung up onto the sorrel again and scouted around the valley, looking for the route the rustlers had taken. He found the trail of the stolen herd leading over a saddle of ground between two large hills. Judging from the tracks and the freshness of the droppings he found, the rustlers were only about an hour ahead of them. The posse could make up that ground by the middle of the day.

For the first time since this whole business had begun, Cole felt confident that it was about over — and none too soon, he added to himself.

Frenchy LeDoux took off his hat and sleeved sweat from his forehead. The warmth of this spring day was growing rapidly as the sun climbed into the sky. Frenchy stole a glance at Alexandra Fisk, who was riding near him. Alexandra managed somehow to look cool, even though she was pushing herself as hard as any of them and had to be quite worried about her sister.

Several hours had passed since the posse had left the valley where the rustlers had hidden the stolen stock. They were out of the mountains now and heading east over the prairie, just as Cole Tyler had predicted. The marshal was a pretty canny gent,

Frenchy thought, and he wasn't sure why Cole and Kermit Sawyer got along so badly. Frenchy saw a lot of qualities to admire in both men. Maybe they were just too much alike to get along, although neither of them would have ever admitted to a thing like that.

Cole held up a hand to bring the posse to a halt. He swung down from his horse and hunkered next to a fresh pile of droppings left behind by one of the stolen cattle. Cole looked up and said, "They're less than half an hour in front of us now. We ought to catch up to them about noon. They're really pushing those animals."

"They keep this up, they're liable to run all the meat off 'em," Sawyer complained. "It'll take a while to fatten 'em back up, once they're back where they're supposed to be."

"If that's all you have to worry about, count yourself lucky," Fisk snapped. "Those men have my daughter and my foreman, remember?"

"I remember," Sawyer said heavily. "That's the only reason I'm puttin' up with you, Fisk."

Cole stood up and moved between the two men. "That's enough," he said. "We'll take five minutes, then we're riding again."

Frenchy dismounted and led his horse over to where Alexandra was getting down from her horse. "Anything I can do for you, Miss Alexandra?" he asked.

She regarded him with an unreadable stare. "You're already going along to help rescue my sister, Mr. LeDoux. I couldn't ask anything more of you."

He hesitated, then said, "Well, there's something I could ask of you, ma'am. Could you maybe call me Frenchy?"

"I suppose I could." He thought he saw a smile tugging at her lips. "But what's your real name?"

The question took him by surprise. "I, uh, I don't generally go around tellin' people my real handle, Miss Alexandra."

"Why not? You're not ashamed of it, are you?"

"Well, it ain't something I brag on, if you get my drift. Reckon it might've been all right had I stayed in Louisiana where there's plenty of other Cajuns, but when I drifted over to Texas I thought it might be better if folks called me something else."

"I won't tell anyone," Alexandra said.

She was obviously glad to have something to take her mind off the danger her sister was in, even for a few minutes, so Frenchy knew he couldn't deny her that. He glanced around to make sure no one was within easy earshot, then said quietly, "When I was born, my folks called me François."

Alexandra smiled. "François LeDoux. I like it."

"Glad you do, ma'am, because I sure don't. I been Frenchy for a long time, and I reckon I'll stick with that."

"Of course. I'll respect your wishes . . . Frenchy."

He liked the name even more when she said it, although to be fair, François didn't sound so bad when it was coming from her lips, either. He decided he didn't much care what she called him, just so long as she was talking to him.

Austin Fisk strode over to them, glaring at Frenchy. "How are you holding up, Alexandra?" he asked his daughter.

"I'm fine, Pa," she said. "Don't worry about me."

Fisk glanced at Frenchy again. "How can I not worry about you?"

She flushed and said, "I can take care of myself."

"Yes," Fisk said dryly. "I'm sure you can."

Frenchy nodded to Alexandra and tugged on the brim of his hat. "Excuse me, ma'am," he said. He turned and led his horse away, unable to make out the low-voiced conversation going on behind him but willing to bet that it had something to do with him. Fisk was bound to be unhappy about the attention Alexandra was receiving from the Diamond S *segundo.*

Well, Fisk might have to just get used to it, Frenchy told himself, because when they all got back, he intended to court Alexandra, no matter what her father — or Kermit Sawyer — thought of the matter.

The posse was on its way again in a matter of minutes, and another hour rolled past as they followed the rustlers. The sun was wheeling ever higher in the sky. It was almost midday when Cole spotted a haze of dust in the air up ahead and pointed it out to the others.

"That's them!" Fisk exclaimed, clenching a fist. "It's got to be!" He kicked his horse into a run and shouted over his shoulder, "Come on!"

"Wait a minute, you fool!" Cole shouted, but Fisk ignored him. The Latch Hook riders followed their boss without hesitation. Cole watched them disgustedly for a moment, then muttered, "What the hell," and waved the others on. They all charged after Fisk and his punchers.

The showdown was finally at hand.

29

The posse caught up to the rustlers in a broad, grassy meadow between a couple of shallow, winding creeks. If they could see the rustlers, then the rustlers could see them, Cole reasoned, so he wasn't surprised when six or eight men peeled off from the group pushing the stolen cattle and dropped back to fight a rear-guard action. Guns began to crash, and a haze of powder smoke was quickly added to the dust in the air.

The long, ground-eating strides of the sorrel carried Cole to the front of the posse, along with Fisk, Sawyer, Frenchy LeDoux, Lon Rogers, and several of the Latch Hook punchers. The hurricane deck of a running horse was just about the worst possible platform from which to shoot, but Cole unshipped his Winchester anyway and guided Ulysses with his knees as he levered the rifle and brought it to his shoulder. The Winchester bucked against his shoulder as it began to boom.

Ulysses ran smoothly enough so that Cole was able to aim better than most. He wasn't surprised when one of the rustlers flew out of the saddle and landed in the limp sprawl that signified death. Everyone was firing now, and so much lead was in the air that some of it had to find its target. Another rustler fell, along with one of the Latch Hook men.

Cole emptied the Winchester, then jammed it back in its saddleboot and palmed out his Colt. Beside him, Frenchy had already drawn his pistol and was firing at the rustlers who met them head-on. For a few minutes, the peaceful meadow became a hellish nightmare of milling horses, gunshots, and screams of pain. The acrid scent of gunsmoke filled Cole's nostrils, and a part of his brain gloried in it. That familiar red haze slid down over his eyes as a killing frenzy gripped him. He had thought that he was beginning to put that part of his personality behind him, but obviously that wasn't the case. He wasn't berserk or out of control. He cut down the rustlers with a calm, deadly efficiency, but a part of him exulted in the danger and death.

The other members of the gang were pushing the cattle as fast as they could, but the posse was delayed only a few minutes by the gunfight in the meadow. Two men had been killed and another three wounded so badly that they were out of the fight, but even heavier losses had been inflicted on the rustlers. Cole managed to reload the Winchester as he galloped after them. He glanced over once, surprised to find that Alexandra Fisk was riding close beside him, a rifle in her hands. He motioned for her to drop back, but she ignored him.

It was her own hide, Cole thought with a grimace.

As more of the rustlers turned back to try to stop them, Cole picked off first one, then another, at a pretty good distance. The outlaws had to be getting discouraged now. Maybe they would give up and avoid any more killing. Cole hoped so. The bloodlust that had gripped him earlier had departed as abruptly as it came, leaving him a little sickened.

He wasn't going to turn back now, though. If the rustlers put up a fight, whatever happened was on their heads.

The posse caught up as the running cattle began to splash across the second shallow creek. Cole snapped a shot with his Winchester and saw one of the rustlers plunge from the saddle to land in the creek with a splash. Nearby, Billy Casebolt's old Confederate revolver boomed heavily and sent another man tumbling to the ground. At close quarters, one of the rustlers charged Frenchy LeDoux and swung his rifle like a club. Frenchy ducked under the swiping blow and fanned his six-gun, the shots coming so close together they sounded like a peal of thunder as they nearly cut the rustler in half. Sawyer, Fisk, Lon Rogers, even Alexandra . . . all of them downed rustlers with their gunfire. Cole expected the rustlers to begin surrendering, but evidently they intended to fight to the bitter end.

Except for a couple of them, Cole realized as he suddenly caught sight of a pair of riders fleeing, abandoning the cattle and their companions. He lifted his rifle, intending to send some slugs after them, but then a cloud of gunsmoke drifted in front of his face, momentarily blinding him. The next instant, a strident curse from his right made him swivel in his saddle as one of the other rustlers opened up on him. Bullets whipped past Cole's head. He fired the Winchester from his hip and saw the round thud into the gunman's chest, driving him backward off his horse.

Cole looked for another target and couldn't find one. Some of the members of the posse were still shooting, but for the life of him, Cole couldn't see any rustlers still alive. Even the two who had fled seemed to have vanished. He shouted, "Hold your fire! Damn it, hold your fire!"

The shots gradually died away. Across the creek, the cattle had run on a hundred yards or so, then stopped in confusion since no one was hazing them on. All the rustlers were sprawled either on the banks of the creek or in the stream itself. There was blood everywhere, soaking into the ground, running into the water in thin tendrils that stretched out and then disappeared but still gave the creek a faint tinge of pink. Holding his Winchester in his left hand, Cole rubbed his right hand wearily over his face.

"Looks like we got 'em all, Marshal," Casebolt said as he eased his horse up alongside Cole's.

"How many men did we lose?" Cole asked.

"Another man killed, and a handful with bullet holes in 'em. Looks to me like all of 'em ought to make it, though."

Cole nodded slowly. "We were lucky. It could have gone the other way."

"Reckon so," Casebolt said. "But it didn't."

Suddenly, Austin Fisk called out, "Catherine! Catherine! Damn it, where's my daughter?" His voice was ragged and thick with misery.

Cole swung around, saw that Fisk had dismounted and was running among the dead scattered along the creek. With all the bullets flying around, it was entirely possible Catherine Fisk and Wilt Paxton had been hit. But as Fisk came to a stop and stood there trembling, he lifted his face to the others and said, "She's not here. Neither of them are here."

Cole dismounted and strode over to him. Alexandra Fisk swung down from her horse and hurried over to her father as well. Fisk caught her arms and asked, "Are you all right, Alex?"

She nodded. "I'm not hurt, Pa. But where's Catherine?"

Kermit Sawyer spoke up, saying, "You should've thought of that before you charged in shootin', Fisk. That was a good way to get that gal of yours killed."

"Damn it, don't you understand?" Fisk demanded. "She's *not* here!"

"Take it easy, Fisk," Cole told him. He turned to Sawyer. "Ride up there with some of the men and round up that herd. Maybe the prisoners are with the cattle."

Sawyer, Frenchy, Lon, and some of the

other men carried out Cole's orders, and a few minutes later Sawyer came jogging back on his horse, his face grim, while the others started moving the cattle slowly back toward the creek.

"No sign of 'em," he reported.

Fisk shook his head. "I don't understand it. I just don't understand it. They took Catherine and Paxton prisoner last night. What could they have done with them?"

Cole didn't want to give voice to the possibility that had occurred to him, but somebody had to. He said, "Maybe the rustlers didn't want to be slowed down by prisoners when they lit out from that little valley in the mountains."

Fisk glared at him. "What the hell do you mean by that?"

"I'm sorry, Fisk, but . . . they could've killed your daughter and your foreman before they ever left."

Alexandra cried out, "No! We were there. We didn't find any bodies."

"There are plenty of ravines around there where they could have dumped them," Cole said.

Fisk shook his head. "No. No, we didn't come all this way just to . . . to get some cattle back! I came after Catherine!"

Cole started to put a hand on Fisk's

shoulder, then drew it back, knowing that Fisk didn't want any comforting from him. He said, "I reckon we can maybe find out what happened to them."

Fisk swung around to face him, wild-eyed. "How?" he demanded.

"I saw two of those rustlers taking off for the tall and uncut while the fighting was still going on," Cole explained. "They're the only ones left alive. If we can catch up to them, maybe they can tell us what happened to the prisoners."

"They'll tell us," Fisk said, his voice shaking with emotion. "By God, they'll tell us, or I'll burn their eyes out!"

To Cole's surprise, Kermit Sawyer made the gesture that Cole had decided not to. The Texan dismounted and grasped Fisk's shoulder, squeezing tightly. "Hang on, Fisk," Sawyer rumbled. "You don't want to be givin' up hope just yet. Could be those owlhoots stashed Catherine and Paxton somewhere. When we catch up to the two who lit a shuck out of here, we'll know."

Fisk managed to nod. He took a deep breath and said, "You're right. But we don't need the whole posse to go after them." He looked at Cole. "I'm going on, but I think some of the men should take this herd back to Latch Hook."

"That's just what I was thinking," Cole agreed. "You and I will trail those last two rustlers, Fisk."

Alexandra said, "I'm going with you, Marshal. I've got a right."

Cole looked at Fisk, who nodded. "Alexandra can come."

Frenchy had ridden up in time to hear this last exchange. He edged his horse forward and said, "I'll be goin' along, too, then."

Fisk glared at him. "There's no need —"

"I want him to go," Sawyer broke in. "I've got a stake in roundin' up the last of those wideloopers, too, since some of these stolen beeves are mine. Frenchy's goin' along as my representative."

"Sounds reasonable to me," Cole said, although he didn't like agreeing with Sawyer again. That was getting to be an unpleasant habit.

"All right, all right," Fisk muttered. "Can we get started?"

Cole nodded and turned to Casebolt. "Billy, you're in charge of getting these cattle back where they belong. Think you can handle that?"

The deputy nodded. "Sure thing, Marshal."

"When you're done, head on back to Wind River."

Casebolt nodded again.

Fisk and Alexandra had mounted up and were anxious to ride. Cole and Frenchy joined them, and the four of them headed east, the direction the pair of rustlers had fled, while the remainder of the posse started the cattle moving toward home.

A couple of days later, the four riders trotted wearily into Cheyenne, the capital and largest city of the Wyoming Territory. In the two years since General Grenville Dodge had established the town to serve as a station for the Union Pacific railroad, Cole had been there several times, as well as to the nearby Fort Russell, which had been built at the same time. Cheyenne had become a boom town with the arrival of the railroad, and even though the railhead had long since moved on, the boom still continued. A shipping center for the growing cattle industry and a supply point for the entire territory, Cheyenne was noisy night and day. The saloons never closed, and neither did the railroad depot or the nearby stockyards. As Cole and his companions rode down the main street toward the Union Pacific station, he looked around at the throngs of people and was glad he didn't have to keep the peace here, instead of in Wind River.

He just hoped that among all the crowds, they could find the two men they were looking for. It wasn't going to be easy.

That same thought must have occurred to Alexandra Fisk, because she said dispiritedly, "Where do we start looking?"

"The cattle buyers stay at the hotels close to the stockyards," Cole said. "That's as good a place as any."

"I don't understand why," Fisk snapped. "Those rustlers don't have a herd to sell anymore. We recovered it, remember?"

"They don't have a herd this time, but maybe they've done business with some of the buyers before. It's possible somebody around here still owes money to them. The trail led here, and they weren't more than an hour in front of us. I think they're still here somewhere."

It was true that once the tracks of the fleeing rustlers had turned south, they had led straight toward Cheyenne. The fugitives had pushed their mounts hard, hard enough to stay ahead of the pursuit, even if it wasn't by much. But Cole knew their horses had to be played out. To continue their flight, the rustlers would have to either trade for fresh mounts — or take the train out of here.

Either way, he and the others were headed in the right direction, because the Union

Pacific station, most of the town's livery stables, and the hotels where the cattle buyers stayed were all grouped fairly closely together. The four of them would probably have to split up to cover all the possibilities.

Frenchy and Fisk could fight over which one of them would accompany Alexandra, Cole thought with a ghost of a smile. He was too tired to grin.

The Union Pacific station came into view. "I'm going over to the depot," Cole said. "Frenchy, you take the livery stables and see if those two have gotten their hands on fresh horses. Fisk, why don't you check some of the hotels and find out if they've been hanging around there?"

"All right," Fisk said grudgingly. "I suppose that makes the most sense. Alexandra, you come with — Alexandra, what is it?"

Cole reined in at Fisk's startled question. So did Fisk and Frenchy. Alexandra had already brought her horse to an abrupt stop and was staring up the street toward the Union Pacific depot. "Look," she said as she pointed a shaking finger. "Just going into the train station."

The three men looked where she was pointing, and Cole saw sunlight flash on blond hair. A man and a woman were just going into the building, and as the door swung shut behind them, Fisk said, "My God, that looked like Catherine!"

"Come on," Cole said, heeling Ulysses into a trot. Maybe luck had been with them after all.

Or maybe not, a small voice warned in the back of his head.

Moments later, after tying their horses outside, the four pursuers strode into the big, high-ceilinged depot. A glance at the schedule chalked onto a board over the ticket windows told Cole that an eastbound train was due at one o'clock. It had to be almost that time now, he thought.

"I don't see them," Fisk said as he looked around the lobby, panic creeping into his voice. "They're not here."

"Let's check the platform," Cole suggested. He walked quickly toward the big double doors on the other side of the room.

His bootheels rang on the planks as he stepped out onto the long covered platform built alongside the tracks. There were quite a few people waiting there for the eastbound, but not so many that Cole couldn't spot who he was looking for right away. At the far end of the platform, Catherine Fisk stood next to Wilt Paxton. Catherine was wearing a dress now, and Paxton's clothes were fresh, too.

They had had time since arriving in Cheyenne to wash off the trail dust from their long ride and buy tickets on that eastbound train, Cole thought. He started to reach out, intending to hold back Fisk and Alexandra.

It was too late. Fisk shouted, "Catherine!" and broke into a run across the platform toward them. Alexandra was right behind him.

"Watch out!" Cole rapped to Frenchy. He veered to his left, spreading out and motioning to Frenchy to go the other way. Cole reached for his gun.

Catherine and Paxton turned sharply, and in the split-second before Paxton drew, Cole saw the horror and hatred on the young woman's face, the surprised sneer on Paxton's. Then Paxton's gun was out of its holster and coming up with blinding speed. A woman nearby saw it and screamed.

"Get down, Fisk!" Cole shouted as he palmed out his own revolver.

Fisk came to a startled halt and reached out to grab Alexandra as she started past him. Paxton's gun boomed. Someone else screamed as the bullet hit the platform and whined off down the tracks. Fisk threw himself down, taking Alexandra with him.

Out of instinct, Frenchy had drawn his

gun, too, and he and Cole fired at the same time, the roars of the pistols blending into one. Paxton snarled and triggered again and then again. All over the platform, passengers waiting for the eastbound went diving for cover. Cole slammed another shot at Paxton, only to see Catherine Fisk slump back with a cry of pain.

One of Paxton's slugs chewed splinters from the platform at Cole's feet. Cole squeezed off two more shots, and Frenchy fired again as well. Paxton spun half-around, red flowers blooming on the breast of the white shirt he wore. His pistol slipped from his fingers to thud to the platform. He went to his knees, swayed there for a second, then pitched forward onto his face.

Catherine pushed herself up with her left arm. The right sleeve of her dress was stained with blood, and that arm hung useless at her side. She let out a gut-wrenching wail and threw herself on Paxton's body, clutching it with her good arm as great wracking sobs shuddered through her. Several yards away on the platform, Fisk and Alexandra were slowly getting to their feet, their faces etched with sorrow and confusion. Neither of them appeared to be wounded.

"Hold it right there, mister!" a voice yelled

from behind Cole. "Drop that gun! What the hell's going on here?"

Cole glanced over his shoulder and saw a heavy-set man with a badge pinned to his vest pointing a scattergun at him. Two more badge-toters, probably deputies of the town marshal covering Cole, had converged on Frenchy LeDoux and were disarming him.

Moving slowly so as not to spook the man with the shotgun, Cole bent down and placed his revolver on the platform. As he straightened, he glanced at Fisk and Alexandra, who were still staring uncomprehendingly at the body of Paxton and the quivering form of Catherine Fisk.

"Take it easy, Marshal," Cole told the lawman. "It's all over, and I can explain it. I don't like it — but I can explain it."

"You'd damn well better!" the local star packer snapped. His eyes widened as he spotted the badge on Cole's shirt. "Say! You're a lawman, too."

"Yep," Cole admitted. "And this is one of those times when I sort of wish I wasn't."

30

"Howdy, Marshal," Billy Casebolt greeted Cole enthusiastically as Cole reined to a halt in front of the office. "Good to see you again. Ever catch up to them rustlers?"

Cole stepped down from the saddle, flipped the reins over the hitch rail, and patted Ulysses on the shoulder. "We found them in Cheyenne," he said to Casebolt.

The deputy's lean face was solemn as he asked, "Did they tell you what they done with Paxton and that gal?"

Cole stepped up on the boardwalk and said, "They *were* Paxton and Catherine Fisk."

Casebolt frowned in confusion and scratched his beard-stubbled jaw. "Don't reckon I follow you, Marshal."

Cole rolled his shoulders, trying to get some of the weariness from the long ride out of his muscles. "Catherine Fisk planned the whole thing," he said. "She never wanted to come out here to Wyoming, so she decided to get enough money to go back east and live her own life. She got Wilt Paxton to fall in love with her and roped him into a scheme to rustle cattle from her pa's spread as well as the Diamond S and get Fisk and Sawyer to blaming each other for it. They were never prisoners of the rustlers at all. They planned all along for that last raid on Latch Hook to be the final one. That's why they cut and ran when we caught up to the herd. Catherine couldn't face going back to her father, not after everything she'd done to get away from him."

A low whistle came from Casebolt. "That's just about the most low-down . . . why, I never heard of nothin' like that, Marshal! You sure about all of it?"

Cole nodded. "Catherine explained it all herself after we caught up to them in Cheyenne and Paxton went for his gun."

"What happened?"

"We left Paxton there . . . in the cemetery. Catherine was wounded in the shoot-out, but one of the local doctors patched her up." Cole inclined his head toward the north. "She's back out at Latch Hook now. Fisk brought her home with him. He wouldn't press charges against her, and since everybody who actually took part in the raids is dead —" Cole shrugged.

"Damn!" Casebolt breathed. "He took her right back into his house?"

Cole nodded. "I hope he's not making a bad mistake. He's liable to wake up some morning with his throat cut and Catherine gone again. But not if Alexandra has anything to say about it. I reckon she'll keep a pretty close eye on her sister from now on — when she's not being courted by Frenchy LeDoux."

"Well, I'll swan!" Casebolt said with a chuckle. "I bet ol' Sawyer'll have a fit if he finds out his *segundo* is courtin' that gal."

"He already knows," Cole said, summoning up a smile himself. He changed the subject by asking, "You get those cattle back where they belonged?"

"No problem," Casebolt said. "Once I got back here, though, I found out there'd been a little ruckus while we was gone."

Cole suppressed a groan. "More trouble? What's happened now?"

"There's Michael," Casebolt said, pointing down the boardwalk. "He can tell you all about it, seein' as it was him what done most of it."

Cole looked down the boardwalk and saw the young newspaper editor coming toward them. He hailed Michael, then strode down the walk to meet him. Michael said, "I'm glad to see you're back, Marshal. Have you got a story for me about those last two rustlers?"

"You first," Cole said. "What happened while I was gone?" An inspiration struck him. "There wasn't more trouble with that medicine show, was there?"

Michael flushed and said, "Well, now that you mention it . . ."

During the next five minutes, Michael explained about the swindle that had been perpetrated by Professor Munroe, Dr. Carter, and their partners in larceny. The story concluded with the death of Chief Laughing Fox, the wreck of the wagon, and the explosion and fire that had consumed it.

"Luckily, all the money they had taken from the townspeople was in the other wagon," Michael said, "so it didn't burn up. Everybody got back what the professor had cheated them out of."

"Where are Munroe and the others now?" Cole asked.

"They, ah, left in a hurry once people started talking about tar and feathers. There was even some mention of a lynching. But Jeremiah said that as long as they paid back all the money, he wouldn't arrest them."

"You could have had them held for trying

to kill you," Cole pointed out.

Michael shook his head. "I thought it would be better if we just put the whole thing behind us."

"Well, that's probably wise. And that's what we're going to do with that rustling business, too."

"Wait a minute, Marshal!" Michael protested. "You promised me the story."

"Nope, I just said for you to go first." Cole held up a hand. "Now, don't push me on this, Michael. Otherwise I might just ask you what you were doing around that medicine show so late at night in the first place."

Michael flushed, stammered a little, then turned and headed back toward the newspaper office. Casebolt chuckled again.

Cole looked at his deputy. "He hasn't said what he was doing there, has he?"

"The boy's bein' mighty close-mouthed 'bout that part of the story," Casebolt said with a grin. "Him and that wife of his'n seem to've made up, though, so I reckon it's best all around to just let things lay."

Cole nodded in agreement.

He was in the office by himself, about an hour later, when Dr. Judson Kent stopped by. After greeting Cole, Kent asked, "How are those bullet wounds of yours healing?"

"They're not bothering me anymore," Cole said with a shrug. "To tell you the truth, I've been too busy to worry about them. Guess I didn't need any of Professor Munroe's tonic, after all. Billy kept trying to get me to take it."

"Well, it wouldn't have done much good, but it might have made you feel better. It was mostly alcohol, you know."

"No, I didn't," Cole said. "But I'm not surprised. I guess folks will leave Medicine Creek alone now and stop bothering the Shoshones."

Kent reached inside his jacket and brought out a small glass bottle. He placed it on the desk in front of Cole and said, "This is what's left from the sample that so-called doctor took from the creek. He claimed it was plain water. It's not."

Cole looked up sharply. "What do you mean, Doctor?"

"I did some more analysis of the water myself after those charlatans had fled from town. It does have a very high mineral content, just as Munroe said. High enough that it could very well have some therapeutic effect, especially combined with those high temperatures."

"Then you figure —"

"That being immersed in that pool really did make Deputy Casebolt's rheumatism improve dramatically. Further treatments might help it even more, might even get rid of it."

"But what about that fever Billy had?" Cole wanted to know.

"There's a French fellow named Pasteur who has theorized that many illnesses are caused by tiny organisms which invade the human body."

"Little . . . varmints of some kind?" Cole asked, trying to follow what Kent was saying.

"You could say that. Pasteur has further speculated that heat can kill those organisms."

"Then that hot water was too hot for whatever was making Billy sick!"

Kent nodded. "It's only a theory, of course. Perhaps . . . it really was magic."

Cole leaned back in his chair. "Well, I'd appreciate it if you'd just keep those notions to yourself, Doctor. I don't want anybody starting another run on Medicine Creek."

"That was my thought exactly." Kent gestured at the bottle of water. "I'll leave that with you."

"What do you want me to do with it?"

"Whatever you deem appropriate, Marshal." With a casual wave, Kent left the office.

Cole sighed. He would never know as much as Judson Kent, would never be as intelligent or well educated. To him, a varmint was something big enough to shoot at, not something so tiny that it could get inside a fella's body and make him sick. But there were all sorts of things under heaven that he had no idea about, Cole supposed. And he would just have to live with that.

He frowned at the bottle of water on the desk. For a long moment, he glared at it, then he reached out, picked it up, and pulled the cork from its neck. There was one sure-fire way to get rid of the stuff — and Kent *had* said it might be good for folks.

Cole lifted the bottle to his mouth, drank down the contents, and put the empty bottle on the desk with a grimace.

It still tasted God-awful. Maybe he needed some Chippewa Tonic to chase it with.

Or at least a beer down at the Pronghorn . . .

ABOUT THE AUTHOR

James Reasoner lives in Aizle, Texas.